For

Enjoy your first bite!
♡ Sharon Hamilton

HONEYMOON
BITE

SHARON HAMILTON

Copyright © 2012 by Sharon Hamilton

ISBN-10: 1495389812
ISBN-13: 9781495389818

DEDICATION

I want to thank my friend and early critique partner, Tina Folsom, for helping me bring my vampires to life. To my Street Team for adopting this author and helping to spread the word. You guys are the best friends a writer could ever wish for in ten lifetimes.

Thanks to my Tuesday Group: Arletta, Kent, Robin, Ronn, and Shane. And to Marlene Cullen for bringing us together in the first place. To Pam and Rochelle for their critical eyes.

Also to my husband for his immortal support and for putting up with the interference from other family members who said, "She's writing what?"

CHAPTER 1

Anne looked down on the sleeping form of her new husband and, God help her, he looked like the first man she would murder. Nestled into his arms was the naked body of her maid of honor.

This made the second time today the bride had caught them together. First was at the reception. In the bathroom.

Monika's dress and Robert's tux were trampled and splayed over the chair and floor, along with a spilled bottle of champagne, cream satin shoes, a long taffeta slip, a hot pink push-up bra, and Robert's new black socks.

"Not exactly what a bride wants to see on her wedding day." Anne spoke without emotion. These weren't the soft lilting tones she'd gushed when reciting her wedding vows that afternoon. Her statement caused the reaction she'd hoped for. Monika bolted up, her eyes crossed but wide open. She clutched a sheet to her chest. Robert scrambled to the floor.

"Don't bother to put your pants on," Anne delivered.

"Honey—Anne," Robert said in his I'm-so-sorry-I-got-caught voice. His tanned face used to melt her insides, like when he smiled and it was if the sun had come out from behind the clouds. But today his charm wasn't going to work. The bride had murder on her mind.

"I'm so glad you're all right. We were—" Robert began.

"I'm fine. I can see how worried you are. Touching." Taffeta and satin rustled as Anne reached down to the handle of her wardrobe roller, stuffed to bursting with brand new clothes for her honeymoon, most with tags still on them. She made sure her money, passport, and airline tickets were still zipped into the top pocket.

"Your dress, Anne." Her former best friend pointed to the red stains down the front. "Is that blood?"

"Catsup. Not blood. Not yet." Anne saw them both flinch.

"Now wait just a minute." Robert climbed back into the bed and put his arms around Monika, but he'd tucked his body safely behind hers. "I'm sorry about all this, Anne. I've been a fool."

Monika turned around and looked at him in a drunken gaze. Maybe she was wising up already.

"No. It wasn't going to work, you asshole. Don't you think your timing sucked? Couldn't you have done it before we did all this?" Anne lifted her skirts as if to curtsy. Robert relaxed and hung his head on Monika's bare shoulder.

Anne grabbed a black rain slicker and rolled her the bag that contained her trousseau out to the hallway. Whispers came from her bedroom. Unzipping the bag, she extracted the red and black outfit she had planned to wear on the plane—the one with the plunging neckline. She locked herself in the bath-room, then shimmied out of her bridal gown and slipped into her new things. Her feet found a comfortable home in her favorite pair of black Crocs, the ones decorated by her bachelorette buddies with little bride and groom charms sur-rounded by red hearts.

No way.

She grabbed Robert's toenail nippers from the vanity and snipped off both the bride and groom, but left the red hearts there. Romance wasn't dead. But her marriage sure was.

Robert stood in the hallway, clad only in his shorts. "Where are you going?"

"On my honeymoon. I planned it. I paid for it. I'm going."

She descended to the ground floor of her house, and then realized her wedding gown was still draped over her left arm. A convenient row of black plastic garbage cans out at the curb for an early morning pick up became the gown's final resting place. The nuclear tufts of stained and shredded white organza looked like tissue paper stuffing for a tall wedding present.

The limo driver waited by the opened door and cast her a smirk.

Second leg of Plan B. So far, so good.

Anne dove in the back seat of the limo and allowed herself to be swallowed by the groaning black leather. She hunched down, bent her knees, closed her eyes, and leaned her weary neck against the headrest as the driver sped towards the San Francisco airport. They rushed down the freeway, leaving the bucolic countryside of Sonoma County behind and entering the thickening traffic and congestion of the Peninsula. Her driver kept looking at her even after she'd told him, for the second time, she would still be going on the honeymoon but *without* the groom.

A glance in the mirror fished out from the bottom of her carry-on confirmed most of her mascara was now located on her cheeks and chin, so she squirted a drop of lemon-scented hand cream into her palm and used it to wipe off the black excess. The driver sneezed, then apologized.

Today, she'd rather smell good than look good. She wasn't going to let a man touch her for, well, it would be years. She was sure of it. Maybe never.

A group of high school kids first stared at her behind tinted black windows, then began a quadruple moon, butts pressed to glass. She eyed their suspicious happiness.

Perfect.

She sighed.

Life goes on. Nobody cares. Get used to it.

How could she have been so naïve? She pondered the events of the day. The wedding had been perfect. Even Robert seemed to get into it a little. They had kissed during their first dance, a nice, long, languid kiss that was probably done to impress the ladies, she realized in hindsight. He had that cat-that-ate-a-hundred-dollar-koi look to him, with those baby blue eyes of his that roamed all over her body when she turned and caught his expression. He was saying something to his friends who were also giving her close inspection.

Had he ever loved her? Just a little? The chill in her heart sent an arctic telegram to her eyes and froze her tears in place.

Does it matter?

Later it had been time for the cake cutting, but there was no Robert anywhere. No one could find him. As Anne looked around the guests, she'd noticed Monika was missing as well. That's when she got a bad feeling.

She was on her way to check the downstairs dressing room again when she thought she had heard something. With her ear to a bathroom door, she recognized the familiar grunts of her handsome groom and the heavy breathing from a well-used partner. The smooth glass doorknob rattled as she slowly opened the bathroom door. It had to be done. She had to see it. See the reality of it, that her husband's faithfulness had lasted less than three hours after they had taken their vows.

Robert was banging Monika in her pale blue gown, her cream slipper-clad feet bouncing in the air while he humped her. Her pert little ass was cradled in the shallow lavie. Monika's eyes grew the size of grapefruits when she saw Anne, and she struggled to sit up. But Robert would have none of it. He was far too focused on the home run, pumping with thrusts that sent Monika's body bouncing between tufts of egg white chiffon.

It was not the ending to her wedding day Anne had expected. She closed the door and heard panicked voices on the other side.

She whipped out the hundred-dollar bill her Uncle Osborne had given her earlier in the day, and with her clutch deeply embedded in her armpit, hailed the sleepy limo driver. Robert had hired one of his regulars to take them first to the house and then the airport. The man had been clearly surprised.

Bet he knows more about my husband than I do.

She had time to kill, and that was exactly the right way to put it.

"Just drive, but get me back to the house before five to pick up my things." She gave him the crisp Franklin bill.

"No, ma'am. I'm paid for the whole three hours until your flight. I'll take you anywhere."

Can you find me a new groom? Someone who isn't a serial cheater?

"Then just take the hundred as a tip. Oh, and go inside and get me a bottle of champagne, one that's opened."

While waiting in the purring limo, Anne found her tears were threatening rebellion, but a look to the crowd of happy revelers made her suck it up. The driver appeared with two bottles of champagne, one corked and draped with a freshly starched white napkin. Several family members had spilled out on the steps behind him and stood there gawking, as if watching a traffic accident.

"Thank you," she whispered as she zeroed in on the frosty neck of bubbly. She took a swig that wound up mostly in her nose.

Her driver stifled a laugh, then commanded their ship out onto the highway, speeding through lush green vineyards arranged in rows so unlike her life right now.

Anne fiddled with the wedding band, but it was stuck. She'd have to get it cut off as soon as she got back.

She'd starved herself for days and now she wanted a burger, one with bacon and guacamole, so she had the driver pull into Burger Palace. With her white dress flowing behind her like froth from a waterfall, she ran barefoot into the popular spot, then stumbled on her shimmering skirt, almost doing a face plant at the order counter.

She managed to get out her order, then sat down and waited for her number to be called, layers of the flounce partially covering an older gentleman on her right, who maintained a brittle smile, and a young boy leaning into his mom on her left, who didn't. In fact, his mother quickly shuttled him elsewhere. Anne twirled her dark brown ringlets, still entangled by tiny crystal clips, and studied the faces in the room all turned toward her. Strangers stood, mostly in shocked silence, or whispered among themselves. Someone tittered.

A bride can't have a burger on her wedding day?

Except this scene had been just bizarre. Checking outside, she was relieved to see her limo driver still maneuvering for a parking spot that didn't block the parking lot entrance.

"Number sixty-seven," the loudspeaker squawked.

Yep, that's me. Number sixty-seven. She wondered what it would feel like to be a number one as she paid for her burger and fried zucchini.

Just for a day, or a night of love. To be cherished and maybe even worshiped, just for a day.

For once in her life, she'd like not to have to share a man with another woman, or worse yet, another man. Was that too much for a girl to hope for?

She got back in the limo, where the driver watched her eat in the back seat, the bottle of champagne wedged between her legs. She dripped catsup down her front and ate pickles from her lap after they fell from the oozing burger, then directed the driver to take her back to her husband and former best friend for the showdown.

But the burger had tasted heavenly. Sinful. It was probably the closest thing to being a bad girl she could ever be.

Well, that had brought on a wave of tears. She'd had a good, satisfying cry, in her wedding dress smeared down the front with hamburger sauce, on her wedding day.

"It says Anne Balesteiri. You are recently married?" The Homeland Security officer, who looked like he could play for the Forty-Niners, checked over her passport and ticket.

In a cruel twist of fate, Robert's mother, the elder Mrs. Balesteiri, had gifted them the tickets and had used Anne's new married name.

"Just today, as a matter of fact."

He looked around to see if he had missed the other half of the happy couple.

"I'm traveling alone," Anne wheezed and gave a casual cough, batting her eyes at Mr. Homeland Security Charles Atlas. Raising her chin, she added, "My husband will join me soon," she said with emphasis on *husband*.

"You're going to have to get that changed." He fingered her passport.

"First thing when I get back, don't worry."

She was itching for a shower to wipe off all the traces Robert had ever been in her life.

The flight to New York was uneventful, except they upgraded a Realtor to the first class seat her husband was to have. Anne wanted to sleep, but the woman just liked to hear herself talk. The stewardess must have guessed Anne's pain from the state of Anne's makeup and her red eyes, because she kept Anne's wine glass filled. In time, the drone of the Realtor's voice merged with the drone of the plane engines, and Anne gratefully fell asleep.

She woke up when the tires hit the tarmac at JFK with a jolt. Her neck was stiff and drool had dried down her chin. After exiting the plane, she hobbled to a nearby women's restroom and washed her face, reapplying makeup and deodorant. With soapy fingers, she tried removing her wedding band, but it was no use. The detritus of her marriage was going to have to stay for a while.

Her carefully coifed curls were tamed, secured with a red scrunchie. She added red lip-gloss and lots of blush. She was a desperate woman, after all. Who but a truly bad person would leave her five thousand dollar wedding gown in a garbage can on the street? She added more red to her cheeks.

Better.

Her cell phone had practically been glowing with calls and messages. Her brother wasn't someone she could ignore. After texting him, saying she was on her way to Tuscany, *by herself*, she asked him to return all the wedding gifts.

Sam: Sis, u OK?
Anne: *&^&*^*%
Sam: LOL That's my baby sister. Now I'll stop worrying.
Anne: Shred the license.
Sam: ??
Anne: The wedding license from the minister. I didn't sign it. It goes away.
Sam: It never happened. Consider it gone.
Anne: Tnx. Luv U. ttfn.

She flipped her phone shut and turned it off.

With a pounding headache, she boarded the nonstop to Genoa at midnight. The glittering lights of New York moved beyond her line of sight in the tiny window at her side. She adjusted the air, turned off the reading lamp and, all alone, in the dark, under the skimpy green airplane blanket, began to cry herself to sleep.

The pink Italian sun timidly poked its afternoon nose into Anne's heart as she exited the airport in Genoa. She was transported to the Swiss Hotel, and within minutes was standing with her bag in the middle of the bridal suite. She took a shower and fell asleep under the cool sheets and heavy damask comforter.

Anne awoke a couple of hours later to a bright orange and purple sunset that bathed the already warm colors of the ancient village square around the corner from her hotel. She passed by open-air cafes crowded with locals, noticing couples holding hands all around her.

Is the whole world in love except me?

Violin music called to her from a neighborhood gypsy café a block off the square. She was going to wait in line, but flickering candlelight that illuminated a chapel at the end of a cobblestoned street caught her eye. She changed course and entered the sanctuary of light as a heavy bell rang, startling her.

Inside, the lonely violin music echoed off carved stone columns in the narthex. The floor was travertine and heavily veined marble in shades of grey, black and sienna. At the front of the church a couple sat, whispering with a priest, their heads bowed. She dipped her fingers into the cool water of the sacristy and, as if they could hear the droplets coming off her fingers, the trio looked up at her.

Anne moved to the side, where a table was covered in garnet-colored votive candles. She lit a votive, and using a stubby yellow pencil from a basket filled with scraps of paper, she wrote her prayer, folded it once, and slipped it under a votive. Her last view up to the nave as she left the chapel was that of the three figures, now standing, ready to leave.

As she wandered the streets of Genoa, the scent of citrus blossoms filled the night air. The dark streets felt oddly safe and familiar. She turned a corner and slammed into someone. She gasped and looked up to see a woman with jet-black hair, dark eyes, and a muscled and toned body. She wore the strong perfumed scent of a woman, and her lips were neon red.

Anne was about to apologize for her distraction when the woman's lips pulled back in a smile, revealing two large white fangs.

Blood pounded through Anne, through her head. Sound muted. Her vision narrowed to focus on the sharpness and angle of the woman's fangs. Her mind eliminated all other thoughts but the terror and havoc those fangs could cause. Her body refused to move. Blotches appeared before her eyes, as if she were having a cluster migraine.

"Your mistake to cross my path tonight, human. Now you'll pay for it with your life."

The woman's words echoed through the empty night but Anne couldn't make sense of what the woman's words. She couldn't run. Could only struggle to suck in oxygen. The vamp seized her body, then tossed her high in the air to let her fall to the ground. A sharp snap and pop sounded and pain shot through Anne. Her mind struggled to make sense of the attack, but all she knew was that something was broken inside her. Bones. Free will. Both.

Anne's scream was cut off abruptly as fangs lodged deep inside her neck. A sweet delirium engulfed her. She thought she heard fluttering in the background, perhaps voices, but the blotches in her vision started connecting with each other and at last, there was only darkness. She collapsed onto the cobblestone alleyway, into the arms of a dreamy sleep that she knew would surely precede her own death.

At least death didn't cheat, she thought just before she lost consciousness.

CHAPTER 2

When the woman had entered the chapel, Marcus had seen her face for the first time. He'd known in his heart that he had found her at last. As she'd disappeared behind a pillar of stone, he'd been thirsty for the sight of her.

This is the fating calling to me.

He heard the chicken scratch sounds as she wrote on a slip of paper, heard the pencil being put back into its basket, and the drop of her coin in the prayer box. The flame that roared to life when she struck a match roared an echo in his heart. Blood pulsed throughout his body, making his hands tingle and his face flush. She was so close to him now. After three hundred years of searching, she had finally arrived in his life. "I've found her at last," he said to his companion and the priest. "My fated female."

He heard the heavy doors at the entrance slam shut, echoing off the ancient stone, as his beloved left the chapel.

Marcus finished his business with the priest, begging off any further entanglements, postponing decisions, duties, and promises, and went in search of her.

As he passed by the bonfire of votives where she had stopped to write, he was compelled to stop. He wove his hands through the air and found the little candle flame that protected her prayer. His fingers were drawn to the stiff cream vellum. He drew it to his nose and drank her scent. He read the words aloud softly:

"Help me find the true love of my life. Help me bring to him all the love that still lives in my soul. Please let me remember the magic and power of this place. Anne."

Could she have been talking about him? As his eyes had moistened and he'd rubbed his forefinger against the words she had delicately crafted in pencil, he'd heard her scream. With horror, he'd realized the fantasy in his heart had put her life in danger. He'd looked around the chapel. Maya was no longer standing beside the priest or anywhere in the building.

He flew through the ancient doors and into the night, tracing the woman's steps, until he came to the dirty alleyway where Maya crouched over his female. In an instant, he was at her side. He pulled the vamp by the hair, turning her face to his. The blood of his female was on Maya's gums, dripping down her fangs and onto her chin. She smiled.

"She is delicious."

How he wanted to end Maya's life right there. The directive not to kill another golden on pain of death was the only thing that stopped him, but he felt the urge to twist her neck and remove her head. Gripping her long black locks at her scalp, he swung her like a hammer toss overhead and threw her as far as he could. She cackled, her voice sending an eerie promise of further evil as she catapulted through the sky, end over end until she landed some distance away. Her ghoulish deed had ruined his life, altered his path forever, and that of the woman he now knew as Anne.

He bent down. His female's body looked pale and fragile. Her dark hair lay across the wet cobblestones, like a matted pillow. The ample mounds of her breasts pushed against her blouse; pert nipples made peaks in the blood-stained fabric. Her waist was small. One knee was bent, with her skirt hitched, to reveal creamy, unblemished flesh that covered her thigh. He cupped his palm under her knee and straightened her leg.

She had sustained a scrape on her forehead, which was bruising, but way too slowly. Her cheek was smeared with grit from the alleyway where she fell. He touched the bite wound on her neck with his fingertips coated in his own saliva. The blood stopped flowing, and she was the color of death. But still beautiful. The sun had set on this human life of hers.

There wasn't any time to consider other options. He opened the blue vein at his wrist, puckered her chalky pink lips, pulled her jaw down to open her mouth, and poured a small stream of his own blood onto her tongue. She would come to life again. If he hadn't been too late.

A minute passed with no reaction. He traced his thumb against her lower lip and blew into her face, whispering the ancient calling. There was always the possibility that the change wouldn't take, that she was incompatible with the vampire blood gene, but he knew she was his fated female, and as such, his blood would heal her as nothing else could. She was getting cold. He rubbed her arms and cradled her against his chest.

All of a sudden, like something out of a fairytale, her body stirred. She arched up, inhaling deeply, but remained unconscious, eyes closed. His Snow White, needing a lover's kiss to awaken her from a deep sleep.

He covered her mouth with his lips and tasted his fated female for the first time. Her coldness sent a shiver down his spine.

I've found you at last.

She would need more blood, and soon, and she would need medical attention. He was sure Maya had damaged Anne's body, possibly gravely. But it was good she was breathing on her own.

Welcome to my world. Our world, my beloved. I didn't want it to happen this way.

She would need undisturbed sleep, away from prying eyes and instruments, and then be given more of his blood. Cloaking them both, he basked in the feel of her head, gently propped against his chest, as he transported her through the night sky to the villa he shared with his sister. The touch of her breasts through the fabric of his silk shirt soothed his soul. She would live, he felt certain. He had given her the only chance she had at another life. As he drew her essence in and allowed it to fill his lungs, her scent coated his insides. Where her body touched him skin on skin, he tingled.

The villa appeared, covered with bright blooming pink bougainvillea that defied the night's darkness. He brushed back her long, dark brown hair from her pale face that remained caked with her own blood. He laid her down in the small anteroom off his bedchamber. The smell of her wasted and violated blood was dangerous perfume. Anger burned a hole in his stomach.

He looked over the body of his beloved. Her full breasts rose and fell with her shallow breathing. His blood had brought a peach blush to her plump cheeks and full lips. Her delicate neck, marred with the wound that still gaped, had re-opened to reveal a faintly throbbing vein under pale flesh. He touched her there, tracing his finger up to her ear, and heard her moan. She must have felt the same delicious tingle he felt that extended up his arm, warming him all the way to his heart. He sifted his fingers through her hair, then positioned her face, rubbed her temples, and watched her arch and take one long, deep breath.

My touch is good for you. Yes, beloved. I will heal you inside and out.

He had hoped someday this little room would be a nursery, had planned it for over a hundred years. How fitting that he'd brought her here. It was her new birth, her new life of forever. She would take her first breaths as vampire here. Close to him, but not yet *in* his bed.

He wanted to lay next to her, naked, to take her in the ancient fating ritual, but he could not risk it until the turning was completed and she gained her preternatural strength. Not until she could look at him with her turned eyes and want him as her mate. He would not force her. But how he needed her!

He summoned his sister, Laurel, who examined his female, then dressed the wound to let it bleed out and purge Anne's body of Maya's poison. Laurel objectively checked the young woman's vitals, something Marcus could not do. He retreated to his bedroom to prepare blood for Anne's next feeding.

Laurel timidly entered his chamber and gave him the news that Anne would live. But Laurel did not smile, and instead told him that the turning had started and taken hold, that Anne was already strong in her new form. But still no smile graced Laurel's lips.

"There's a complication, brother," she said.

Marcus didn't like the dark timbre of her tone.

"Come, and I'll show you."

Laurel opened the door and the two of them approached his female, lying naked under a down comforter. He wished he had been the one to remove her clothes. He was jealous of even his sister's touch upon Anne's fragile skin. But he would not take what she wasn't conscious to give her consent to. His fingers fluttered in the glorious feel of her deep breathing, just above her face, as he bent to touch the lips that would soon give back the flame of their eternal love.

Before his fingertips could caress her mouth, Laurel stopped him, gripping firm bony fingers around his wrist.

He stared at his sister's cool steel blue eyes. Had he overstepped his bounds?

Laurel studied him as she raised the woman's left hand and showed him the wedding ring.

She is married?

Envy and anger shot through his body. How could someone take from him what he'd been waiting for all these years? Who would dare do such a thing?

Laurel lowered Anne's arm and tucked the comforter up around her neck, straightening her brown curls still caked in blood. With a finger to her lips, Laurel guided Marcus through the archway to his bedchamber and closed the door.

"This complicates our position here, Marcus."

The words hung like weights attached to his heart. "Yes. I'll pay the price if I must. No reason for you to suffer. Once she is out of danger, you should leave and not know anything about her."

"No. I mean the marriage. She is not free to be your fated female. She belongs to another, Marcus."

"But the fating . . . I *feel* it, Laurel."

"And I believe you, but she is taken already. You know you will have to ask permission. What if her husband is human?"

Marcus's huge frame collapsed to a sitting position on his bed. He glanced around the room. He had hoped tomorrow or the next night he could begin to spend eternity here with his fated female, at last. He would lovingly guide her, show her their ways. Bring her to life, to a life he hoped she would cherish and make her own. Give her time to feel the fating, and then they would mate, mate forever. He felt trapped in a fantasy of his own making.

His insides felt hollow as he spoke. "Then I will not touch her until I have permission. I will ask them immediately, after she has fully accepted the turning."

"But you gave her life without their permission."

"Yes. I had to protect her." He looked up into the gentle face of his sister, his biggest supporter. A woman who had not yet found her mate, who devoted her life to making him comfortable. Her long face and quietly beautiful features never needed makeup, and she wore none. Her peach skin had a natural glow, framed by a perfectly heart-shaped mouth. Her long shiny light brown hair was tied back in a chignon.

They had spent the last century easing each other's pain with a deep devotion and filial friendship. She had been his constant companion and kept him distracted from the fact that he had not yet met his fated female. If Marcus was right about Anne, Laurel would soon be left alone. He opened his arms to her and she kneeled to his embrace. "We'll figure something out," he whispered to the top of her head. "Maybe I just won't tell the Council everything."

Laurel separated, but remained kneeling in front of him.

"The Council will know what you've done. You can't hide this for more than a day or two."

"Yes, but by then, you'll not be suspected of helping," he said as he stroked her cheek with the backs of his fingers.

"Is this worth the risk to you?"

"It is fated. I wasn't given a choice but to answer the call to save her. Maya forced my hand."

"As she does every time when it comes to you. The woman will claim your soul yet."

"Her time will come," he said. He stood, transferred a catheter to another bag, and resumed draining more blood, handing Laurel two full bags. "I must be protector first. Warrior second." He pumped his forearm up and down. "Thank you, Laurel, from the bottom of my heart."

"I only hope when I find my fated male it doesn't cause me the amount of pain this is going to cause you. And everyone around you."

"And then I will come to your aid, if needed." He patted the top of her head. "Go tend to your patient, sister. Tell me she needs my touch, my blood."

Laurel moved back to where Anne lay, and gave Anne Marcus's blood. As minutes passed and the last drops drained, Anne opened her eyes and became fully conscious, inhaling deeply as if she'd nearly drowned. Marcus watched from the crack in his bedroom doorway.

"Where am I?" Anne whispered, suddenly looking at the plastic blood packet hanging from the stand.

"You're at our clinic," Laurel answered. "A private clinic, dear."

"Where?"

"I think very near where you were . . . attacked." Laurel picked up a chart and began to write in it. "May I have your name?"

"Anne Bal—"

Anne. Marcus whispered it, but noticed both women looked to the crack in the door. Had she heard him?

"Well, Anne, you are very lucky we came upon you when we did. I'm quite sure you would have died in that alleyway tonight."

Anne searched the room, her eyes darting over sterile instruments and a jar of bougainvillea blossoms Lauren had placed on the counter. Marcus knew she would think this odd for a hospital room. Her gaze rested on the stand that held the bag of blood.

"I needed blood?" she asked at last.

"Yes. You were drained to within an ounce of your life. How do you feel?"

Anne clutched the blanket close to her, and then looked under it.

"I'm naked. I guess a little cold."

"You feel well enough for a warm shower? It might do you some good, but only if you feel up to it."

"Oh, yes, I'd like to get clean, get all this . . ." She fingered the long curls matted with dark red blood.

Laurel helped her fragile, naked body up. Damn. She was still wrapped in that damned comforter. He longed to see her naked form. Anne allowed Laurel to escort her to the bathroom so she could wash up. Marcus had to work not to throw himself in there and rip that blanket off.

Anne, I could warm you, warm you in ways you can't comprehend.

"Are you sure you're okay?" Marcus heard his sister whisper.

"Yes, oddly."

"We use lots of lemons here, so I have wonderful smelling lemon soap and blood orange shampoo. But keep the bandage on your neck for overnight."

Laurel closed the bathroom door and shot Marcus a disapproving frown. She scooted him away and closed the door behind her as she whispered her disapproval, "Voyeur! Mind yourself."

She barred the door to his prying eyes and listened, waiting for her patient to finish. He returned to his bedchamber to retire for the evening, alone.

Marcus knew Laurel would make a good sister to Anne, in time. His fated female was going to need a confidant if they were all going to survive together. He heard the loud click of a lock and knew Laurel had intended to keep him away from her tonight.

He smiled at the thought. Nothing could ever keep him away. Not now.

Anne had been convinced she was in an outpatient treatment center and had decided to stay overnight and until mid-morning the next day. She was dosed with another infusion of the blood cocktail she'd received the night before, and the blood seemed to heal her further. Marcus wanted to join them for breakfast, but Laurel insisted he not. Anne didn't finish her eggs, but took three glassfuls of blood-laced orange juice.

"What is this? It's delicious."

"I put a spot of my sweet tomato puree into the orange juice, along with some cranberry juice. Unlikely combination, I know, but our water here doesn't taste very good and this masks it."

"Never had it before. I love it."

Laurel explained they were a neighborhood center run by a charity that tended to victims of street violence, alcoholics, and drug addicts. Marcus overheard her tell Anne they liked to operate outside the jurisdiction of local police, but offered her the chance to file a report, which Anne declined.

"You're going to feel a little different, as you heal. I have given you our 'miracle drug,' formulated for this very purpose. It aids especially in the healing of skin scrapes, and . . . puncture wounds, like those on your neck," Laurel said.

"But she bit me."

"No, I think you hit your neck against a couple of sharp objects, perhaps some glass, as you fell against the curb. In these dark places at night, it is easy for the imagination to fly."

Marcus could tell Anne wouldn't argue, but she didn't believe Laurel one bit.

"You may hear strange sounds—even think your hearing is changed. And you might have more difficulty sleeping. You'll have the desire for more . . . protein, especially meat, which would be good for you right now. But stay indoors at night. And don't wander around alone."

"But I am alone."

"Forgive me, but I see that you are wearing a wedding ring. Surely your husband must be curious where you spent the night last night?"

"No. He's back in California. I am here alone."

"Most unusual for a woman to be traveling alone."

"It wasn't planned that way. It was supposed to be my honeymoon. I was married just two days ago."

"Ah, then perhaps it would be better to go back to him, now that this has happened?"

Marcus's hands balled into fists and he clenched his jaw. The thought of his woman going back to the arms of her husband in California filled him with fury. How could a true and honorable man allow his new bride to travel unaccompanied?

"No. I'm afraid the wedding has been a huge mistake, so I'm going on without him. I planned it, paid for it. I've always wanted to drive the coast of the Mediterranean, and I'm going to do it. All alone."

They watched her walk away from the villa down an uneven street. Marcus wanted to go with her, help with her new life, but knew it was unwise. He hoped Maya didn't know Anne still lived. Watching her disappear around the corner was one of the hardest things he'd ever done.

"She is lovely, Marcus. A perfect match."

"Yes. I felt that the instant our eyes met."

"But I wonder, will it be enough?" Laurel was always the practical one.

"It has to be," he answered, and put his arm around his sister. "It just has to be."

"Then there is hope for me yet, brother."

"Always. There's always hope. I'd almost given up, but now there's a bright future."

"I must pack. You are sure I shouldn't stay behind for a few more days?"

"No, Laurel. It's too dangerous. Best only one of us is exposed to it. I don't want you anywhere around when the summons comes from the Golden Vampire Council. And they *will* summon me."

Bright pink bougainvillea covered the villa. He did think the flowers bloomed brighter this morning. As soon as Laurel was distracted with her packing and left the house, he would find Anne again.

CHAPTER 3

When Anne had awoken in the hospital that morning, it hadn't taken long for her to learn she was now able to hear through walls and smell things from far away. The cacophony of conversations rolling around in her head made her dizzy.

Her flesh felt firm and smooth, as if stretched over cool marble. Colors were intensified. She could even smell the droplets of water holding fast to the walls of the clinic's stainless steel sink. Even the wind had a woodsy taste.

The nurse had said things would change, and she would need protein. She was absolutely starved for a burger. All meat. No bun.

She made her way back to her hotel, stopping at a kebab vendor on the way and devouring four skewers of hot lamb. With each step she took, her muscles seemed to expand and harden. The smell of jasmine and lemon blossoms created a heady elixir. She let her hair down to fall over her face and neck, enjoying the sensual caress.

And she was horny as hell.

By the time she made it to the hotel room, she felt like showering again. She stripped and stepped inside the marble alcove, luxuriating in the feel of her own hands caressing her skin as she squeezed her breasts and pretended a dark lover was suckling them. She placed her fingers between her legs and stroked herself, causing spasms to twist her body inside out. As if some dark lover pressed himself against her back, she felt addicted to his scent, the smell of his need of her. Looking behind her, all she saw was steam. Anne wanted him.

Who was this dark fantasy man? Where did this image come from?

The new clothes the nurse at the clinic had given her even smelled like him.

Anne had made up her mind not to get involved with any man until she could heal, but now, in her newly aroused state, she was in need of a man as she never had been. She was steeped in dangerous and wicked thoughts of tasting and *mating*. Not sex, but *mating*, needing it like an animal in heat. She felt stronger than any man she met on the street, but ached for the man that would tame her, breed with her. A dark instinct was gaining dominance over her emotions.

I am in season.

Marcus should have left her alone, but he couldn't. He was drawn to her body just as if there were tethers connecting them, tethers he would gladly wear. Chains even. He didn't care.

But that was a foolish thought.

Having done his duty by seeing her safe return to her hotel, he could have just walked off into the misty streets like any number of gentlemen coming home from a rendezvous. But he couldn't help himself, and instead stood under the blooming pear tree outside her hotel room. He needed to feed in her arousal, bask in her desire. Her scent worked like a homing beacon, a searchlight over the dark and dusty waters of the last three hundred years. He wrapped himself around the lamppost to keep from *tracing* a path to her. He had to be careful. She was not fully available, though he knew she belonged to him. And though it burned a hole in his soul, he stood strong and drank of this bitter cup.

He heard water. Anne was showering. He saw opportunity.

He traced to her bathroom, and, without showing his form, invisibly watched her naked body for the first time. He then wondered how long he'd be able to contain himself but couldn't bring himself to leave.

She bent over, extending her hand to feel the warmth of the water, and then adjusted the brown fluffy curls of her hair with a clip. He would buy her a diamond-encrusted one, he thought. He would be the only one allowed to lace his fingers through her hair and remove that clip and have her locks fall down over his chest as she released herself to him in every way possible.

Her white body glowed like alabaster, evidence of her recent turning. She had strong legs with ample thighs and a bottom plump enough to fondle, to knead into submission. The juncture between her legs was bare, something he hadn't seen in a hundred years, since that woman in France. The lips of her peach dripped with hunger. He could tell they were swollen, needing release. They needed to be suckled.

He watched her raise one leg up over the tiled lip of the shower and disappear into the steamy warmth. She began rubbing her porcelain skin with the lavender-citrus shower gel provided by the hotel. He found himself in front of her as she backed into the showerhead, water cascading down her neck and shoulders. She smoothed the luxurious gel over her slick breasts. And then she reached between her legs and washed her sex.

If you were mine now, you would lie in my arms, covered with my scent. It would bring you pleasure and you would never want it to wash off. Anne, I can give you this . . .

As if she heard him, she smiled, rinsed off, and turned several times, giving him a full view of all of her. He could have taken her twice or three times in the shower. They'd stand there, locked in ecstasy, until the water ran out. Or until they had to feed. And they could do that too, but that would be for the bedroom on the satin sheets he'd picked for that occasion.

His cock was turning to concrete.

She brought a hand to her core and inserted two fingers there. Her mouth opened and her eyes closed as she pleasured herself. He knelt before her, his face just an inch from her sex, his lips opening as his tongue extended and he invisibly swiped a lick from the slit her fingers had invaded. She shuddered and then moaned. She was *feeling* something.

Remove your hands. Let me do it. As if she heard him, she floated her hands to her sides, fingers splayed, and widened her knees to accept his gift.

It took his breath away. *Can she sense me? Does she know I am here?*

It was impossible. But he knew little about the fating process. Perhaps she did sense him after all. He'd had thousands of sexual partners, and the only time this happened was when he was glamouring a human female, trying to help her adjust to his strong sexual needs and size. But he wasn't using his glamour now on Anne, and yet she'd opened herself to him completely.

He inhaled, taking in the scent of her juices, then let his tongue slip aside her pink lips and tasted her bud.

She jumped.

He extended his tongue behind the knob and slid the length inside her labia to the dark passage, where one day he would plant his seed, where he would send his son to be born. He blessed her with a kiss and a prayer, charming her body to accept the gifts he would bring her. The thick cream she gave him tasted like honey and lemons. In that instant, he almost felt like he could live off it.

"Oh, yes," she sighed. "Oh, my God, yes."

You are mine, Anne. Soon. You will be mine.

His own erection was causing him pain. His thick cock was thrusting against his wet breeches, begging to be released. Marcus knew it would have to wait, but how much longer? His member stiffly disobeyed, and he knew it would be strong enough to rip the fabric of his pants. If the head of his penis came in contact with her opening, there would be nothing he could do but plunge in. And then he would have sacrificed both of them for his own desire.

Abruptly, he pulled away from the shower, turned his back to her, and exited to the hallway, then stood and waited for her. He stared at the closed bathroom door between them like it was a twelve-foot stone fence.

Done with her shower, she walked naked from the bathroom, unconscious of how she delighted him. He was jealous of the thirsty pink towel she tamped all over her skin. He could hear the hairs of her forearms press back as she rubbed and damp dried herself. In the mirror over the dresser, she examined her pert nipples, pinching herself and feeling the weight of each bosom in her palms.

And then she climbed onto the bed. Marcus could still taste her peach, which was now displayed before him as she crawled to a mound of pillows at the headboard. He had to adjust his pants as his erection was near erupting, demanding fulfillment.

Marcus watched her ass rise up and then lower slowly down, as if she was dreaming of riding his shaft and sliding down the length of him, feeling every inch penetrate slowly. She settled on the bed sheets, and, mercifully, fell asleep. Had she not, he might have had violated her, violated their eternity together.

He traced back outside and stood, looking up to the window but still feeling her pink lips on his tongue.

Dangerous. He wondered if he could speed up the process, have her come to him early, but still make it a natural selection. He would have to be careful. Eternity was at stake.

CHAPTER 4

Anne could not believe the changes going on in her body. She could hear things streets away. The conversations blended over each other and confused her. She heard the breath of little birds and the scratch of insects climbing up tree limbs.

But the biggest problem for her was her insatiable appetite for raw meat. Her first purchase, cold calf liver, she ate so quickly she left bloody stains down the front of her shirt and scared passersby. She quickly bought a T-shirt at a local vendor and made it home to the motel room before the stains could bleed through.

The obsession to feed also kept her awake. She couldn't sleep, and when she did, dreams haunted her and made her waken, her body tingling as if remembering the touch of a lover.

She knew she was not human.

But a vampire?

No. She decided the answer was no.

Have I contracted some blood disease?

Perhaps the clinic wasn't what it was supposed to be. Perhaps the drug the nurse had given her didn't work properly and was too weak against the raging disease taking over her body. She decided she would get fully sated, give in to the desire to feed, and then go in search of the clinic and see if she could get some answers.

She heard the heartbeat of every person she passed on the street. Even children. She found herself attracted to men her own age. Her eyes involuntarily flirted with them, made them stop, check her out.

And she found she liked it.

She felt powerful. Unafraid. Unsure what was to come, but stronger than she had ever been in her life, and capable of defending herself against anyone.

She gave up her quest to find the clinic, winding around the narrow streets and seeing building after building that looked familiar, then rounding a bend and finding herself lost again. She looked for the little church, but couldn't locate it.

Resigned to follow her itinerary, she began her trip along the Riviera, traveling the narrow highway and switchbacks, overlooking the blue water of the Mediterranean speckled with boats. She stopped to buy meat every few hours. The more she ate, the clearer her vision became and the easier it was for her to tune out conversations so she could understand what was being said around her.

One morning she woke up next to a man in a strange apartment. One look at his fully clothed body and she knew they had not had sex. But his neck lay at a strange angle, and two dark puncture wounds invaded the flesh above his jugular. She knew.

I have killed. I have become a . . . a . . . vampire.

She was filled with disgust. But as she looked at her face in the bathroom mirror, her skin had taken on a glow unlike one she'd ever seen. Her hair was shiny. Her lips were dark red, her breasts felt full.

She felt satisfied. The urge to feed had lessened. But the urge to mate remained.

Marcus was summoned three days later. He had been discretely watching Anne as she made her way along the Riviera, and wasn't of a mind to leave her side yet. He could smell her attraction for other men and it pained him a little.

At first, he was concerned when she did not feed. He watched as she gulped down several ounces of raw liver at the *boucherie* in Nice in front of a horrified tourist crowd. Anne took no notice of this, which was how he knew she was unsatisfied. She counted sailboats at the harbor, counted pigeons in the church squares. She busied herself with visiting every chapel and church that called to her with bells, like she was summoned. And in a way she was. She was searching.

Is she searching for me?

He was greatly relieved when she finally did take her first feeding just before leaving France. And then the next night she did it again, although she seemed to enjoy feeding from younger, attractive men.

But after her feedings, the nights belonged to him. He waited until sleep overtook her, and then he traced next to her body and pleasured her with fingers and lips and his tongue. He used glam to keep her in an aroused sleep while he satisfied her sexual urges without sex. Marcus paid no mind to the fact that his sexual urges were going unfulfilled; he needed to make sure she was spent. He did not want her doing something she would regret, now that she fed. Now that she was so close to strange men every day.

Marcus felt he could travel now, go back to Italy to face the Council. They had not been forthcoming with their reasons for his summons, but he knew it was not good. And their timing was horrible.

Maya was seated in the large chair before the Praetor's desk. A vacant chair next to her was where Marcus had been instructed to sit. Maya's face was beautiful, as always. She maintained a smug smile and cool demeanor. Obviously, she had spoken to the Praetor and had worked something out with him beforehand. This didn't bode well for Marcus.

Praetor Artemis was not in a jovial mood. He was a few years older than Marcus in terms of appearance but was in reality easily three hundred years older. He had strikingly good looks and an impressive countenance, which felled the ladies right and left. He had been wise to steer clear of Maya, but on force of personality, they were a match. He also had never taken a fated female, enjoying every available unattached female, and it was rumored he'd slept with some of the council wives as well. Not that anyone would tell.

"Marcus, Maya has brought something to my attention. Naturally, affairs of the heart are private matters between two people." He attempted a smile. "I try not to get involved in things I am not a direct party to."

"I see." Marcus hoped his eyes showed Maya he was completely cold to her. He masked even his anger.

"The boy is now almost six years old," Praetor Artemis continued, directing his attention to Marcus, "yet you have not publically taken responsibility for him. He has known you, but as a friend of his mother's. He perhaps has some inkling of who you really are."

Maya's face was radiant. Marcus noted how someone else's bad news seemed to be good for her. His bad news. She gave him a devoted, sufficiently demure smile. His stomach churned. He wanted to sink his fingers into her neck and rip her throat out.

"It is time the boy got to know his father. It is time you acknowledged the fate between you two."

"I will not. I am not ready."

"Yes, Maya has told me just a week ago you met with Jacobi and had made arrangements for the ceremony at the Chapel. Why was this not acted upon?"

"Praetor, I do not wish to cause you or the boy or Maya any pain."

This seemed to distress Praetor Artemis. His eyebrows drew down in a frown. "Well then, what is the problem?"

"Maya has told me we are fated, yet I don't feel it."

"But she bled for you, bore you a child."

"I admit to having fondness for Maya and the boy." He lied about his feelings for her, but the boy was sweet and did look just like him. "But I have not felt the fate as she does."

"The bleeding is never wrong."

"I have no explanation for it. But I have found my fated female, and I believe Maya has hidden this fact from you."

Her eyes went red with anger. She stood abruptly. "What the hell is this? How dare you say this to me?"

"Maya, sit. I must hear him out." The Praetor was upset as well. "We will get to the bottom of it immediately." He motioned for Marcus to continue.

"I was preparing to meet or address the fate put upon me, one I did not feel. But, as you have said, much time has gone by and the boy is growing up. I had resigned myself to accepting the responsibility of claiming him into my household, and take Maya as well—"

"You act as if you are taking in a charity case," Maya yelled. "I bore your son! Your son! No one ever forced you to bed me. You bed me several times a day for years. It must not have been too unpleasant. You are a dog, but you will pay for your cowardice."

"It isn't cowardice. I don't feel you and I are fated. I enjoyed our time together, but never thought we were fated lovers. And I never took from you or made the oath."

"Is this true, Maya?" the Praetor asked.

"I told him when I bled. I told him I was pregnant with his child. We were exclusive unto each other, or, at least that's what he told me. I thought in time he would bring the oath and take from me. I thought he was a man of honor. Apparently, I was wrong. But my son is paying the price. Our son, Marcus! How can you be so cruel?"

Marcus did feel for the boy. He could have been a father to him, but now there was Anne. "Maybe there is something wrong with me, but I believe I am fated to another. Maya knows this. She tried to kill her."

"Tried?" Maya's face went white.

"She practically drained her," Marcus said, his voice cracking from the emotion.

"Maya fed on your fated female? How did this occur?" Praetor Artemis looked back and forth between the couple.

"You thought you ended her life. But she lives." Marcus was not happy to reveal this obvious surprise to her. But it had to be done.

"You turned that little trollop? You did it just to avoid your responsibility. Does she now bleed? Were you going to tell the Praetor and me that you made two women bleed for you, Marcus?"

"No. She has not adjusted. She is married to a mortal and I will not interfere with her vow of marriage."

"This complicates things. How was it, Maya, you fed from her?"

"Tell him, Maya." Marcus smiled for the first time. "Tell him what you saw."

"She came into the chapel while we were talking with Jacobi. She must have been lost, and so stupid to go out alone, unprotected." She flashed a hard look at Marcus. "I followed her. I took her in an alleyway. I was hungry." She sent her chin out in a huff.

"Ask Jacobi," Marcus responded. "I saw this woman and I immediately told both of them I felt the fate come over me. I declared it. Maya tried to destroy her. She tried to come between her and me. That carries with it punishment. I ask that I be released from this obligation to Maya and the boy in exchange for this violation. I need to sort out my true feelings for this woman, and her for me."

Praetor Artemis nodded his head and scratched his chin.

"You cannot be serious, Praetor Artemis. This is blasphemy!" Maya spat out.

Marcus tried one more time. "You have my word. If it is not meant to be, I will return to Maya, and, if she will have me, I will accept the oath."

It had been decided after a meeting of the Council that Marcus would have to wait one month after Anne's turning before making himself visible to her. And he would have to verify she intended to be divorced. Affairs of the heart were always given a cooling off period, and one month was a mere flick of the eye to the immortal golden vampires.

Marcus agreed to allow the child to live in his home in a shared custody arrangement but refused to live with Maya. He would begin to father him, train him, as a proper father should. This part would not be difficult to do. He had genuine feelings for the boy.

But more importantly, Maya was permanently bridled, enjoined from doing any harm to Anne on pain of death. She was furious with this decision and Marcus knew she would do everything in her power to bend the rules to suit her liberal interpretation of them. Although not accepted into her new family, Anne was a now a golden vampire, one of the rarest breeds in the universe, and had to be protected at all costs since Marcus could not interfere with her life.

He could not wait until he could get back to Anne and make sure her habits weren't getting her into trouble. Although vampire, she was still an innocent, and it would be days before he could begin to properly train her. He traced to the Island of Majorca, where Anne had rented a room in a converted monastery, which was now a hotel.

Yet, he still wondered about the boy and Maya's bleeding. No, blood was never wrong. There was no precedent anywhere that Marcus could remember where one man had been fated to two females. Try as he could, he just didn't feel anything for Maya.

He put the worry aside as he anticipated finding his female again. He was counting the minutes until he could appear to her in the flesh. Would she recognize the fating as he had?

So much to look forward to.

Just twenty-one days to go.

CHAPTER 5

Robert bolted up in bed. Something was wrong. Sun streamed in through the windows of the dingy motel room like an unkind nurse had switched the light on for an unwelcomed evaluation. He had no idea where he was. Didn't remember checking into the place. He waited for a minute, listening, waiting for who knows what, and then he realized it. His neck hurt like a son of a bitch.

He rolled out of bed and felt the back of his throbbing neck. His fingers came back bloody.

Now what the fuck happened?

With his left hand, he rubbed just under the hairline and found that area swollen, tender, and probably black and blue. The front of his neck was bulging with little bumps too.

I don't remember a goddamned thing about this.

It was a week after the disastrous wedding. He was beginning to get tired of Monika's constant begging for his time, although at first he'd been thrilled. They'd had a little row, so he and Gary had gone to the topless bar and picked up a couple of girls. He'd spent the night with the dark-haired one. At least, he thought he had. Surprised to see the bed sheets stained with spatters of blood, he mumbled to himself, "Whose blood is that? Mine?"

The girl's side of the bed wasn't even warm. She'd ditched him. He didn't even remember falling asleep. Could he have hurt her? Could the blood be partially hers?

This was way over the top. Things were getting stranger by the minute.

He heard a sound from the bathroom and wondered if perhaps she was still there. He walked on tiptoes, naked, to the bathroom, then stood still. Christ. Even his pecker was sore.

Overuse.

He couldn't remember how many times he came. It was like he'd gone going in and out of a drunken stupor. The girl was insatiable, he remembered that. He couldn't remember her name or even what she looked like, except for those red lips and a funny smile. And she liked to lick him . . . in places. If she was in the bathroom, would she look like some of the girls he used to pick up in a dark bar who were uglier than sin the next morning in the light of day?

Robert, you need help.

The bathroom door squeaked open from a gentle touch of his palm and he found the source of the noise. A cotton curtain flapped in the breeze of an open window.

His shoulders dropped as he sighed, scratched his scalp at the back of his head, and endured the dull pain.

If any of the boys heard about this, they'd have thought he had a guardian angel. What any one of them wouldn't give for a woman like his date last night, what's-her-name hot pants. Totally horny, easily turned on by the slightest little thing he did. It really was too much, he thought as he stepped into the bathroom.

And then he looked in the mirror.

The front of his neck was red, scarred with little red bumps. Then he turned to the right and was horrified to see large purple hickies the size of his thumb all around the backside of his neck, extending well down to his shoulders. He knew she'd been extra frisky, but he hadn't felt the pain. She had sucked and almost bit him.

Fuck me! There was something not right about this. And then he wondered, what would Monika say? What about Anne?

But of course, it was too late for Anne.

He'd have to get some Neosporin. The wounds on his neck were getting uglier as the minutes drew by.

I'm in some kind of time warp. So much has changed . . .

Just a week ago, on the night before their wedding, the night of Robert's now-infamous bachelor party, he felt lucky to have gotten Anne to marry him.

He'd nailed her on their first date two years before, something of a ritual for him with his sexual partners. But Anne was a keeper. He always knew he would treat his keeper different from his other, former girlfriends. She had a healthy sexual appetite, although still not his equal. But she was innovative, and although inexperienced, willing to learn. He liked that in a woman. In time, she would make a real honest-to-goodness sexual siren, and probably would stay that way even after they had kids. The thought thrilled him.

The years during their courtship and engagement were some of the best of his life. He was halfway convinced he would be able to be faithful to her. This was something that had eluded him before in all his other relationships. But Anne was a better person. He hoped some of her goodness would rub off on him.

Not that he was completely faithful to her during their engagement, which was something he saw as a warm-up to marriage, not necessarily a commitment. He'd tried, he told himself. He really had tried. But he seriously thought it would be impossible to be a one-woman man until his marriage. And then, well, he would see.

He looked in the mirror and was embarrassed to admit his faithfulness had not lasted more than a blink of an eye.

"Too much excess. Got to stop drinking. Need some new friends," he said to his reflection. Gary was pulling him down. Monika too.

Making me do stuff I think twice about later. It was like he was an unruly teenager all over again, now in his late twenties.

Why?

Robert opened a plastic bottle of water on the cheap dresser and took stock of his situation as he swirled down the cool liquid, satisfying his parched throat. He had a strange metallic taste in his mouth for some reason. Images of his bachelor party surfaced. He chuckled and let them flood over him.

He had been showing the guys brochures about their trip planned along the Mediterranean. It had been Anne's lifelong dream. They would pick up a car in Genoa and drive all the way to Spain. They would spend the last week in Majorca at a converted monastery, once owned by a Hollywood couple.

His old girlfriend, Monika, had dropped by the house. Well, she wasn't really his "old" girlfriend, since he'd fucked her the week before and just about every week before that.

The party was just beginning and Monika was game, so she went along with the eight of them. Not before everyone was sworn to secrecy, of course. In exchange, Monika promised to do them all—so everyone would be in trouble together.

Only thing Robert insisted on was that they all wear condoms. No telling where some of his friends had been. No need to tempt fate. That would be just stupid. He was pretty sure Monika was a very bad girl as well. He did not want to bring an unnecessary wrinkle to his new bride's beautiful forehead.

His best man and the other friends at the party were happy for him. He knew they all doubted this marriage would work out. But Anne trusted him. And as long as she didn't find out about his activities, and so far Robert didn't think she did, she would continue to trust him.

After all, he did love her.

Robert was notorious for his dumping scenes, and the makeup sex that could go on sometimes for weeks before the final straw. And that usually happened when the girl found out there had been someone else all along. His friends had warned him about Anne, that she wouldn't be so easy to fool. He was convinced this was "it" and committed to making the rest of his life more meaningful than the first part.

But he didn't see why that night he couldn't have a little fun. After all, he was not yet a married man. Almost, but not quite.

The black limo pulled up and one of his groomsmen shouted out they were ready to leave. Robert had just taken his prearranged place with Monika, which was first. His cock fully sheathed and ready to pump into her. No way he would be denied. He wasn't going to waste a perfectly good cherry flavored condom just because the driver was five minutes early.

When Gary opened the door to make sure Robert heard the call, he found the groom riding her hard. Gary got the finger for his efforts.

"Unless you want to jump in, get the fuck out. Have him drive around the block, twice," was Robert's response. Monika's breasts were bouncing as he pumped her. He loved the way her little soft pillows of flesh rippled with each thrust.

Gary gave the instruction and the room was cleared with a clamoring of hoots and hollers and heavy footsteps down the stairs. Then Gary came back to the room and stripped off his shirt.

"Monika, honey," Gary began, "this cowboy might get you off, but I'm gonna make you sing. You deserve better."

"Oh, that's right Gary," she teased. "Give the groom a little competition. I like him all hot and bothered and trying real hard. Ah . . . I feel him rising to the challenge. Oh. That's nice, baby."

Robert grunted as he stroked her, turning her to her side for deeper access, one of her legs over his shoulder. "You bet your sweet ass. You want more of me? Can you handle more of me?"

"Look what you'll be missing. I'll be fucking all your friends, Robbie. Just think about me every day. I'll be fucking them while you are on your honeymoon. I'll be so sore I can barely walk. We'll compare notes when you're back." She locked lips with Robert, who kept thrusting. Their private conversation was too soft for Gary to hear, so he stepped closer. Monika held out her hand.

Gary presented his cock and she grabbed it, squeezing him hard. She leaned over and put him in her mouth.

"Hey, Robert. Wanna flip her over so I can get a little more action, if you don't mind?"

With a big hand under Monika's belly, Robert flipped her forward and then entered her from behind. He left his hand between her legs to finger her clit. She moaned long and hard.

"Oh, here it comes, sweet cheeks." Robert said to her ear as he pulled her onto him. "I used to call you 'Moana.'" Robert leaned over, "Make that sound for me, baby."

She did.

"Come moan all over me, Moana," Gary said as he thrust his cock into her mouth. The two friends faced each other and grinned.

"Hey, this is the best, man." Gary said.

"Nothing better. If the girl's willing," Robert lowered his face to Monika's ear again, "and Miss Moana is always willing"—which elicited a shriek—"isn't she?"

"Oh, yes. Oh, yes. Oh, God," Monika mumbled through her sucking lips.

"Don't tell me, sweetheart, show me," Gary whined. His blond hair and big white teeth made him look the part of the lifeguard he was. "Oh, man, you have a nice tongue." His fingers were clutching her red hair, which fell long and loose over his thighs.

Robert began to shudder, thrusting to finish.

"There it goes. Your last fuck as a single guy." Gary said to Robert's grimacing face. He lowered the tone of his voice as he addressed her. "Monika, honey, you get off? I want to be sure you got off."

She moaned.

Robert looked at her ass as he pulled out. He would miss that ass. "Yea, I'm pretty sure she got off. She just can't talk on account she's got her mouth full." He went into the bathroom to freshen up.

Gary was getting close.

"You want it in the ass?"

"No!" Monika suddenly rose up to her knees. Gary took the opportunity to grab her breasts.

"You know, honey, no reason you need to get dressed tonight," he said as he squeezed and pinched her nipples. "You got eight guys gonna keep you real warm. I might have you twice, if you're nice. And I think you're real nice."

"Shut up and fuck me."

"Never argue with a lady." Gary muttered. He grabbed the box of condoms and prepared himself. Monika rolled over to her back and he began his vigil. Foreplay wasn't necessary, as the limo was honking downstairs.

Robert came back, towel in hand, rubbing his crotch. He stroked himself a few times, watching Gary and Monika, but he couldn't get hard, so he dropped the towel in the bathroom and got dressed. He watched them the whole time.

"I'm giving pointers, Monika," Gary rasped. "Notice what a difference the size makes?"

"Uh hum," was all she could say. She watched Robert as he dressed. The groom understood from the look in her eyes that she had wanted to be the bride. He saw a tear or two before she managed to wipe them away without Gary seeing them. This private moment touched something in Robert's heart, and surprised him.

"You're a good girl, Monika, honey. Thank you. That was real nice." Robert smiled. He meant every word. He walked out to the living room. "Any century now will do, Gary. I'm waiting down at the limo."

He was greeted with cheers. There was a triple-X DVD playing and the guys had popped some champagne and beer. He crawled in front by the driver.

"Hey, Charles. Thanks for taking us out tonight."

"No problem, Mr. B. Are we all here, then?" The driver had been on assignment for several of their parties.

"No. Gary's coming, and there's the girl."

"Right."

Noise erupted from the back at the sight of Gary, who strode fully clothed from the house but tugging a bare-footed Monika along, who wore only one of Robert's shirts buttoned halfway up the front. Robert looked at her nice legs and pink toes and sighed. The driver chuckled.

"Looks like you're gonna have a little fun too," Robert said to the driver.

"Oh, no, I don't touch the merchandise when I'm on duty."

"But you can look, right? She likes it when you look."

The driver laughed again. "Yeah, I can look. That's my favorite part nowadays. I'm happily married."

"Yup. That'll be me tomorrow. But not tonight." Robert punched the driver in the arm and went to join his friends in the back.

Monika was already on another lap. The sound of a belt buckle clanged as they sped off to the topless bar.

When they pulled back to the house at five AM, Monika was asleep in the back, curled up into a ball. Half the party was asleep too, overcome with alcohol and excesses of the evening. The coke had run out. Time to go to bed for a couple of hours.

Robert picked Monika up and carried her inside. Gary made a space for her on the couch but Robert went right past him to the bedroom and closed the door.

Yeah, he'd been an idiot, he thought. Anne's brother practically decked him the day of the wedding after the bride left in their limo. Gary got so ripped he knocked over the cake, not that there were many guests left to eat it. The DJ kept playing like the orchestra on the Titanic. The place looked deserted. To make matters worse, he caught Monika in a lip-lock with some dark caveman who liked to dance the bear hug. She'd fainted in his arms and the guys laid her on a settee in the dressing room, in her blue maid of honor dress. Too much champagne, he thought. They'd all nearly left her there passed out.

But he'd gone back and brought her to Anne's house. *That* sexual liaison he remembered. Vividly. Unhurried, like the one earlier in the day in the bathroom, but just as urgent. God, he loved fucking Monika. And in a way, Monika made him a better man too. He didn't feel dirty for loving her, and he knew he truly did. Hell, he loved them both.

And then Anne had walked in. He never wanted to see his lovely Anne look at him like that again. Woke him up from the fantasy that he could just go along without making a choice. Saw the reality of the pain he'd caused everyone.

He thought about her place. He'd always liked it there. Maybe she would give him another chance, although he admitted he didn't deserve one. Anne was looking more attractive the less available she was. He began to think he was budding a conscience.

Something messed up with that.

He'd have to mend his ways. Maybe start going to meetings again.

Fuck that.

He knew he was slipping into an abyss. Now it was getting dangerous, and bloody.

Robert shook his head and swore under his breath, slammed his palm down on the coffee tabletop.

He was forgetting things, too. First, he'd cheated on his wife, and now last night he had cheated on Monika. He was going to have to figure out what exactly he wanted and stick to the plan. Getting Anne back was Plan A. But he knew he had a much better chance with Plan B.

CHAPTER 6

Anne opened the heavy wooden door to her room, a converted cell in an old monastery. The Majorcan summer night air was warm and fragrant. Maybe she could float. *Something to try another time.* Just five days into her change and she was still getting used to her new self. Tonight she needed to feed—a need that would not be denied or it could get dangerous. And bloody.

She loved the sounds her feet made as she lightly skipped along the moon-lit cobblestoned street. The cool smell of dusty stone houses was pleasant.

She could even smell blooming jasmine and orange blossoms from miles away. She was still adjusting to the sensory overload that was now her daily challenge. Pulling a deep purple satin cape about her neck, she drifted down the cobblestoned streets of the village, high atop the hills. If it weren't two in the morning, she would be able to see the ocean, but she could smell its salty air. The unmistakable rusty scent of blood arrived not thirty yards in front of her.

Men.

A whole group of them. Young. Virile. In their peak of health. Her favorite kind.

Her first few attempts to feed had been pathetic failures, and she'd barely enough to satisfy her needs. She'd ruined clothes until she learned she could get her feeding done as they were showering.

She didn't have the desire to kill, just to feed, but her first few attempts ended in death for the human, sadly. If she took someone expendable, like a street drunk, she could get high from the alcohol, or worse, from the drugs in their system. And she hated eating while the smell of urine, vomit, and weeks-old human sweat filled her nostrils. She had indeed been cursed those first few days until she learned how to leave the humans alive. Then she discovered several other things she liked about her new form.

For the first time in her life, she wasn't afraid of anything. She was able to process every little detail of a scene, even down to the smallest pebble. She could hear the footsteps of small bugs that lived under rocks and the whir of bee wings, the language of crickets and mating calls of frogs in the rain. Liberated from all her doubts and concerns for her own safety, she felt sexual arousal constantly, especially when she caught a particular scent that lingered near her. She'd been aware of it in her bed, in her shower. She'd feel it curl around her like arms of a lover and she'd basked in the tingly feeling it brought her ultrasensitive skin.

She had no idea what kind of being she had turned into. One thing she knew for sure, she certainly was not human.

She studied the five handsome twenty-something young men who stood before her, probably out for a night of dancing and drinking. Anne sensed they were looking to satisfy their sexual appetites. That worked.

She picked out the tallest, and handsomest male in the group. The alpha, she thought. He was so sexy the way his confident, loose gait carried his muscular body straight to her. His dark brown bedroom eyes perused her over, and yes, she had to admit, her nipples tightened so hard they hurt, and she felt the delicious wetness in her panties as her sex vibrated to life.

Hands on her hips, she smiled back at him. The others hung slightly back, gawking. This alpha was the stud, the legendary one.

Perfect.

"Hi there," she whispered. The boys were animated. They registered she was an American and spoke among themselves.

Alpha rubbed his palm against his chin, then swiped his fingers across his lips and made no mystery of focusing on her cleavage. Anne flushed at the attention. She was hungry too.

"It is late and you are alone in a dangerous place," he said in English with a thick Spanish accent. She liked the way his Adam's apple bounced up and down his tanned throat as he spoke.

"But I've found you. Will you save me?"

His friends laughed enthusiastically. Alpha was wary. "You do not look like a professional—"

Anne urgently stepped to him, then rubbed her breasts against his clean white shirt opened two buttons too low. She noticed the golden cross tucked in his dark chest hair. "I am not a professional," she said, "but are you?"

The boys roared. Whistles and catcalls laced the air. Alpha searched the smiling faces of his compadres, who encouraged him. At last, he inhaled and took a long, slow look into her eyes, then dropped his gaze down to her chest. His half smile showed a delicious dimple on the right. In a husky voice he answered, "It has been said a time or two."

This was good news. She craved him even more for his bravado. She saw the flush cover his face and the rush of blood heading down to his groin. The scent of his blood was laced with tangerines and red wine. He stood tall, his chest extended, showing her he was all male, that he was capable of pleasuring her in surprising ways. She liked that.

Without taking her eyes off his, she extended her hand. She touched his cheek and watched it deliciously flush his skin again. Then she moved her palm to rest at the side of his neck, underneath his muscled jaw line. His pulse was strong and intoxicating.

"Can you show me around and then take me home? Are you up for that?" She rubbed the length of him with her other hand, ignoring the whoops and hollers of the other boys. He stood before her, caught in the web of her glamour, every delicious drop in his body trying to jump ship. Her effect on him was obvious: he would do anything she wanted him to do to pleasure her.

Anything.

Marcus stood alone in the shadows, fully cloaked, and hung back well away from the crowd. He watched Anne lean in and kiss the tall male. As difficult as it was, he couldn't take his eyes off her. His hands fisted as he saw the male place his palms against her backside, and then creep into and under her wrap to find her flesh.

She is mine.

The erection in his pants was getting uncomfortable. He could send an erotic wave toward her and make her so horny she'd ignore the stranger and run up the little hill, straight into his arms, where he could finally claim her.

Anne and the young Spaniard were fully engulfed in a deep kiss, exploring each other's bodies. The young man's group moved away, clearing their throats and making whistling noises, but getting no response from their tall friend. The group evaporated into the streets. Anne and the large male were alone, surrounded by warm night air. Would she remove some of her clothing? Show herself to him before she took his blood? Marcus hoped not, but knew well about the new erotic forces making her do things she wasn't used to.

Either way, he was bound by duty not to interfere. This was to be his curse of the moment. All he could do was watch. She was a married woman, and the possession of another man. A mortal man who didn't deserve the heavenly gift of her body and all its charms, someone incapable of understanding what her needs were or that she was created for a higher, more powerful love. A love only Marcus could give her.

The male nuzzled her breasts. For one brief moment Marcus saw the magic of her flesh exposed to him in the moonlight, saw the beautiful mound, now glistening wet from the stranger's probing tongue.

She lets him have his way with her. Will she open her other parts to him as well? Marcus was filled with unspeakable sadness. He had to do something.

He double-checked his cloaking, then moved to stand behind her and was immediately charmed by her sweet vanilla scent, which brought his groin to life. He reached an invisible hand to her shoulder, to touch her there, or perhaps her neck, to feel the fullness of her soft dark brown curls, to beg her to feed from him instead. Her name stuck in his throat and he whispered what only he could hear, "Anne."

The ache in his chest intensified as he smelled her arousal. He placed his lips to her ear and pretended she could hear him tell her of his need for her. Of his centuries spent waiting, longing for the one woman created for him. His fated female. Marcus needed to pour out his melancholy so he could purge himself forever of this burden.

You are here at last. See me, Anne. See and feel me. Feel how I love you, have always loved you.

He wanted to think her sigh and the sultry smile on her lips came because she somehow knew her fated male stood behind her, ready to open the doors to their love, arousing her need to partake of the ancient ritual for their kind.

The male was expecting sex, and he had shoved her skirts up, seeking her core with his long fingers. This was to be Marcus's right. He felt her swoon as the man's finger traced over her pleasure button. He could smell her wetness, her need for sexual release.

He whispered to himself again. *Anne, it is I you need. Let it be me who pleasures you, makes you moan hour-by-hour, day-by-day. Let it be me you crave more than the blood in any vein. Crave my blood, Anne. Drink of me, and let me fill you with eternal pleasure. It is our fate. Our destiny together.*

Marcus felt the hunger for blood rise in her chest, the smell of the glamour that came on just before the feeding. It would calm the human, would transform the bite into a memory, make the male think he had the best sex of his young life instead of what it really was.

She came at his neck with fierce determination. She was so beautiful. So strong. So demanding. And Marcus knew he could meet every one of her demands. Only he could do it, he thought as she brought her thigh up over the male's hip. They collapsed to the ground. Marcus kneeled at her back, rested his head there and smelled the scent of her flesh, listening to the blood from this male rush in to fill her cavities, bringing her strength, life.

Yes. Make yourself strong. Take the blood and join me forever.

He had waited three hundred years. He could wait just a little more. But just a little.

Anne felt aroused and unsatisfied, even though her craving to feed had subsided. Something about the dark young man in her arms sparked a tender chord in her heart. She brushed the curly hair from his neck and licked the two puncture wounds there, following it up with a kiss. She'd discovered yesterday if she licked any wound, it would heal immediately. It was a nifty trick.

This young stallion was delicious—in every sense of the word. His chest rose and fell, the golden cross glinting in the moonlight like the delicate twinkle of an angel's kiss. Her fingers scanned his full red lips as she looked into his closed eyes.

He would wake up soon, probably with a hard-on, and, as she confirmed this, he started to stir. She undid his button fly and slid his pants down one hip, then raised her skirts so he would think they had just been intimate. As she felt his hardness against her abdomen, she found she did feel intense desire. But it wasn't for him, exactly. And it wasn't for Robert either.

He awakened. She smiled, giving him the satisfied glamour of a woman who had been pleasured by a skillful lover. "Thank you," she said, and kissed him.

His fingers gripped her skirts, drawing her against his groin. "Uno mas," he whispered, *one more time.* He buried his head between her breasts, which were flaming hot with desire.

"Lover, as much as I want to, I can't. I must go before my husband misses me." She displayed her ring.

It was a lie, but she didn't need entanglements.

Pain registered in his face, sending a frown and a worry line between his eyebrows. His silky lashes glistened as he squeezed her breast and took in his last look at her warm flesh.

"Where are you staying, then? I must see you again," he whispered to her chest. He groaned and pushed his cock against the black lace panties she wore, dangerously tempting her.

She was not going to have sex with this tall, dark Adonis of a man, even though he looked at her in a way that thrilled her. She would need another feeding tomorrow. The timing would work out nicely for her.

"I will meet you tomorrow night, if you like, but not late. I'll meet you here at six, after dinner."

He threw his head back and laughed. "Dinner? I don't eat until nine or ten." He kissed her apple-shaped breast, licked her bottom lip, and then covered her mouth. "But I will meet you here tomorrow night, and take you to dinner afterwards," he whispered between kisses. "We will dance with the gypsies, and then I will take you to my bed, and—"

"Do you have a shower?" she interrupted.

"Of course."

"Good. You will take me to your place, and then I must leave. I go to bed early and leave the next morning. Sorry."

Now it was her time to frown and kiss his right temple. His pulse roared back strong, nearly recovered. She saw visions of feeding on him while he pleasured her with his cock, of her allowing him to feed on her. She was wet all over again as a little orgasm tickled her insides.

So it was arranged and they kissed as he thanked her for the evening of sex he thought he had. He reluctantly let her go, lingering and begging one more time, which Anne sidestepped with a sweet kiss. She was thrilled she could take a wet feeding in the shower tomorrow. No mess that way, but no sex either. The thrill of being naked with him fueled anticipation. It would be the first time she'd feasted on someone for the second time.

He watched her adjust her skirts and re-button her bodice, but at the last minute tore it open to feast on her breasts again. He would have been a wonderful lover, she thought, if that were what she was looking for.

Am I looking for something? Someone?

Yes, she thought. She was certain it wasn't her husband, and it couldn't be this young stranger.

But who?

So many things had changed. She wasn't afraid as she walked through the wet streets all alone. She heard people inside rooms eating food, arguing and making love. She heard children snoring in their beds. Dogs barked as she passed and she found if she sent them a gentle message they would quiet.

Very odd. But not unpleasant.

She found it easy to run up the narrow steps to the room. She used her heavy iron key to unlock the door, which groaned open. In the dark, she undressed. Did she see a figure standing below under a streetlamp, perhaps looking up at her?

She blinked, rubbed her eyes, but this time all she saw was a swirling white steam coming from a grate embedded in the stone sidewalk.

Anne slipped into the sheets naked, loving the sensation of cloth against bare skin. She pinched her nipples and turned her face to the light of the streetlamp. Her sexual need was driving her crazy.

Perhaps I'll let him tomorrow. I'll try feeding and fucking at the same time.

As she scanned the room in the early morning hours, hoping for another erotic dream to overtake her, she suddenly felt sleepy, as if a warm breeze had floated over the back of her neck. She felt protected, as if arms held her warm and secure. She would live forever. She could live and die in his arms. Whoever *he* was.

Marcus had been standing outside the Monastery Hotel under a streetlamp when he saw her figure in the darkened window. His body absorbed the swirling white misty air, hiding him from her sight.

He'd made sure she got home safely, walking behind her as tears streamed down his face with need as he'd smelled her arousal and knew he could satisfy her. As she prepared for bed, he traced to the Spanish lad, her intended meal for tomorrow, and made sure he would not be physically able to keep his appointment with Anne. Then he'd come to her as she lay naked and full of desire. He'd pleasured her until she said those words that haunted him now:

"Take me."

And he very nearly had, too. He'd sucked at her peach and vibrated her core with his tongue, making her come, and beg for more.

Her sexual appetite was growing by the day. He knew it wouldn't take long before he would no longer be able to satisfy her with just oral sex. She wanted *him*.

He would make sure tomorrow's feeding, the last before her trip back to America, would not take place. He had disabled the young Spaniard—not permanently, but enough so that he wouldn't be able to keep his appointment. Anne would have to feed on a stranger.

As he lay invisibly spooned behind her, awash in the scent of her flesh, her hair, her juices, he reminded himself to be careful and not get too carried away, though his animal side was rattling the cage to get out. He sighed and placed a gentle kiss on the back of her neck.

How in the world am I going to last another twenty days?

Marcus was good as his word. Anne returned to California and he continued to check up on her by day and appear, like in a dream, at night.

He purchased an estate property, suitable for royalty, in the countryside north of her, with over a thousand acres of some of the finest grapes in the valley. He brought the boy Lucius with him, and started his instruction by telling him of the ancient stories. About fating. About the blood. About the choice he would take at puberty whether or not to turn vampire or remain human. He treated the boy as his own. It helped to pass the time until he could contact her and appear in person.

And on the thirtieth day from the imposition set by the directive, he stood in line behind Anne at Starbucks, hopeful he could now put an end to a bitter-sweet chapter in his life and open a new one. A chapter that would bring him joy and all the wishes his heart desired.

He hoped.

CHAPTER 7

"Does your husband know about your appetites?" From behind Anne came a gravelly male voice that sent shivers down her spine. The screams of the Starbuck's espresso machine made her wonder if she'd really heard the voice. But the male scent of him was impossible to miss. The hairs at her neck stood at attention, telegraphing urgency. The sensation extended well beyond her waistline. Time stood still before she could bring herself to turn around and fall under the warm gaze from this tall dark male that covered her.

Not man. Male.

He held her gaze as she stood, transfixed, unable to move or to speak. That was the way it felt. Being held. "I'm sorry?" she blurted out finally.

"Don't be sorry, my dear. It's a simple question." The ends of his lips curled up at the corners. When he inhaled, his chest extended, and he appeared several inches taller. Then he exhaled and she was covered with the same musky scent, incapacitating her, wrapping around her like a warm shroud. It was familiar.

She heard mournful viola music drip with slides and rifts that pulled on her heartstrings. She felt dizzy. Did she hear him murmur a groan? Or maybe it was a small earthquake? Probably an ordinary person wouldn't hear or feel it. But she did.

Anne was on alert; this male took liberties with her feelings.

What a crazy thought. Ridiculous.

He leaned forward, grazing just the edge of her forearm with his warm hand. An electric spark pricked her. He leaned against the counter and looked at the barista, not her. "I'll pay for the lady's drink."

She noticed the strong pulse at his neck. *Healthy. Smells wonderful.*

"And what would *you* like, sir?" The young barista was pert. Anne didn't like her perfect white teeth. That and the fact the girl's shirt was made for a ten-year-old, showcasing her pierced bellybutton.

"I have all I need." The rumbling words sparked shivers again down Anne's spine. He said it just next to her ear, barely touching the small of her back . . . He was facing the barista, but deep inside Anne knew the words were meant for her ears only.

"You didn't have to do that." Anne suddenly found the urge to speak.

"My pleasure." He removed his hand and gave a slight bow.

A bow? No one had ever done that before. Anne had just fed. She wasn't hungry enough to play the game this afternoon, having gorged herself on a salesman who liked to eat garlic fries. His blood was thick with fat globules she could almost see as well as taste. But it went down smooth.

So maybe she would play along. This stranger might be a good candidate for a snack tomorrow. She had never fed twice in one day. She wondered what being too full would feel like in her current state. It would probably make her horny. Well then, maybe she should reconsider. She should do a wet feeding. That way she wouldn't have to be too careful, could gorge herself on him. He'd be wonderful to look at in the shower, and his hands might do something unexpected to her. Something memorable in a string of unmemorable feedings.

His hand gently touched the small of her back again, and she allowed herself to be ushered to a corner table, flanked by two purple velvet overstuffed chairs. They sat, facing at right angles to each other. The counter girl called out Anne's drink. He was up and walking over to pick it up for her before she had a chance to react.

She watched him cross the coffeehouse like a thirsty traveler eyeing a pitcher of water. He was probably six foot six. His dark hair was pulled back in a short ponytail. His black leather bomber jacket showed his nice ass and those long lanky legs that went all the way to Heaven. Even for his size, he appeared graceful. Unassuming. Confident. And the nicest looking male from behind that she had ever seen.

And then he turned, holding the little white paper cup with two fingers, the other ones splayed out, large as antlers. She could see how long his fingers were, how substantial. She envisioned what those hands could do to her. But as sexy as he was, he also made her mouth water to feed.

His prominent jaw line sported blue-black stubble. His strong pulse would be no problem at all, but she would have to bite a little harder to crack the skin. Maybe he would let her take him slowly. Then she could kiss other parts of him in between while his heart pumped more of the blood she craved. His lips were bright red and full. She would enjoy sucking them, licking them. Perhaps biting them.

His eyes found their way to hers, and when she met his gaze, she became self-conscious of her thoughts, as if somehow he could read her mind. Anne told herself it was her craving for blood that caused the almost sexual attraction for this male. After she fed, surely she wouldn't feel this way, she thought.

He delicately deposited the white cup in her hands. One finger touched and almost rubbed against hers. She thought she was imagining the touch, of course. Between her legs, a warm pool had formed. It was a curious place to feel hunger, a hunger of another kind. She blushed at her erotic thoughts.

"You like cappuccino?" He seemed intrigued by the idea. Dancing eyes, all over her upper torso, his breathing steady but deepening.

"Yes. I need the caffeine in the afternoon."

That little hitch in his throat, almost like a moan of surprise. "And here I thought your cheeks were flushed and ripe from a good meal." Those black eyes peered right to her soul. Almost as an afterthought, he smiled, and the dark became brown, ringed with a coppery color that drew her in.

I'll play your game.

"Yes. After a big meal, I get tired sometimes."

He nodded. "I remember that."

Anne looked out the window. This was beginning to feel dangerous. She grabbed her drink and stood. He stopped her by placing one hand on her wrist. His action was soft, but deliberate. *This male won't be denied.*

"Please, sit just a little longer. Then I'll let you go home to your husband."

"Go? You'll let me go? What kind of talk is that? I think . . ." She began to rise again, but his firm grip on her forearm stopped her.

"Hear me out just a bit." He did appear to be begging. Could it be she saw a flash of pain there? *No way.*

"How do you know I'm married?" she snapped out, letting her impatience show.

"You wear a wedding ring." He fingered her ring slowly, sensually. She let him touch her, perhaps a bit too long. She was going to correct his misconception but decided to leave him thinking she was protected by another man. Safer that way.

But was she looking for safe?

There was an obvious physical attraction between them. She had not felt this before, not since before she was made.

"Do I know you?" she asked, ignoring the comment about her marriage.

"No. Ask it another way." The huskiness of his voice made her ears buzz, like he was brushing his lips across them, like they were in bed whispering unmentionable things to each other.

"Do you know me?" Her eyebrows rose at the ridiculous suggestion that seemed to be planted in her brain from somewhere else.

He very lightly nodded, his obsidian eyes flashing. "Oh, yes. I have waited a long, long time for you."

"Okay, that's it. I'm outta here." Anne jumped up, her coffee in her hand. She slung her purse over her right shoulder and stormed off. He followed her outside, keeping pace like they were walking in unison. She stopped suddenly.

"Look. Whoever you are, I will call the police if you don't leave me alone."

"And tell them what?"

"Tell them there is a very strange male following me, bothering me."

He groaned again. The ground beneath her feet rumbled when he did that. "I like that you say male."

She backed up, raising her palms up and out in his direction. "Please, please leave me alone."

"Agree to meet me here tomorrow at this time and I won't follow you." He smiled. "I promise." He held his hand over his heart. Anne felt a small tug at her own, as well as an ache down below.

"Alright," she said, willing herself to say no when her body wanted to say yes. She'd wrestle with her decision if she could just get away from him right now. This coffee house would have to be forever off her list. "Tomorrow at four. But I will call the cops if you don't stop this, this, *way* you are being—"

He grabbed her upper arm and pulled her close his chest. She struggled, but he held her tighter the more she wiggled, and yet she enjoyed the physical play between them. No matter how hard she fought, he would win. She softened and heard his sharp inhale. The spice on his cheeks was a familiar scent to her and, relaxed her just enough so she wouldn't collapse entirely being so close to him. He leaned down and whispered into her ear, "Go for now, little one. But as for leaving you alone, there isn't a chance in Hell that will ever happen. See you tomorrow."

And then he was gone. Just gone. Nowhere to be found. She turned around and around and there was no trace of him. No car leaving the parking lot. No door being opened. Just the normal day all around her.

She was hungry and scared. She liked feeling both emotions equally.

She knew it was going to be forever until four o'clock tomorrow.

A feeding would take up the next hour. Only twenty-three more to go.

CHAPTER 8

I n Robert's 1948 Oldsmobile, and with an hour to kill, Anne cruised through the parking lot. Driving the Olds was like gliding on an overstuffed horsehair couch on wheels. She loved the green bomber and how positively ageless and invincible she was. She counted all the cars on her first pass, then did another pass and separated out the sedans and SUVs. On her third run, she counted all the red cars, then 4-wheel drive vehicles. She had a list in her mind of the other things she could count, like the number of whitewall tires, cars with sunroofs, dirty cars, top ten cleanest cars. But then she saw the man she'd met the day before drive in. He was a full five minutes and thirty-seven seconds early.

It was hard to miss his black Ferrari as it roared into the parking lot. She memorized the sleek vehicle's every detail. She noticed things more than ever before, ever since the turning. The change her body created a compulsive need to count things, just for fun, but especially when she was hungry.

And she'd come hungry.

The man parked the low-lying vehicle and somehow extricated himself from the driver's side. Anne thought he must have been almost supine while driving the beast. A nice, classy beast, though. Like the driver. Dark-haired men with nice cars were becoming a lethal combination, usually for the man. She wet her lips as her pelvic muscles tensed.

Anne was weighing how it would feel to feed on him when he spun around and pointed to a parking space beside his and smiled.

Let the games begin.

She aimed her old green bomber three spaces away and parked. He was there by her door as soon as she had collected her keys and her purse. He opened the door for her. That was kind of a nice touch. There were so few men who knew how to be polite these days. Too bad.

He held her left hand, helping her slide off the light brown fabric of the front seat. The old tank was so high, Anne's small frame had to drop the remaining six inches or so until her feet settled on the ground, barely touching his. Her right knee nudged his left thigh as she slid, initiating a buzz that traveled up her spine. She balanced on his hand like a bird perched on a golden bar. His firm grip kept her steady while he looked over her shoulder and scanned the sleek lines of the vintage car.

"I like your vehicle," he said, still holding her fingers.

"My . . . husb—soon to be ex-husband's, actually. A '48 Olds fastback."

The man released her, stroked the backside of the forest green metal like he was caressing a lover.

You're in trouble if you don't stop this. Everything he did reminded her of some sexual play.

"Gets terrible gas mileage and it smokes," she added.

"Ah, but makes quite a statement, doesn't it?"

Anne shrugged, but she had to admit, that's one of the reasons she liked driving the Olds.

He was still admiring her Olds. "I like old things. And I love cars." His eyes sparkled as he looked down to her. He completely blocked the sun.

Anne peered around his massive frame and nodded to his black Ferrari. "You like fast cars. How many vintage cars do you have?" she asked, sure he didn't own one like the Olds.

"Fifty-nine." He smirked and added, "but not a single Oldsmobile. You must take me for a ride in it sometime."

She wasn't sure where this was heading, so she shrugged again. It was Robert's legendary car, the one he nailed all his girlfriends in on their first date. Unfortunately, she learned this after she'd been conquest number one hundred and something. But for now, it was hers, since Robert had given the Olds to her as an engagement present. And though Anne knew her relationship with Robert was at an end, she felt she deserved it after what he had put her through. She could understand why a guy would love the roomy back seat. She did too.

His white long-sleeved collared shirt gaped open at his throat. Hard to miss the thick pulsing vein so large she could almost smell it. It was the size of her little finger. He was making it easy for her, showcasing all the highlights of his body. He seemed to enjoy the luscious look she gave his neck. She would have to be careful. Not a good idea to give this guy too many clues as to what turned her on. And she was hungry. Famished. But Anne sensed an exotic, sensual danger lurking between them. She wasn't sure if this was dinner or a date.

After he closed her door, he stood back and gave her the once over. Apparently she'd passed the test, since his gaze fluttered slowly, lingering on parts he liked best, traveling down her whole body and back up again without missing a single detail. He smiled.

"I can buy you coffee, or we can take a drive." Although she doubted he could hurt her in her now powerful state, she thought it unwise to go off with this strange male. And her curiosity about this meeting was taking a close second to her desire to feed.

"Coffee is fine. Just remember what I said yesterday." Her voice didn't sound convincing.

"Oh, yes." He put his massive palm at her lower back again like he had yesterday, and the lead her to the café front doors. "You were telling me you would call the police if I didn't stop . . . being this way." The last part he had said as he leaned over, brushing her ear with his lips.

Damn but it was hard to pull away from him. Everything inside Anne wanted to lean in so she could have a proper kiss. On her ear. Anywhere.

"You invade my space before I give you permission."

"And you don't like it?"

Oh, God. It was hard to lie to him as well.

"No . . . n-no. I don't." Anne could tell he knew what she was thinking.

He held the door open and smiled. "I know what you like," he said as she grazed his chest with her shoulder. "Go find us a seat, okay?" His voice followed behind her.

Anne found the corner with the purple velvet chairs available. She already thought of it as *their spot*. This was not a good sign. To vary the routine, she sat in the other chair this time. Her throat was parched but her pulse quickened with the anticipation of their conversation. Being in the proximity of this man made her feel as if she'd just fed. Her heartbeat so loud she thought anyone in the room would be able to hear it.

He walked across the floor with confidence, the object of everyone's attention. He appeared oblivious he was attractive to both sexes. Anne wondered if he liked both men and women. But when his dark eyes flashed up to meet hers, all was answered. She was convinced he wasn't interested in any other man or woman. He was interested in one woman only.

Me.

Being the object of his attraction was just as exciting as it was scary. She accepted the cardboard cup with its plastic hat, which was dwarfed by his enormous hands. He sat, crossed his long legs, propped his on the arm of the chair, and rested his cheek against the third and forefinger of his right hand.

With difficulty, Anne tore her eyes away. She sipped her cappuccino and looked around the room. She caught furtive glances from other women who tried to look away before they were detected snooping. But his gaze was locked onto her face. At least, when he wasn't looking at her neck.

He leaned forward and put the tips of his fingers and his palms together, elbows resting on his knees. "So, here we are at last."

"Yes. What is it you wanted to talk to me about?"

"I find it funny I am at a loss for words. There is so much I want to say."

"Oh, come on. You don't look like the type who usually gets scared. You look like the one who does the scaring."

He threw back his head and laughed to the ceiling. She smiled in spite of herself. Watching his lips curl, the dimple at the left side of his mouth and the dark sparkle in his eyes as he focused his attention on her mouth, warmed her whole body.

"True," he said in a soft rumble she could feel deep in her chest. "Very perceptive."

Anne's heart did flip-flops. He was so gorgeous to look at when he smiled. But her need for blood was rising. Now she wished she had fed beforehand so she could concentrate. She was about to count his eyelashes but removed her gaze from his face and instead counted the tufts of carpeting at her feet. It would be impossible to savor him like she'd planned. Her need for his blood was making her ravenous.

And horny as hell.

He held out his hand, palm up.

"Excuse me?" Anne scowled at his impropriety. "I'm not going to sit here and hold your hand. I am still a married woman." She was beginning to convince herself some of what she said was true. There was safety in having him think she was married.

"Give me your hand, Anne. I wouldn't do anything to hurt you, ever. You know this already."

"No. You promised you would behave."

"I am behaving. This is me behaving, believe it or not."

"Then I would hate to see you when you misbehave." Anne knew it was a ridiculous statement. "Don't say a word." She warned.

He chuckled behind a smile.

She looked around the room for help, or for any distraction to the steadfast gaze he was flooding her with, a gaze that made all of her sensitive body parts tingle. She sighed. "Oh, alright. Here." She stuck out her hand.

He took it quickly, held it in both his, warming her cool, sweaty palm. His fingers massaged and kneaded her knuckles. His touch released tension like he knew exactly where she was stiff, like he knew every sinew and muscle of her. His hand was twice the size of hers. She could imagine those fingers working at the tops of her shoulders, down her spine. Other places.

God help her. His touch made her feel wonderful all over.

"Anne, like I said yesterday, I have waited for you a long time. Over three hundred years." He gave a little squeeze to her hand. She took it to mean he knew it was a bit much to take in.

And it was. Anne looked at her fingers, which had become intimately entwined with his. His eyes were pure golden brown now, tethering her to him in some ancient way. Part of her screamed to run for safety. The newer part of her kept her glued to the chair.

"You going to explain this? Don't you think I deserve it?"

"Forgive me. I thought that perhaps . . . well, I wasn't sure how you would take this news." He bent and kissed the backs of her fingers.

"You mean if I believed your story, which I don't?"

"Search your soul." Those three words felt as intimate as if she was standing in front of him naked. Did he know what was inside her soul? How?

She'd been wondering if she indeed had a soul, with all the changes coming at her so fast these days. Maybe he would have some answers. Curiosity was beginning to out-position hunger in the war for her attention.

"So, who am I . . . to you?"

"You are my fated female."

Fated female! What the hell is that? Like I'm born and bred for him? Like I belong to him? No. This isn't happening.

"Why are you so thick-headed? I have told you at least three times, I am married." The more she said those words the more ridiculous they sounded, but her protestations didn't seem to stop him. "And what does this mean, fated female?"

A couple of students reading at the next table looked up. Her voice had carried. Anne pulled back her hand and refused to look at him. But she did want to know what he was dying to tell her. She knew her life would never be the same after this conversation.

"I know what you are, Anne."

And there it was. "I asked you before, how do you know my name?"

"I told you yesterday, I know you."

"But I don't know you."

"Then I will formally introduce myself. I am Marcus Monteleone." He nodded his head carefully while lowering his eyes.

Something fluttered inside her chest at the sound of his name. "I'm Anne B—um, Morgan. My maiden name is Morgan."

"Yes. Nice to meet you, Anne."

"This doesn't answer any of my questions. What is a fated female?"

"Do you want to continue here, or—"

"Here is fine. Please continue."

"You have undergone a recent change. I know about that."

"And how would you know about that?"

"Because I am the same. The same as you."

A mixture of relief and fear filled her. Finally, she'd met someone she could talk to about the event that occurred in Italy a month ago. She was afraid of finding out the truth about what she was. She knew she was not human. There was a part of her that didn't want to know what that really meant. She would use this chance to ask anyway.

"So what exactly am I?"

"You are one of a golden vampire. Goldens are very rare."

"*Vampire.* Okay." She held out her hand into a ray of sunlight flooding through the coffee shop window. "See? I don't seem to catch fire, and being in the sunlight isn't at all painful."

She saw his eyes dance with something more than humor as she waved her hand around in the sunlight, twisting her fingers and arm in different directions, demonstrating for him.

He raised his fingers to touch the same ray of sunlight, then smiled when he noted her watching his fingers glisten in the bright light, unharmed. "As I said, you are *golden* vampire, like me."

"As opposed to the dark ghouls that run around in rags all the time and sleep in coffins? The ones that can't come out in the sunlight?"

"Exactly. Actually, some of the dark vampires are among my best friends. But each breed usually stays with their own kind."

He was struggling with words. "We are able to live in the sunlight. But we still need to feed. We mate for life. We have children who are born and raised human. They make the choice whether to remain human or turn when they enter puberty."

"And so you chose to become vampire. You were born human?"

"Yes. Just like you. I had a normal human childhood."

"But I *was* human. Neither one of my parents was vampire. My kind *is* human."

"Not any more, Anne."

The truth of his words wounded her. He was right. No longer was she anything close to the same woman she was when she left on her honeymoon. She could pretend. But she could never go back. She was permanently altered. And now would live . . .

Forever?

"But, I prefer to live as a human." Anne knew she had it in her to adjust. No one had to know. And she didn't have to join any weird vampire coven, either.

"You will need help," he said.

"I've adjusted just fine, thank you very much. So far."

He nodded and then smiled back at her with those eyes and she wilted. She felt her will, her control waning. His body sat before her like a magnet, drawing her into some dark, strange journey she hadn't asked for. She'd been made, not born this way. Someone had stolen her human life from her. As much as she didn't want to admit it, she needed information. How had this happened?

"There are things you must be curious about, Anne. Let me help you."

She wasn't sure she trusted him, regardless of the undeniable attraction to his lean body and the way she felt just listening to his voice, feeling his presence, his strength.

"Look. I acknowledge I am no longer human, thanks to that bitch who almost killed me in Italy. Do you know her, as well?"

"Unfortunately, I do. Her name is Maya."

"Well, if she's part of your little group of friends, no thanks. I'm much safer on my own. Your crowd's a little too dangerous for me. I'm better off in the company of my own kind, as you say. My husband and my family . . . of origin."

"He cannot protect you. I can."

She agreed with him. Robert would never be able to protect her, even if she wanted him to. He was a louse and a coward. Always had been.

"You talk about protection. Why wasn't I protected when I was attacked by this woman?"

"She won't hurt you again. She has been enjoined from contacting you personally. She's bridled."

"Bridled, as in a horse?"

"Yes, similar. 'Restrained' may be a better word."

"So then it's up to me to protect my family and friends from her kind?"

"Our kind," Marcus corrected her.

"I don't want anything to happen to Robert just because I had a bit of bad luck."

"I understand. But others might cause him harm as a way to get to you."

"I do care about him." She could see Marcus wasn't convinced.

"Yet you don't live together," he said.

"No. We've had some difficulties." She examined her nails, removed an invisible piece of lint from her skirt.

"Are you truly married to him, Anne?"

"How do you know my name?" She looked up at him and felt his pulse race. She could hear his beating heart. And he felt hers beating in tandem.

"Answer my question and I'll tell you."

"What question?"

"Are you still married?"

Oh, that.

"Technically, probably not." There didn't appear to be any reason to deny what was obvious to him.

"You renounced the ceremony?"

"You mean the wedding? You talk funny."

"Forgive me." He laid his palm against his heart and inclined his head slightly.

"Yes, I renounced the ceremony. But Robert has been a little stubborn about it. He's not quite given up. But legally, I don't believe we are married. And I sure as heck don't feel married."

"Why do you wear his symbol?" Marcus pointed to her ring.

"I can't get it off."

Marcus chuckled, revealing the crease at the side of his mouth that was so damn attractive. "Would you like me to help?" Now he looked like the Cheshire cat.

Anne caught herself gasping for air. Fear mingled with attraction and made her stomach churn. "I'll have a jeweler do it."

Marcus nodded his head slightly. "You put your own husband in jeopardy the longer you are near him. Don't you ever fantasize feeding on him? You could kill him, you know."

I've already had that thought. Every day.

"I think I have more control than you give me credit for. The reason I feed is so I can be strong. I may not want Robert as a husband, but I wouldn't want him to come to harm, would you?"

Marcus gave her one of those confident smiles. "You have no need to worry about me. I will not cause either of you harm." His gaze drilled his words into her head.

"Who then? Why is he in danger?"

"I'll explain it later. Trust me, as long as others think he is your husband, he is in grave danger."

"Then I will protect him. And I am going to live my life as a human. No one but you will know about this. So, you see, you need not worry. I'm all taken care of."

"What will you do when people notice you do not age? What will you tell them, my pet?"

"I'm not your pet. Look, all this is new. I'll figure something out."

"Don't you want children?"

"Yes. Someday."

"What will you do when you don't get pregnant? You can't be tested or your secret will be revealed."

"I might be able to have children. I don't see why not. I'm healthy, just eccentric in my eating habits." It felt good to say it, even though she knew he didn't believe her.

"Do you bleed?"

"Excuse me? Don't you think that is a little personal?" She couldn't believe he had asked her about this.

"How can you get pregnant if you don't bleed? Do you bleed now?"

Anne waited a minute before she answered. "So what? I've skipped a cycle. I can't be pregnant, but I don't see why I couldn't. Maybe I will when my body gets adjusted."

"If you were with me, you would bleed."

"This is getting to the point where I feel like I should leave."

He covered her hand resting on the arm of the chair. Anne could see the tenderness he was trying to convey.

"I wish you wouldn't. I would like the chance to earn your trust. To become your . . . friend."

"I thought you said I was your fated female."

"Well, that is what I feel. Clearly you do not, yet."

"No. And I'm not going to allow even the hint of that thought in my head." As she said this, she saw his body covering hers on a bed with black sheets in a room lit by candles. She knew she wouldn't have to be careful not to hurt him. She saw him feeding on her neck as she fed on his. Her face flushed. He smiled.

"Are you spying on me? Following me around? At night?" Her cheeks flushed as she recalled her erotic dreams.

"Oh, yes, I admit it. But don't worry about your safety. I'm actually going to help you protect your husband. There are those of our kind who don't think you should be married to a mortal. People are watching you."

"I think it's creepy so many people want to insert themselves into my life. What did I ever do to them? Why me?"

"Because of who you are and what you represent."

"Well, I want to be left alone. To live my life as I see fit. Without all this baggage. I didn't ask for this."

"I believe you. I promise not to interfere. But, Anne, you must accept the fact that you have changed, and you need someone to help you along with this change. I would like to be that person. I will promise not to be inappropriate. You won't do anything you don't want to. You won't be unfaithful to your 'husband,' if that is your choosing. I won't ask that of you."

"I do have questions, but I don't think this is a good idea."

"Let me earn your trust. I won't ask you to compromise your standards. I am discreet."

Like hell you are. You're about as discreet as an ambulance with a screaming siren running through a playground filled with children. The things I think about when I'm with you. I seem to not have a will of my own.

Anne fiddled with a seam on her jacket. She noted Marcus had five buttons on his shirt, all mother of pearl, except that one which was slightly grey in color and didn't match the others. And then there might be another mismatched button, but it was tucked into . . . into . . . wait. There were thirteen people in the coffee shop and they had made twenty-six espresso drinks in the last fifteen minutes, which meant they sold one hundred four espresso drinks an hour, at an average price of three dollars and sixty-five cents, that would mean $379 and thirty . . . no . . . sixty cents per hour just on the espresso . . .

"Please?" His words brought her back to their conversation. "I have nothing but the best of intentions. Honest."

"My better judgment says no."

He leaned forward and collapsed his fingers together, which he then tented on his lap. "Trust your heart, then."

There it was again, the battle between logic and emotion. She looked up. There must be something else that needed to be inventoried. She started scanning the room again.

He placed his hand on hers. "Stop counting."

She stared at him, stunned. How did he know?

"Have just a little trust in me. I will not hurt you in any way, and I won't have you do something you will ever live to regret. Ever."

"You promise?"

"Absolutely."

"I'm still not convinced."

"That's my job."

She knew he would not have any trouble with this. The tough front she was showing was in actuality paper-thin. Her resistance was futile. "This meeting turned out much different than I thought it would. I don't usually talk to strange men."

He chuckled. "Not polite to talk with your mouth full."

"That was awful! Stop that." But she was smiling inside and couldn't help but show him on the outside.

"Well, this was a good start. It's good to see you can find the humor in our . . . our . . . situation." He patted her hand but did not grab it. "But one thing can stay as planned."

"And what is that?" She watched a glow cover his face. His full, deep rose-colored lips curved up at the ends, forming a seductive smile and showing just the tip of one white fang. He had no right to look at her that way, to melt her to the core. Unable to help herself, she focused on those lips as he formed his answer.

"I am still willing to be your meal."

CHAPTER 9

"And where would you prefer this feeding to take place, my pet?" He was very close to her, just outside the café entrance.

"Look, Marcus. I know you are trying hard. It bothers me when you call me pet. It feels inappropriate."

"I understand."

They did not touch, but the heat from his body was warm and intimate. Anne would have to say intoxicating. The sound of his voice was velvet. She had the urge to lean closer to him. His breathing was new to her, but becoming familiar the longer she stayed in his presence. She could pick out the unique resonant sounds deep within his chest of his inhalation and exhalation from a crowd of fifty men, at a distance across the parking lot. A group of teenage girls tittered as they scanned his large, looming frame bent over hers. He didn't pay them any attention. A young couple waiting in line inside the store turned and looked back at them several times.

"I will pick a place, then."

He led her to his car. The instant she sat down in the rich black leather upholstery his scent enveloped her. She caught a glimpse of him through the windshield as he made his way around the front of the car. And then he was inside.

The area between her legs throbbed. Her panties felt moist. She was lost in this sensual pleasure, aware of the thin line between the two kinds of hunger, one for blood and one for sex. This male could satisfy both.

His fingers grazed her cheek. His forefinger traced her lips. She parted her lips and let her tongue barely touch the tip of his finger. He moved his hand along her jaw line and turned her head to face him. He whispered, "Do not be afraid. Please trust me." His eyes had that copper ring at the outsides of the irises, which pulsed to his heartbeat.

She was at the edge of losing her consciousness.

The roar of the car made her jump. The Ferrari was a beast, a living thing, demanding attention. Demanding to be driven. By a strong male. This male. This male who thought she was his female.

Each time the car jerked forward, centrifugal force pressed her body back against the molded seat, and each time her head was jammed into the headrest she felt the thrust of a male inside her. Marcus didn't try to drive carefully. His reflexes were perfect. He drove with confidence and command. Captain of her ship. Keeper of her soul. God help her, he was both.

They drove up the freeway as other cars scrambled to distance themselves from the Ferrari's powerful lunges. About twenty minutes later they had passed a town square surrounded by shops, and then turned left out into the valley floor, which was covered in vineyards, lush and verdant.

"See, Anne, the grapes are still green." He slowed down, leaned across her, and pointed out the window so she could see the clusters glowing in the early July sun. "Some of these will be deep burgundy in color within just a couple of weeks. The change happens fast."

She nodded her head. He pulled back his arm and she felt the airspace in front of her grow cool.

"Everything changes, turns. The leaves turn colors. The grapes. The grasses in the fields. Even the sky turns from blue to gray to black, and then back to blue again."

She continued nodding, accepting the lesson.

Teach me more. Her insides ached for a touch from him. She rested her hand on his as he maneuvered the gearshift lever. She felt the rumble of a groan emanating from his chest.

"You touch me, female. You touch me."

"I couldn't help it."

He pulled over to a gravel trail that led through a rusted gate he clicked open with the touch of a button on the dashboard. They climbed a small hill. He positioned the car so they could see the rows of vineyards stretched before them. The beautiful sight brought tears to her eyes. She was filled with emotion—both confusing and delicious.

"I will kiss you now, my female."

She should resist, but found she couldn't lift a finger to stop him. He leaned toward her face as she parted her lips. "Anne. Just say Anne," she barely got out just before her breath was taken away.

His lips on hers made the ground tremble. He was warm and seeking. There was not an ounce of hesitation in the way his mouth claimed hers, in the way he angled his head to gain more access to her. The suckling between them became more forceful as their tongues danced. He chased her, and she was so willing to be caught. She was aware of the faint smell of his light citrus cologne and the harsh sound of his breath as he tasted her.

They parted for air, then repositioned their bodies to face each other. The car was unforgiving and the leather seats groaned. Her back and thighs were wet with the sweet sweat of arousal. She looked into his dark eyes but could not see the copper there. She studied his lips and mentally willed them to take her again. He must have known because he reached for her again.

After a long moment, Anne put her hand to Marcus's cheek and brushed her thumb over the prominent bone under his eye, then lightly rubbed her three middle fingers over his mouth to feel his breath there. She licked her lips, then touched the sharp tip of her fangs on her tongue. She was desperately hungry for him now and wasn't afraid to show it.

He moved her hand open so he could kiss the inside of her palm. He followed that kiss with others up to her wrist. His tongue traced the blue vein that throbbed there. The question was in his eyes before he said it.

"May I taste you?"

She inhaled and nodded.

He closed his eyes, then very lightly pricked the vein with one sharp fang. He drew upon her. Her palm went limp but then pressed against the side of his face as she offered her wrist to his needy mouth.

He didn't take much. She almost wished he had taken more. Sensing this small snack could be dangerous, she allowed the moment to pass. He kissed the skin and left it slightly red and violated.

"How do you feed?" She wondered why she suddenly wanted to know.

"I have a delivery service bringing me fresh blood daily. I don't like to hunt. I am like you that way."

She watched his tongue lave over the little red marks on her wrist and suddenly wanted the marks to show so she could trace her fingers over her sensitive flesh and see he had been there.

"But Anne, you will feed from me."

"Will I be satisfied feeding only from you? I mean, can we each keep each other satisfied?"

His face broke into a warm smile that lit up the afternoon. "In time, I hope to be able to satisfy your every need. But the answer to your question is we could do this for a short—a few days or maybe a week. However, one of us would need outside blood or else we would begin to get tired and perhaps age. You can feed from me without having to hunt, for the time being." He leaned over and whispered in her ear, "And I hope you will be fully satisfied with my blood."

Anne knew she would be. Her lips were anticipating the taught texture of his skin. Her fangs ached and her throat was thirsty for the rich coppery taste of his life force.

"Come, it's time, my p—... Anne." He smiled and got out of the car. It took an eternity for him to walk around the front, to come to her side and to open the door. He gave his hand, gripped hers, and pulled her from the vehicle. The car seemed to shudder as it released her.

When she fully stood, they faced each other but did not touch. She felt the heat from his body as he carefully kept the space between them. She knew he did not want space between them. She understood the sacrifice offered. The gesture made her both grateful and stimulated. He dropped her hand.

He pulled out a quilt from the rear of the car, wrapped it over his arm, and then held his other hand out to her to walk alongside him. They were at a hillside vineyard, and as they walked among the vines, Anne frequently turned to look at the display of the valley floor below them. Everything was alive and growing. Everything was green and golden, bathed in sunlight, as if she were looking through a tinted windowpane. The view and the moment were perfect. She felt the happiest she had ever been. The setting felt like Tuscany all over again.

Marcus spread the thick quilt down between the vines and sat. She stood above him.

"You may take me, Anne, but except for a little taste you've been permitted, I will not feed from you. I only do that when I make love, and I will not ask that of you today. You won't have to worry about stopping. Come." He held out his hand and she took it, then stooped to her knees. He put her hand on the buttons of his shirt and left it there.

She unbuttoned the first one. He watched her in silence. Then she unbuttoned the second one. She looked into his dark eyes and felt his pulse quicken at the touch of her fingertips on the skin of his chest. She peeled his shirt back to the side and slid her hand up his neck, feeling the strength of the blood flow there. The touch of his skin gave her little jolts of pleasure. His eyes showed her his complete surrender.

"Take me," he begged, his voice husky as if he were barely able to speak. "You will see it won't take much to satisfy."

Anne wished his hands were on her breasts.

Marcus heard her words of apology, words she didn't need to say. Just the same, he loved hearing them.

"I will try to be gentle. I'm learning." Anne flashed her dark eyes at him. Her eyebrows rose, making shallow creases form above the bridge of her nose. Her silky eyelashes sparkled and fluttered, fanning his cheeks. His desire flamed for her, just as he expected.

"You won't hurt me." *Though I wish you would.* "Don't be afraid to bite deep and"—he got distracted by her pouty lips—"suck hard." His voice trailed off, wavering. He wasn't anxious to hurry the touch of her lips, the feel of her fangs in his flesh. He had waited three hundred years and could wait a few delicious minutes more.

Marcus lay back on the blanket but did not draw her to his chest. She was not yet his to possess. Anne adjusted her body, carefully leaning on him as if she could hurt him. Her long brown curls grazed his bare chest for the first time, sending him into ecstasy. He knew, but she didn't, that in lying down she would have to press her breasts to his chest in order to feed. He could have merely seated himself in a chair and had her come at him from behind.

I am not sorry for this little deception. I am not a gentleman. I am a scheming rake. But he wasn't crossing the line. Not yet.

With his gaze fixed deep into hers, he saw her quick little inhale when she scanned his chest, felt the side of his neck, and then inhaled his scent. He felt her change focus from lover to ravenous female in need of feeding. Her eyes swept up to the side of his neck, taking in his thick pulsating vein. He let his blood hammer hard and course lower, into his groin. Her thigh moved in response.

Swallowing first, she lowered her chin, then took a deep breath. When she placed her right palm against his exposed pectoral muscles, he felt her warmth all over his body. Her fingers lightly dusted his skin. Her breath came over him, timid and demure, belying something deeper inside. She hungered for him. After one last check and his nod of approval, she lowered her upper body onto him, laced her fingers through his hair, and then pulled it aside, giving herself full access to his neck. He got a glimpse of her fangs just before her lips touched him. He grew thirsty. Thirsty for her blood.

And then she bit down on him.

The fating was unmistakable. Her lips pressed against his skin and she suckled, drawing his life force into her body. It left him feeling delirious, invincible, and ageless. He felt the dust from years of loneliness fall away, as if he'd stepped into a warm shower. And then something wonderful happened.

She moaned.

Reflex action made him raise his hand, wanting to press her into him deeper, but he stopped just before he could touch the small of her back.

At last! Worth the three hundred years of waiting. My fated female drinks of me. She tastes me. She needs me.

The warm elixir, his life force, moved over Anne's tongue and filled the caverns of her soul. What she drank almost didn't taste like blood, but rather like a fine brandy, laced with something else that was more emotion than taste. She felt every cell of her body plump up with the vitality of his liquid, then scream for more. She felt places that had withered and her body and soul suddenly become alive and supple.

She slowed down the taking to make it last and found that she could savor him. She moved one knee across his lap, which lightly grazed across his bulging pants. His shaft came alive with the stimulation. He groaned and pressed his cheek to hers. She straddled him and very carefully set herself down, placing her sex just above his. She tingled where her mound touched his erection.

She inhaled one more time and took the last bits and found, with relief, she could stop without draining him. This was the first time she had been satisfied without taking life. Nothing had ever felt better.

She kissed the two holes in his skin. A tear came to her eye at the sight of the damage she'd caused him. He pulled her with both his hands face to him, then rubbed the tears from her cheeks. His mouth came over hers. She sighed into his kiss.

"Oh, God. Thank you. That was so wonderful," she whispered, "I never knew about this."

His serious eyes almost looked sad. "It has been a long time since I first had this dream. You have no idea how wonderful it is to have my female love the taste of me."

He put his hands at her hips, then moved her over his crotch, watching her. She let him, and let him slide one hand up under her stretchy top. His fingers brushed across her nipples, which hardened and knotted under the flimsy fabric of her bra. She arched up at his touch. She drew close to an orgasm. Every part of her body was more sensitive than ever before.

He withdrew his hand. "I've made you a promise. I will keep it."

"Yes, thank you." Anne looked down. Somehow, she had become shy.

"With my blood inside you, you will experience strong erotic dreams tonight."

Anne knew exactly what he meant. She was starting to feel the sexual intensity coming already. But there was no desire for anyone but this man before her. Just an empty room. Waiting. Waiting to be filled with the scent and body of this man.

She bent down and kissed him again. He slid a finger up her thigh to the front of her panties, then rubbed her through the thin fabric. He could have dipped a finger or two under the elastic at the leg and felt her sex, but his hand remained still. He started to remove his hand, but she held him there, rubbing his hand against the thin fabric of her panties. But he did not violate the trust, even though he must have understood she would not deny him. He pulled her back from the brink.

"Someday, Anne, you will be mine in every sense of the word. Until then, you can take me as often as you like. Drink only from me. I don't want you in the company of strange men. It is safer this way." His finger continued to rub her sex. "I promise I won't hurt you. I will protect you and the man they call your husband. But drink only from me, promise?" He removed his hand and held her face. "Promise me?"

"I promise."

CHAPTER 10

M arcus drank his best red wine and warmed himself by the fireplace in his study, alone. The flames soothed his nerves. He saw her face coming to him, rising above him as she felt the power of his passion coursing through her veins. He hadn't wanted to take her home, but he'd promised not to interfere until he was given permission.

He felt the red bumps at the side of his neck where Anne had bitten him, noting that the swelling was going down. He almost wished the wound wouldn't heal, but rather stay in all its painful glory, a living legacy, a celebration of the love he felt for this woman. She had tasted him and wanted more. And he had so much more to give her. For the first time in decades, he was filled with joy.

Tonight she would feel the full force of his blood in her body. He had decided to let her experience it without interference. He wished he could go over to her house and share her passion. He thought about what they would do some day when they mated in the ancient way of the goldens, and his hard-on increased to painful proportions.

He pressed the bumps again, a little harder this time, until it hurt. He wanted to relive that moment when her fangs had crossed the threshold and had taken something from him and made it a part of her. A part of his body would now be inside hers forever. Nothing else in the universe compared to the thrill of her feeding. And she had promised to use him as her sole source of sustenance and energy. He now had even more of a reason to live, to serve her. His new purpose would help soothe his anxious libido.

He looked down at his cell phone. He'd given her an identical phone so she could call him when she needed him. He'd programmed only one number into it: his.

She does need me. I bring her life's blood. I will fill her every need in time.

He rubbed his thumb over the plastic face piece as if he could will it to light up and ring with her beckoning. He could always go find her in the meantime. He had been finding her on his own for over a month now. But some time tomorrow, she would call and ask for him, as her vampire hunger overrode what was left of her doubt.

He doubted she would sleep at all tonight. It was risky, knowing her friskiness could put her in harm's way, but she'd promised only to feed from him. She would promise much more when their love came to full bloom, when he could claim her, but for now, this little victory was all he had. He'd wait. Even the genetic pull he felt toward her, his fated female, was delicious, albeit painful. He didn't want to make himself unwelcome. It was important she be the first one to reach out.

Anne bought extra pillar candles. She opened the Cabernet. She would put the steaks on later, after she called him. She had dropped by Victoria's Secret on her way back and had bought a new black lace bra and panty set. She'd come home, showered, washed her hair, shaved everything she could, and rubbed her body down with almond butter cream. When putting on makeup, she did her eyes darker than usual and used red lip plumper in a cherry flavor.

She removed her robe and felt the wickedness the black lacy underwear that squeezed her breasts and barely hugged her peach, which was bruised with desire. She wished it wasn't so hot, or she would have built a fire. But there were enough candles around for two fires, since she wanted to spend the evening naked with him, and watch the flicker of light caressed his skin.

She lit the row of pillar candles that sat on the window ledge behind the couch. Then she lit the ones on the coffee table, then ones in the guest bathroom. She lit the three candles on the tumbled soapstone vanity top in the master bath, and then moved to the bed. She was bent down, match touching a white ginger pillar wick on her side of the bed, when she noticed the burgundy red glass votive and the scented reddish orange candle contained in it. She had not put it there.

Holding the end of the wick, she raised the little stubby candle from its glass holder and read the foil label on the underside.

Blood Orange.

It shouted, "I am here. I wait by your bed at night."

His blood was in her veins, filling her with a sexual desire she hadn't felt in years. She welcomed the change. She felt it as a gift given by someone who truly cared for her. It was a simple fact. Marcus was a welcome guest, and she was thrilled just thinking about seeing him again.

She set the candle back down in the holder and lit it.

Thank you, Marcus.

There was no answer.

But first, she had one more thing to do before she could lose herself in the evening. She needed to set up a meeting with Robert for tomorrow. She needed to put that chapter of her life behind her so she'd be free to—what? She picked up her cell and dialed Monika's number.

"Hello, Anne? Is that you?" Monika's voice seemed far away.

"Tell Robert I need to meet with him tomorrow, at nine."

"I don't know anything about this," Monika replied.

"I'm sure he'll fill you in. Will you tell him?"

"Yes. Anne, I am so sorry about what has happened. Robert and I—"

"Forget it, Monika. I don't want to hear it."

Anne was grateful for the silence at the other end of the phone.

"Monika?"

"Yes. I understand."

"You need to get ready."

"For what?"

"Robert is going to need a place to stay, to save him from himself."

"Not sure what you're talking about."

"He has a lot of stuff. But I'm keeping the car." Anne hung up. One thing to tell Robert he would have to find another place to stay, quite another to tell the other woman. She was proud of herself. There wasn't an ounce of regret in her body.

She stripped off the sheets on her bed and threw them in the washing machine. She added the new silk sheets she'd bought this afternoon and had washed in lavender soap. They were still warm and filled the room with fragrance.

Anne closed her eyes. She concentrated on the way Marcus's lips felt on hers as she pushed the number "8," which automatically dialed his number.

He picked up at the first ring. "Anne. Is everything well with you?" There was an edge of concern in his voice.

"Yes, Marcus."

He exhaled in relief. "Good. I'm glad. How do you feel?"

In truth, she felt the best she had ever felt in her life. "I feel fine." It was an understatement, but she didn't want to seem too eager. Would it scare him off?

His rolling chuckle starting a buzzing in her ears, like he was blowing on them. "I had hoped you would feel more than fine . . ."

"Yes. You know how I feel."

"Do I? Tell me. I want to hear you say it."

"I. Feel. Wonderful." There, she'd said it. "Thank you."

"My pleasure."

Anne felt her face flush at his words. Everything in her body attuned to the vibrations coming from his words. "Listen," she began. Why was she so nervous? "I was putting on some dinner and wondered if I could have the pleasure of your company?"

He uttered something she couldn't make out. The happy ripples of his laughter trickled down her spine and warmed her.

"You hungry so soon?" he asked.

"Is it too soon? I'm *starved.*"

"That makes two of us."

"I have a couple of rare steaks I would like to share. You do eat rare meat?"

"Only the rarest."

"You didn't tell me I would feel this way. Positively wicked. Dangerous. Am I dangerous, Marcus?"

"Yes and no. To me, no. To others, like your husband . . ."

"Almost-husband," she corrected.

"To all your human family and friends, you are dangerous."

"As in, I could harm them?" She was enjoying playing with him.

"I promised I'd help you protect your husband. I won't violate that promise."

"So you—the man I've known for less than twenty-four hours—are someone I can trust, and my non-husband, who I have known for three years, I cannot?"

"That's about the size of it," he said into the phone. "But I've searched for you for three hundred years. Don't forget that part."

"I found your candle. I thought you might want to watch it burn with me."

"Next time I'll have to bring a bigger one."

"You've already saved his life, you know."

"Robert? How is that?"

"I admit to having unkind thoughts towards my almost-husband. But it wouldn't have been fair to make you visit me in a jail cell, now would it?"

"Inconvenient is the word I was thinking," he said.

"He actually did me a favor, didn't he?"

"I hope he'll do you one more by releasing you from your vows."

"He already discarded me, Marcus."

He was silent. Then he whispered, "You shouldn't feel . . . discarded."

"I'm needing to feel wanted right now. Can you do this for me?"

The warm breath at the back of her neck carried his words. "I shall devote my whole life to it, I promise."

CHAPTER 11

Marcus put his arms on Anne's bare shoulders as he stood behind her and kissed her neck. She shuddered as if she were cold, yet her body was burning like a torch. He brought his arms around her chest and she leaned back against him. She pressed her cheek next to his, as if seeking his connection. He'd thought she'd be more afraid of him.

Fated. She feels it too. She is mine, after all.

He turned her around, then smoothed a hand down her chest, tracing the space between her breasts with his forefinger. He eased his fingers underneath the satin bra. His fingers grazed over her nipples. She leaned back, making him hold her up with his other arm.

"Are you hungry now?"

"No. Yes." She began to cry. "I'm confused. I feel everything . . . stronger."

It made his heart ache to see this. He pressed her face against his chest, and she sobbed as he stroked her hair.

"It is a lot to take in. That's why I'm here, to guide you, to keep you safe. Ease you into this life of ours. Perhaps you had too much this afternoon. In time, you will adjust."

She looked up at him, her eyes filled with tears. Her lips called to him. "I don't want to adjust."

"You will learn how to deal with the fullness of this passion, in time. It's overwhelming at first." He loved how her tears danced in the candlelight, like the sparkle of diamonds he would buy her.

"I don't want to learn how to deal with it. I want to feel this way forever." She stared at his lips, her tongue coming to the edges, as if seeking to taste his mouth. He gave in to her, covering her quivering lips. Her supple body melted against his frame.

He understood fully the new, confusing emotions she was experiencing and the intensity that grew in her flesh by the hour. He was suddenly grateful for the more than three hundred years he'd had to prepare. He'd always thought the wait as a curse, when in fact it had been a gift. Anne was young in her new life. And just a few hours had passed since her first taste of her fated male. She was in need of a satisfaction he was not prepared to give her tonight. In his world, the fating mark would be followed by a night of beautiful sex. But he was enjoined from this claiming. He wanted to be very careful. There was eternity at stake.

He picked her up and sat down on the couch, with her in his lap. He could smell the heat of her passion. "I like these new clothes," he said, hooking a finger through the ribbon of the black thong at her hip.

"I'm overdressed." She begged him with her eyes.

"Insatiable. I had hoped it would be so."

"You knew." She lightly covered his lips with hers and whispered, "Take them off me. Rip them off me."

"Anne, I cannot . . ."

"Don't tell me what you cannot do," she said between kisses. "Do what you can. Please, I need your hands and mouth on me. *Please*." She laid her head against his heart. Her hand slid underneath his shirt to fan out over his burning chest. She unbuttoned one button and kissed him there. Her little tongue wickedly played with his nipple.

The fact she was consumed with his nearness and the heat of his body sent him into his basic primal nature. He felt the pain of knowing he would have to stop her, but secretly hoped he did not have the strength to. He could not have asked for a better partner. Anne had taken to her new appetites like she had missed them her whole life. He hoped he could teach her fast enough to keep her from getting bored.

"I am flattered you wish to cook dinner for me . . ."

"But you don't want . . . food," she purred to his chest.

"Perhaps a little wine. But dinners are a bit different for us now." He smiled with his lips closed. He found it amusing she had forgotten she was trying to entertain him as a human man.

"A little taste then, Marcus."

"Yes, of course . . . Anne." This he could give her. He would never deny her the taste of his blood.

Her bite was almost a tickle. She supped his essence but was not greedy. He felt her heartbeat race as his blood hit her system and her passion rose.

"You want me?" She looked at him with those deep eyes. "You want me, Marcus?" His hand had found its way to between her legs. His long forefinger was tracing the mystery of her sex over the panties. The muscles at her lower belly contracted. She arched into him. "More."

He tore the ribbon and her panties went limp. Her pelvis rocked back and forth, calling to his groin.

She turned and raised one knee, giving his fingers access to her. "Do you want me?" she asked again as she guided his hand to close in on her mound.

"Yes. But I cannot take you yet."

"I release you from your vow."

"You're not released from yours. So I must uphold it."

"But he has. He has chosen Monika. I am released."

"He must release your vow, not your body."

She sighed.

It was difficult for him to know that he could satisfy her every need, but was not allowed to do so. He'd not yet been given permission. "Soon, soon, my pet."

She raised her arms up to his neck and pulled his head down, then kissed him. She demanded to know his mouth with her tongue. She found his fangs. Her tongue eased over one sharp point, lightly piercing her own skin, and she moaned. A single drop fell to his tongue and he swirled it, mating with hers. The taste of her blood was sweet, and it heightened his passion.

"Careful, careful, pet."

But she wouldn't be denied. She raised herself up to straddle his lap. Her white breasts shone in the candlelight as she arched and undulated in his crotch. He found himself groaning as his cock rose in response to the feel of her warm body massaging it through his jeans. He touched her nipples and then squeezed them with his hands. She was perfect for him, filling his palms with the flesh he had missed for centuries. He kissed the nipples, and then suckled them, grazing one with a sharp nick. He lapped the single drop of blood from her like it was the last on earth. He could feel his resolve and control vanishing. He wanted her, wanted to fill her with his seed. He could not bear the thought of being without her for even a minute.

"Marcus, take me. Please take me." His heart soared with the words, words he thought he might never hear. His hands moved up and down her back, then he kneaded her buttocks as she leaned into him, arms about his neck, squeezing her breasts together, pressing them into his waiting mouth. She rose up, tilted her pelvis over one of his hands that had drifted down her front side to between her legs, and spread her folds by using his own fingers. He rimmed her opening, stroking gently. He felt the slick muscle of her opening and breached her with his first two fingers, indulging in the warmth and wetness there. She moved her sex back and forth, allowing him to massage her clit with his thumb.

She was fully orgasmic, moving to his ministrations of love. He felt her muscles clamp down on his fingers. A new wetness thickly rewarded his efforts.

He whispered in her hair that covered the side of her face, "I have a place I want to take you. Will you let me trace us there?"

"Trace?"

"May I show you how we can travel together?"

Her large eyes scanned his soul. He felt her trust and the blissful experience of her need. She nodded. He stood and held her thighs around his waist, then moved her so he was holding her sideways, one arm under her knees.

"Hold on. Sometimes it gets cold." He set her down, then brought a throw from the couch and placed it around her shoulders. It was his excuse for touching her while covering her lovely body. She nodded again and, laid her head against his chest.

There was a flapping sound as they instantly transported to the sacred temple pool. He set her down at the top of the stairs that descended into the water. Steam rose. A faint smell of oranges and spice lingered in the air.

He started to take his clothes off. Anne let the blanket fall to the tiled floor, then stood naked before him. His erection throbbed. She finished his undress. Each piece of his body that was revealed to her brought kisses. He had never felt so worshiped. No woman had demonstrated her desire for him in such a manner.

On her knees, she encircled his cock with her fingers and looked up at him. She took him into her mouth, the force of her tongue wrapping around his shaft, calling forth a hardness he had never experienced in his ancient lifetime. It was heaven.

Fated. We are fated. It has to be.

She worked over his skin, sucking and caressing him, making him harder, the blood expanding him still. She dug her nails into his buttocks to push him deeper into her mouth. She gasped, and he felt her need for his seed as she drew him in and out with her wet lips. Her moans nearly made him explode. He was desperate to release into her mouth. She paused, the look of need in her eyes, confirmation of what she wanted from him.

He could not speak. His passion flared as she studied him, let him see her desire. With her mouth all over his throbbing cock, her tiny fangs grazed the flesh. The small wound wasn't painful. She drew him in deeper and sucked again, which drove him over the edge. He spilled his seed deep in her throat. The edges of her lips curled up as she swallowed him again and again. He felt her body temperature rise.

She was hot with lust, and she refused to stop. Her skillful mouth and tongue worked on him again, urging his full member on. She rubbed her sex against his leg. He smiled and motioned for her to rise up.

"I am thrilled beyond belief, my little pet, that you have such an appetite." He smoothed the hair back from her forehead and kissed her there. She claimed his lips, pressing her sex into his thigh and rubbing back and forth.

"Ah, Marcus," she sighed into his open mouth, "I will never be able to get enough of you."

"Well, you have only tasted blood these past weeks. We don't want to upset your delicate stomach."

She shot him a questioning look.

"My semen is an aphrodisiac, as perhaps you have noticed, especially for my fated female."

She flashed him a sinful smile. "Then you must not give me so much."

It truly was a wicked thought. Impossible to accomplish as well. He chuckled at her humor. *Fated. Comfortable with me completely.* He took her hand and they walked down the steps into the pool together. Her face became radiant in the light, the ripples of water casting golden ringlets onto her skin.

"What is this place?" Her eyes were wide, excited.

"It is special to our kind. We call it the Pool of Grace. It's where we go to wash our conscience, our bodies of impurities, where we confess . . . things."

"What things?"

"You will see. Soon, my love." He knew she wouldn't be satisfied for long with this answer, but was grateful she had no more questions.

They dipped to their necks into the warm water. She encircled his waist with her legs and wrapped her arms about his neck. She pulled out the leather string that tied his hair back and let the black curls fall at the sides of his face. She kissed him, showing him her hunger for his body.

"Oh, God, I confess I love this man, this man's body. Forgive me for wanting him so."

"Yes, my pet. I'm yours. I'm yours forever." But he did not take the oath. He stopped just short. He wanted to complete the ceremony, wanted to bind them together for all eternity when he was at liberty to do so, when the words could take hold. When it was real. Oh, God, how he wished for that moment now. But he would have to be patient. Just like he told her. *In time.*

He set her on the steps and watched as the golden waters glowed against her body. He put his hands inside her knees, which parted for him at his slight touch.

"I wish to pleasure you. I wish to do more, but this is all I can tonight. Please enjoy what I can give. I hope it is enough."

"Then take all of me you can, please. Take all you can, Marcus."

Her folds were pink and hot for him. She leaned back on her elbows, watching him approach her, her eyes wide and dancing.

I've waited centuries for my female to need me like this.

He needed to see her desire and abandon for him as much as his cock needed to spill inside her.

He slipped his long forefinger into her dripping sex. She arched back, breasts reaching to the sky. He massaged her with gentleness, rubbing over her button, causing her to jump with each little friction. He was thrilled to see her spot swollen and bright red. She moaned as he took forever to tickle his next finger up inside her. His other hand squeezed her nipples. Her warm pink breast filled his hand with the flesh he craved. She jerked as her pleasure began to build.

Anne sat up onto his fingers, pressing her sex against his palm, squeezing his fingers with her muscles. Marcus felt the need to satisfy her fully as she rocked herself back and forth on his hand, looking into his dark eyes. He smiled, loving the vacant stare she gave him when she began to climax, sweat beads collecting on her forehead and on her fuzzy upper lip. That lip needed to be taken, he thought as he bent down and slanted over her mouth. He tasted the salt of her sweat and his fingers completed their thrusting until she fell backwards, but he caught her with one hand at the small of her back, that place where he had touched her in the coffee shop. Her scream was exquisite.

"Ah, yes, my pet. But I am not done with you."

He seemed to have piqued her attention. She raised her head to look at him, a question written on her face. He smiled. *Good, she was not expecting more.* His insides were roaring in flames. He could not get enough of the sight of her, spread before him under the lights. Water dripped and splashed, and the warm moist fragrance of orange spice and sex floated on the air. He licked his lips to taste the salt of her sweat.

He lowered his mouth to her mound and kissed the bare pink flesh. Her lower lips were soft as a newborn's skin as he teased them apart, running his tongue along the meaty dark pink of her insides. She was fruit of the gods to him—the elixir of life was the taste of her orgasm. He placed one of her knees, then the other, over his shoulders, then knelt on the steps before her, his head deep between her thighs. She clutched his hair. He knew she was pulsing with pleasure that grew inside her with each lap of his tongue.

"Oh, Marcus, Marcus, please. Please take me." Her voice was soft and more breath than words. He heard her perfectly.

"There is one more thing I can do. Oh, sweet Anne, I wish I could do more." He moved his lips to the side of her sex in the little hollow between her labia and the top of her thigh. He replaced his tongue with his two long fingers inside her, twisting them, causing her to gasp. He first kissed the little hollow area, and then bit her hard, drawing blood.

She went wild. Marcus wondered at that moment whether he might not be able to contain himself. But he forced a stop and kissed the redness he'd left behind while her body still shuddered from her orgasm. He slowly lapped up the juice from her sex, then sucked her with his lips and tongue.

"I could live on your taste alone." In his dialect, he whispered some of the ancient love poems he knew, calling forth the goddess of her womb. He would teach her these words in time. In time, she would say them back to him. In time.

In time.

She dropped her knees, then leaned forward and wrapped herself around his body. He floated with her across the pool. Their lips caressed each other's, their hands explored and rubbed. Marcus wanted to put his shaft inside her, but that would be on another night, when he was given permission to take her in the ancient way of their kind.

They lazily wafted around the pool. She was now looking at the white gazebo structure overhead and the stars in the background.

"Don't count them. I am all you need," he said, smiling.

"I don't think I can. I seemed to have lost the ability." She smiled, as if shy.

"Then you're satisfied, my pet."

CHAPTER 12

"It pains me to leave you." Anne could hear the crackling in Marcus's voice and the catch in his throat. Sun had invaded her brightly wallpapered bedroom. She rolled over to entangle their legs again, loving the feel of the hard length of his lean body against hers. They'd stayed up all night. First at the temple, then from the early morning hours until this glorious dawn in her own bed. The satin sheets still smelled of lavender as she moved about. But there was also the scent of their mingling love.

"Then don't. Don't leave me, Marcus." She tried to reach his neck again, so he lifted her small frame and held her by her buttocks as she straddled him. She kissed him, begging him to resume their passionate play.

He cupped her face with his enormous hands. "Even immortals rest sometimes. Last night you wore me out, little one." He placed his hand on his chest. "My heart feels like it is going to burst. But there are some things that have to stay the same for awhile. There is much we need to talk about."

His warm smile made her hot for him all over again. She could see herself spending days in bed with him. "But I have only just started."

"Yes." He chuckled deeply, drawing her body to his. "I can only imagine what you have in store. That's what I'm talking about." He put his forefinger on her nose and tapped it. "You have much to do today." He held his palm up to his eyes, looking at the fancy watch he wore on his wrist. "In fact, you'll start in about three hours. These things you must do on your own. It is a big day for you."

"And for you," she said.

"And for Robert." Marcus did not smile when he said this. She had told him Robert was coming to the house to collect his things. They both knew it was important that he recant his vows.

"He will be safe with me. I'll help him with the packing. I could probably move everything for him!"

They both laughed. "He is lucky you are so strong." Marcus kissed her along the sensitive part of her neck just under her right ear. "So deadly beautiful." They kissed again.

She could tell he wanted to say that she belonged to him. She ached to hear it. Anne traced the pectoral muscles of his chest, circling a nipple. "Marcus, what do I have to do to be . . . released, so we can . . . you know?"

"He must agree to let you go. He has to declare it. I must hear him say it."

"Doesn't the fact that there is no license on file satisfy the requirements? I'm not legally married."

"You swore an oath in front of witnesses. The paper is not significant. The oath has to be taken back."

She slipped her fingers along the bulging muscles of his abdomen. "And you have to hear the renouncement?" She continued counting his ribs, running her fingers up and down his chest.

"Um hum." She kept up her fiddling. "Counting so soon?" he asked.

She nodded and sighed. "I'm a hopeless case, aren't I?" She felt his eyes on her as she reveled in the glory of his tanned chest, kissing his nipple in order to feel his flesh on her lips one more time. "Can a golden vampire want . . ." She looked up at him and saw his warm brown eyes pulling her to him again. Resisting him only made the experience more delicious. "Is it a bad thing to want too much?" She gave him a pout, knowing what it would do to him inside.

She felt his body lurch. His erection, unfulfilled, persistently looked for a way inside her.

He laughed. "I have never heard of a golden vampire dying from exertion in the arms of his fated love, but somehow I think if there was a first, I could claim it."

"And then I could bring you back to life, as you brought me back."

Marcus stiffened. "Anne, listen to me. You must never do that. You must never create new life that way. That is forbidden, you understand?"

This new revelation concerned Anne. There was so much she did not know. Could she accidentally do something that could cost either one of them their lives? She suddenly felt vulnerable.

"Then, Marcus, you must teach me these things. Please, I don't want to make any mistakes."

"Yes. We must begin your training tomorrow." He drew her to him again. "We have a lesson, then we play, okay? It has to be in that order."

"Then I'll look forward to recess." She kissed him again, wrapping her legs around him.

After Marcus left, Anne stepped into the shower. The water trickling down her body made her think of the temple and her evening with Marcus. Just the thought of him between her legs, hungry for her, tasting and drinking blood there, made her little nub pulse. She rubbed it in slow circular motions, her eyes closed. Willing his mouth there, willing his tongue scraping over her pinkness, perhaps taking a tender bite . . .

The shower curtain abruptly parted, and she was caught in Robert's gaze. He looked angry. He had reason to be. But not for the reasons he knew about. His neck was a solid mass of bruises, some of them very dark purple. He looked like he was wearing a collar of black raspberry jam. Anne almost laughed.

"You called Monika last night and woke her up."

"Robert!" Anne crossed her breasts with her arms and turned away from him to hide her nakedness. He disappeared behind shower curtain after yanking it closed.

"I still live here," he whined.

"We're fixing that today."

"You called for me, over at her place. You needed me."

"I called her," Anne shouted over the top of the curtain, "before . . . dinner . . . and told her to confirm you're coming over here today to begin the move. I didn't wake her up, Robert. It was the middle of the afternoon."

"Yeah, well someone called at one A.M. this morning. Someone with heavy breathing."

"Absolutely *not* me. I was . . ." She couldn't tell him what she was doing. She felt her cheeks blush. "Maybe it was one of Monika's boyfriends you don't know about."

Robert swore.

"Weren't you there? With Monika last night?"

"No."

"So what happened to you? Who did that to your neck?"

"Long story. Gary and I . . ." Robert's voice trailed off. "We went out and met some girls . . ."

Terrible timing. Now you decide to be a little honest with me. You dog.

"Ah, so that explains your wounds." The thought pleased her.

"Wounds?"

"Your neck," Anne said as she turned off the water and took the towel Robert offered her through the curtain. "Thanks."

She secured the towel around her and pulled back the plastic curtain. Robert's sad eyes scanned her face and shoulders. "Looks like someone repeatedly stabbed you with a pencil," she added. "You got any vampire girlfriends I don't know about? Not that it makes any difference to me."

He squinted and sucked in air. Then he cursed and left the bathroom, slamming the door shut behind him. Through the wooden slats he yelled, "I'll talk with you when you're out. I'll wait in the living room."

Anne slipped into her bedroom, dropped the towel, and dressed quickly. The cream-colored terrycloth still smelled like Marcus. She straightened the satin sheets on her bed and got another whiff of him. She missed him already. Her heart flipped.

She found Robert sitting on the living room couch, one knee over the arm.

He sipped from a mug of fresh coffee. "Damn, I sure do miss your coffee."

Too late. Way too late, Robert.

"I'll bet. I'll bet you miss it real hard as you bang my former best friend all over our house."

"You don't have to say things like that, Anne. Only makes things worse between us."

"How could it be worse, Robert? There is no *us*."

Robert nodded. "Okay. I get how you feel."

"No, you couldn't possibly know how I feel." She heard his heart skip a beat, saw the vein tense at his neck. She held no attraction for him. Just for his blood.

Got to get this over with quickly.

"Forgive me, Robert, if I indulge in a little resentment, seeing as how my best friend was fucking my husband. My husband who should have been enjoying his wedding day with his wife instead of that bimbo."

He turned and faced her.

"She's not a bimbo."

"So, just what is she? She's your girlfriend, the girlfriend you chose over your own wife?" Anne was getting riled, in spite of her desire for control. Was this anger something she would have to be careful of? She felt the fangs in her mouth extend slightly. *Calm down. He doesn't understand.*

"We decided to end it," Robert said. "We talked about it this morning."

"What?" Anne stood there in shock, listening to the sounds of the shower drip. She also heard the lovemaking going on across the orchard, the dog barking on the back porch three streets over, and the bees talking among themselves as they buzzed and hovered in apple trees. She could hear all this, and yet, her world suddenly seemed so small.

"That's all you can say, 'What?' Not exactly a ringing endorsement for my former role as your husband."

"No, you were never really my husband."

"And you in there feeling yourself up. Who were you thinking about, hmm? You have a new boyfriend? So soon?"

"Soon? You, the one who said 'I do' and then banged my maid of honor? What do you care?"

Anne was confused by Robert's comments. Monika apparently was smarter than Anne thought. The mere idea of Robert moving in probably had sent her former friend into a panic. She would bet almost anything except Marcus's life that Monika broke up with Robert, not the other way around. Her admiration for the slut went up a notch.

"I want to talk it over, see if we can work things out. Maybe go to counseling." Robert's eyes were contrite and pleading.

Oh, God, no. This can't be happening. She realized what she had longed for was now beginning to happen—just when she no longer wanted it.

"Sit down, honey." He patted the area beside him. She sat in the cotton flowered overstuffed chair across the room. Robert shrugged and hung his head. He rubbed his face with both hands, suddenly reached for the ceiling, stretching and letting out a large groan.

How hard could this be, she wondered, finally telling the truth? But she guessed whatever Robert had to say wouldn't be one hundred percent the truth. Not like Marcus.

Marcus.

The pain in her heart, the need to be enveloped by Marcus, brought tears to her eyes. She wished she were sitting on his lap. She wished she had his strong neck and chest to hold on to. Then perhaps Robert could see he didn't have a chance. Perhaps he would no longer delude himself that Anne would take him back.

So this is what he's thinking.

But that wasn't happening. Marcus had left her alone to clean up the mess that was her marriage. And now the worst possible outcome was in front of her. Robert wanted to apologize and come back. She could read it all over him. She had hoped he would say something that really pissed her off so that she could just get him out of her life quickly.

She wanted to add a couple of puncture wounds to those hickies on his neck, but that would mess up everything.

He stood up and came over to where Anne sat. He kneeled and put his hands on her knees. His eyebrows arched in forced sincerity.

She did not soften to him. He probably didn't expect her to cave, either. Anne thought his blackberry collar ridiculous and she stifled a laugh.

"Annie, honey, I have been a real fool," Robert said. "I've had the best thing any guy could want, right under my fingers, and I've not appreciated it. God, I am so sorry, honey. I love you so much."

Anne stayed stoic. She was unprepared for this.

"I want to make it work out between us. I want to make it like it was before we got married. Remember that, honey? Remember how we were so much in love? Remember how we found each other, how we just loved being around each other all the time?"

She reached for her memories. Seemed so long ago when the sound of his voice, his laugh, thrilled her. "Yes, I do, Robert. I felt that way at one time. But no more. Something tells me you never did. I don't think you ever stopped seeing Monika."

"No, I did. When we went skiing in Canada, and other times too."

"Damn it, Robert, she was a whole country away!" Anne got up and went into the bathroom, slamming the door and locking it behind her. She was beginning to get hungry and she didn't want him to see it. She didn't trust herself.

Robert followed her. He leaned against the wooden door and whined, "Anne, honey. I am a complete idiot. You are always the one I loved. Look, if I could cut my pecker off for you, I would."

"Go away. I want you to go away. I want you to move out, today."

"No, honey, I can't do that. I love you too much. You'll change your mind. I'm gonna try real hard. You'll see."

The thought of Robert trying really hard was almost laughable, if it wasn't so sad. She recalled her evening last night with Marcus. She smiled and shook her head. It would be impossible for her ever to forget Marcus.

Help me. Help me out here.

There was no answer.

CHAPTER 13

Robert sat in the cab of his pickup, staring at the outside of Anne's little place that had been their love nest. At least, up until the wedding the place had been their love nest. Now it was something else entirely. A fortress. A series of locked doors keeping him from talking to her, smiling at her, reasoning with her.

Anne was so different now. She was unshakable in her resolve. He'd had to work to catch a few shirts and another pair of jeans that she had thrown at him. He had begged her not to throw his cell phone, so she'd lobbed it for the easy save. And when he had asked for the cell phone charger, she'd thrown it, aiming for his head. Her arm was as good as any pitcher he'd ever seen, and he even felt she had held back. God, she was beautiful when she got angry. And so strong, too. Why was it he always loved the girls he could never have? Then when he did get one, like Anne, he'd go and blow it by running around.

His life had gone to shit in just a month. Just over a month ago, he had Miss Monika—and as much of her as he wanted as often as he wanted. And he had the woman who had agreed to be his wife, had agreed to share his life with him, and who made him feel like a better man even though she went on their honeymoon without him and claimed the marriage was null and void.

A minor problem.

He wondered why it was that way, how some women seemed to bring out the best in a man and some others, well, they brought out something else.

When they first met, Anne had been everything he looked for in a woman: smart, sexy, and delighted in making him happy. She was always helping out kids at some teen center or at the home for battered women where she volunteered. He had done a little free work for some of these women, replacing windows and doors destroyed by abusive boyfriends or husbands. He kind of loved being a good guy. He had no trouble staying away from those poor women. After all, he wasn't a complete rat.

It was almost like there were two parts of him, the good part, and then the bad part. Anne always fed the good part of him.

He had to admit, he wasn't ready to give up that part of his life—the good Robert. That's why he hoped Anne would change her mind, would come around, like she had before their wedding. He thought she knew about some of his dalliances. But she had been occupied with planning the wedding those past few weeks before the Big Fiasco, and hadn't seemed to notice anything. So Robert had taken the opportunity to roam. And the more he did it, the more the other side of him seemed to pull him harder. He thought one of these days he would change; he'd wanted to keep to the good side permanently. But he sure as hell wasn't there yet. He really was not to be trusted. He just wished Anne wouldn't dismiss him and would give him a second chance.

In the last thirty-plus days, he had gone from having both women to now having none. And how the hell was he supposed to get female companionship when it looked like his last date had been with a gorilla? A gorilla that liked to bite? His neck hurt like hell, too. He could barely turn his head.

How he wished Anne would open that front door and take him back, wearing something black and sexy, like what that woman or last night. How could he have been so dumb?

And Monika was acting funny too, with all her toys and experimental things she wanted to try all the time. He was beginning to think maybe she didn't like his taste anymore. He always had to put something on that smelled like some tropical fruit.

Am I losing my touch? Am I that boring in bed now?

He started the truck and drove off, but not before checking in his rear view mirror, hoping for the sight of Anne running down the street to stop him from leaving. Damn, she'd looked good, healthy and flushed in the cheeks, bright red lipstick that looked way better on her than Monika.

No, the street was empty. No Anne. No second chances this time. He'd try to call her later. Maybe she would change her mind.

He was not sure where he would be spending the night. He decided to keep trying to call both women. Hopefully, one of them would let him in. And then he could do the grateful sex. He was good at it, had lots of practice.

But more than likely, judging from Monika's demeanor on the phone this morning, he would be bedding down at Gary's. He dialed his best friend. When Gary answered, he wheedled, "Ah, Gary, I might need a place to stay tonight. Neither woman is speaking to me. Can I bunk with you if I can't get through to either of them?"

There was silence.

"Gary, you there?"

"Holy crap, Robert. What the hell happened?"

"I don't want to go into it. It kinda hurts." This was true.

"How'd you manage to get them both mad at you, Rob?"

"Incredibly bad timing. Look, I've got a full day, but I'll buy dinner or drinks if I can stay there tonight."

"You're on. I had no plans, not that I didn't try. Hey Robert, Anne divorcing you?"

Great. Just great.

"Not that I blame her, no offense," Gary added.

"You asshole. Shut up, Gary."

"Look, I'm single. You're the one that went off and got married."

"Her brother says we're not even legally married."

"What's Monika's beef? She never seemed to mind before . . ."

"It's a long story. What do you care?"

"I don't. I was just wondering."

"Gary, you piece of shit. If you touch either of them, I'll come over there and go caveman on you with my baseball bat." Except that his bat was at the house he couldn't go into, but the threat sounded good.

"No worries. Who do you take me for?"

"Gary, let's face it. You're just like me."

Robert walked into his construction office. His doting secretary, Elena, took one look at his neck and dropped her coffee cup.

"Oh, Jesus, Mister Robert." She made the sign of the cross. "You have had a fight. Very unfair. He bite you. Very unfair fight, Mr. Robert."

"No, Elena, there was no fight. Don't worry. I'm fine."

She made the sign of the cross again just for good measure. She waddled down the hall, mumbling, then went into the bathroom and closed the door.

Robert checked himself out in the mirrored Budweiser sign over his desk. The color on his neck was intensifying. *Great.*

On his way to one of his job sites, the local police, stopped him for speeding. He pulled out his license and registration. This was one gargantuan fucked up day, and it was only 10:30 AM.

"Can I see your license and . . . what the hell happened to you? You okay?" The officer bent down to look into Robert's eyes. The policeman was about the same age as Robert, but he looked about as straight arrow as they came. Probably went to church regularly, too. Ex-jarhead. *Just my luck.*

"It's a long story. My date got carried away last night."

"Was she pissed?"

Robert's heart sank. He was hoping it didn't look that way. Like he'd been punished. Rather like wearing a scarlet letter. He cursed himself for being so stupid. All these little lapses in judgment were adding up rapidly and were scaring him. If he wasn't careful, his bad luck could stick around for a while, decide to nest in his life.

"Maybe she was mad." Robert handed over his license and registration. He sat and waited while he got checked out. He wondered what the code sign for hickie was. No doubt some dispatcher was getting a laugh at his expense. Suddenly the bench seat in his truck wasn't very comfortable. Several long minutes later, the officer returned.

"Mr. Balesteiri, your license has expired. Just last month. So, I'm going to write you up for that too. You were doing fifty-seven in a thirty-five zone." The officer seemed to wince before he continued. "Look, fella. None of my business, but I'd keep my mind on my driving, and not whatever else you were into here." He pointed to Robert's neck, then smiled.

"Uh huh." Oh, great, now even the cops were giving him advice.

"Better start paying attention to those little warning signs." He handed Robert back his paperwork and passed over the thick leather pad with the citation on top for him to sign. "That piece of art on your neck doesn't look normal. Did she cost very much? Were there two of them? Bet they used hand-cuffs too." His face was grim, with just a hint of a smile.

Robert almost choked on his own tongue. "My date, you dumb f—Christ. I said it was my date!" This had gone from bad to worse.

"Uh huh. Okay then, someone might say you'd been abused. You might look into that. Men get abused by women every day."

"Sure, thanks."

"It was a woman, right?"

"Of *course* it was a woman! I've already told you it was my date . . . not my girlfriend or my wife." He was a little embarrassed by the revelation.

The officer started to chuckle, shaking his head. "Yeah, that's what I thought. Two women."

Dumb shit. Keep your opinions to yourself. He handed the officer back the pad, swearing under his breath, and took the pink ticket with a scowl. He hated having his manhood questioned. He'd never had to pay for sex in his life.

He knew the ticket would be a whopper. He needed that like castration with a dull knife, although it might solve some of his problems. Now *that* would really hurt.

He pulled up to the jobsite and his long time employee, Enrique, came out to greet him. They were like brothers, having played on the same baseball team in high school.

"Ah, that's fucked up, man. Look at your neck. What happened?"

"Nothing. I don't want to talk about it."

"Jeez, you try to hang yourself or somethin'?"

Something like that.

"You gotta put some ointment, some cream on it, man."

"Look, Enrique. It's none of your goddamned business. I can take care of myself, thank you very much. Now, can we talk about work?"

"Okay, well, I'm glad you're here. The missus is real unhappy with the win-dows, Mr. B. She's gonna talk to you. I think she'll be here in 'bout a half hour."

Robert looked at his watch, only to see a bare wrist. His watch was at the house. He cursed for about the fifth time today. "Uh, I gotta go get some mate-rial for my other site. I can't wait for her. Can you handle it?"

"Nah, Mr. B., she wanna talk to you, man. She's real unhappy."

"What about?"

"Her son, you know the kid in college? Well, he has some construction experience, you know?"

"Yeah."

"Well, he came by yesterday and told her the windows is in backwards. I wasn't watching the guys too good, I guess. The ones I looked at were okay."

Robert went over to the site of the addition. Everything looked fine in the kitchen, but, sure enough, the windows in the bedroom had been installed in reverse. And now he'd have to pay his crew thirty bucks an hour to correct it. He took out his glass marker and put an X on seven windows.

"Hey, get these changed right away. She's right."

Enrique was already rounding up the guys. A little red Mercedes two-seater drove up before Robert could get into his truck.

"Mr. Balesteiri, Mr. Balesteiri." His client was making a beeline for him. On the other side of her, a lanky teen with hair too long joined her. Mrs. Watson was on a mission. She was a well-put together forty-something MILF. Her breasts were expensive. He couldn't help but stare at them. He got hard, even though he was fairly sure he would be punished for it. *So welcome to my life.*

"Good morning." He gave her the grin and the stance in his blue jeans that had earned him the job. "You look lovely today, Kimberly."

His words had no effect. "You are behind schedule. We wanted to be in this house well before Thanksgiving. I've got to order all my stuff and I can't until the walls are finished. We aren't going to make it."

"Don't worry about it. We've got lots of time. Barring something unforeseen, a supply hang-up or something out of my control . . ." This usually worked. Anything could be excused and deflected off him if he could blame a subcontractor or supplier. She stopped him.

"Putting in those windows backwards doesn't help our situation." She stepped up closer to him, close enough to remind him that she could be grateful in special ways if he played the game her way, but not too close to alarm her college-age son. Her voice was soft and low. "You know, Robert, you were chosen because we had the most faith in you. You weren't the lowest bidder. But my husband and I liked you the best, thought we could—*work* with you the best." She sighed.

Robert knew it was because *she* liked him the best. He had to admit, he did enjoy a few afternoons getting to know the lady's tastes, not just in design.

Then she leaned forward and stared at his neck.

"Good Lord, what is that?" She pointed and spoke so loud the entire place stopped working to look. He shrugged. A smile of bright recognition crossed her beautiful face. "You are a very naughty boy, Robert."

Actually, he was thinking about the fact that all he had done was to lie there. The woman had been the naughty one. She hadn't let him do a thing. When he tried to get up, she'd pushed him back down on the bed with such force the pressure of her hands almost caved his chest in.

Oh, God, I'm screwed. Will this day never end?

Mrs. Watson had renewed interest in the sight before her. "You know, I have some changes I want to consider. I'm tied up tonight." She fluttered her eyes and smiled, probably so he could get the full import of what that meant. She was a very literal person, as Robert had discovered earlier. "But tomorrow night I'm free. I don't think Charles would mind me going over the changes with you. He has a meeting that will go until late."

"Um, sure, Kimberly." He leaned in and whispered, "What about your son?"

She smiled wickedly. "Sometimes he likes to watch."

Robert said goodbye and drove to his next construction site. He was pleased to find things in much better shape. They were actually ahead of schedule. There was a bonus in the contract to finish early, something he hadn't been able to get in the Watson contract. At the time, however, he didn't care how long the Watson project took, as Mrs. Watson's appetites in the sexual arena were voracious.

Best of all, at this project site, no one gawked at his neck. He was beginning to feel like his old self again. Until lunchtime.

When he walked into the Apple Box Diner, the air took on the weight of a funeral procession. The usual jovial crowd stopped talking and followed his gait with quiet stares. They were somber. Robert felt like someone had given him advanced billing. He felt eyes staring at the back of his head, at his neck. Pissed him off.

He sat in his regular booth. His favorite waitress, Adele, came over with a coffee cup. "You eating alone today?"

"Yeah. Thanks."

"You gonna make me ask?"

"I'll have the regular." Robert always had a BLT with a green salad on the side.

"Dummy, I meant your neck tattoo. Can't say as though I've seen one like it before. And I've seen a lot."

Robert knew this to be true. He had dated Adele in high school, back when he was a star baseball player. Back when his life was normal. Back before two women had rejected him in one day, one of them being his wife.

He shook his head. "I think I'm going to explode if one more person asks me."

"You okay? I mean, that's quite a statement."

"Mind you own god-damned business, Adele." She did, retreating to behind the counter.

He looked around the room in time to see several people turning back around so as not to be accused of staring. He rubbed the back of his neck and felt soreness there too. *Even the back of my neck?* He didn't even remember. Must have happened when he passed out.

Robert ate quickly and then got up to leave.

"Bye, darlin'. Don't do anything I wouldn't do." Adele winked and flashed him an orange-lipped smile. Robert remembered those orange lips. He had dreamed about them almost his entire senior year. He glanced at his receipt and noticed Adele had written her phone number prominently in red pen. He looked back, but she was already reaching for something under the counter and was bent over, her cute little ass displayed for his view. She was wearing a black garter belt that held up her black stockings under her blue uniform.

He liked to think about things in baseball terms. *Two hits, two outs, two errors, nobody left on.* Things always came in threes. He was looking for another hit, not an out. But he would be grateful if this day could end without another major incident. His ego was just as sore as his neck.

When he finished his workday, he picked up his mail at the local post office. He opened a letter from the bank and discovered he'd been overdrawn again and had accrued some $260 in overdraft fees. Damn. He'd forgotten to deposit a check. Another little lapse had cost him some money. This needed to stop.

He got to Gary's about six. He was beat. In his arms, he cradled the few things he had bought. He could hear the loud music about ten doors before he got to Gary's apartment. Gary was in a party mood. He always played country western when he was ready to go out.

Robert had to knock twice before he got an answer.

"Hey, partner. Look at you!" Gary surveyed Robert's neck. "All branded up. You are some sore little puppy."

There was a limit to Robert's patience. He threw his clothes down on the floor and grabbed Gary by the collar. "Quit it. Not another goddamned word, Gary, you hear?"

"Hey, don't get the wrong impression." Gary extricated himself from Robert's grip. "I was just trying to make light of a pretty ugly situation." He pointed to Robert's neck.

"Okay, I'm leaving." Robert bent over to retrieve his precious stash, but Gary stopped him.

"Come on. Take a shower and get some clean clothes. We're going out tonight. I'm not going to make you pay."

"That's good." And it was, he thought. Things were finally starting to look a little brighter.

When he found out where Gary wanted to go, his assessment how things were looking up changed. The Double Eights was a topless bar in the seedy part of town, attached to an adult bookstore. The scene of his bachelor party loomed large in his mind. Robert had done some work for the owner, who looked more like a priest than a person who would own such a place. Robert knew what went on in those little rooms in the back, the "chat rooms" as they called them.

When he had worked on the remodel a couple of years back, he had found an assortment of toys and pieces of underwear or paraphernalia like he'd never seen before. The owner had tried to do a trade for services before paying him, which pissed Robert off. But, eventually he got paid. He would have taken the guy to small claims court, but he didn't want it published in the paper. Anne never knew about this particular job and he wanted it kept that way. He wasn't a fool. With Gary, he entered the dive, which smelled of male sweat and smoke.

The girls looked good tonight, no doubt due to his circumstances. He was grateful for the darkness there too. Easier to hide his neck.

They chose a table in the corner, but with a good view of the two lighted boxes with the dancers in them. Robert never could eat up at the counter. It just didn't seem right to have some woman's ass that close to his green salad. Of course, his mouth had done worse. He simply didn't like to confuse his needs. That's why Monika's flavored condoms annoyed him so much.

The salads were passable, prepackaged in cellophane and obviously not made on site. Thank God. The only items of protein were hot dogs, sort of a house specialty. In more ways than one.

He lathered his with mustard and had just taken a huge bite when a black-haired vixen made her way over to their table. She sat on Gary's lap. Robert could tell she really was looking at him and had wanted the vantage point from Gary's side.

"Hello, darling. Ain't you cute?" Gary had no trouble talking to strange women, especially those that would sit on his lap without permission.

"Cute? Wow, it's been a long time since I've been called that. I think the last time was when I was a girl of ten or so." She smiled. She had huge white teeth and the reddest shiny lips Robert had ever seen. She wore black velvet stretch pants with a red satin baby doll top that scooped low, showing her breasts. They were bigger than Mrs. Watson's, but all flesh, no plastic. They were luscious. She caught him staring and didn't seem to mind a bit. Neither did he. He quickly finished his mouthful and wiped his mustard-covered lips.

"I think you're just drop dead gorgeous." It was a cliché, but the tired line seemed to work on her. The girl smiled dreamily as Gary's paw found sport down the front of her blouse. The red satin rippled as Gary massaged and squeezed her substantial breast.

Robert got hard immediately. He shifted in his seat.

Gary bent down, descending into the oblivion of her cleavage. Her eyes got deep and dark as she looked at Robert and licked her lips. She made sure he got the message she liked to be nuzzled. And in public. She was telling him she could do other things too, most likely with expert ability. Robert wanted her more than he thought possible on a day like today. Well, maybe it was because of the day he had that made him want her. But it didn't really matter. He had to have her. She was more than willing. He didn't want to share.

Gary whispered something in her ear while his other hand found a home between her legs, which she kept tightly crossed over his. God help him, but Robert wanted to part those legs. His cock felt like a heat seeking missile and her sex was the target.

Gary made the arrangements. The girl had an apartment nearby. Robert thought that would be best, just in case Anne stopped by Gary's to talk as she sometimes did. He felt bad for about a minute, then realized Anne had kicked him out so he was free to roam. No way was he going to be made a fool of by those two women. He would end the day on top, literally.

She brought them to her apartment. It was clear she was a pro. Her place looked more like a seduction stage than a living space. She offered them the use of her full bar. She didn't ask for money. Robert didn't know what had been agreed on, but Gary was the expert with call girls.

They each took a long necked beer from her refrigerator and popped them open. They sat on her command and watched as she peeled off the layers of her clothing. They were both squirming in their seats, eyes lapping up the scene.

When she stood before them, almost naked, her perfectly formed breasts of double D variety staring straight out them, she undulated her narrow waist and started to slip down a black thong panty, moving her hips from side to side in a figure eight pattern. Robert noticed she looked directly at him. She leaned forward to remove the little article from her ankles, her breasts full and extended towards him. Gary was enjoying the view from the back just as well. He stood, then came behind her and rubbed against her ass through his pants.

She rose up and leaned back against him, but her gaze stayed on Robert. Gary's hands were all over her chest, squeezing her breasts. Her heavy breathing and that dark stabbing stare at his groin told him she was becoming aroused. She licked her red lips with the tip of her tongue, her eyes still pinned to Robert.

Then she turned and kissed Gary. Robert saw Gary's hands on her white bottom, his fingers dimpling her skin. She looked over her shoulder at Robert before she reached down and caressed Gary's member through his pants.

Robert felt drawn into her like a moth to the flame. Something told him he was about to have the greatest sex of his life. He never liked the truly bad girls. This would be his first. He sensed he would never be the same afterwards.

She parted from Gary and reached out her hand, the red fingernail polish shimmering. It matched her toes. It matched the red of her tight nipples. It matched her wet lips. Robert grasped her fingers like they were a lifeline. She walked to the bedroom, hooking Robert behind. They left Gary in the other room. Robert didn't even look up to see if this was okay with him.

Everything in her room was red. She clicked a little black device and some sultry music began to play, laced in with some kind of Gregorian chant. There were candles lit everywhere that seemed to come on with a flick of her fingers. He knew he was about to have a full-on religious experience.

She dropped his hand and leaned against the door. With a click, it locked. "You're the one I wanted," she said.

"Well that suits me just fine." Not sure why it mattered, he asked her, "And what do I call you?"

"Maya."

Robert thought to himself. *Three hits. Thank God it's a hit, not an out.* The girl knew how to treat a guy right. She didn't even ask him about his neck, or look at it once. He realized just before his lips covered hers that at last his day was looking up.

CHAPTER 14

T he next morning, Marcus was out in the vineyard inspecting his grapes
when Maya suddenly traced behind him. She leaned against him, then
threaded her arms around his chest, squeezing her breasts against his back. At
first he startled, then willed himself to relax a bit, not wanting her to see how
uneasy he was around her. She had not used the formal protocol of asking if
she could visit. She had just appeared.

"Marcus, have you no space in your heart for me? For our son?"

He turned to look at her face, which was beautiful as ever. Her generous
bosoms were heaving. They were hard to miss. He unpeeled her arms from
his around waist. He was trying to be gentle, calm, but everything about her
spelled danger. He remembered their bedding, how he never could lose command of his faculties out of fear of her. Their relationship was intensely sexual, but he couldn't say it was very pleasant. And he couldn't feel love for her,
although he had tried, for the sake of the boy.

"How is Lucius?" It was about the only subject he could discuss with her
openly.

She sighed, twirling a lock of hair between her fingers. "He's fine. But his
mother is hungry. Hungry for a real man's touch on her flesh. Hungry for his
love, for his bite. Only one man can do that for me." She flashed her gaze up
to meet his.

Maya was about Anne's size, only a darker version of Anne. He had always
been attracted to shorter women, but only if they were powerful. This woman

was *too* powerful for him. And there would be no other now that Anne had appeared in his life.

"Who tends to him when you are . . . traveling?"

"My mother. And I'm not traveling. I've taken an apartment in town, not that it makes much difference. The month is up and you've not claimed her, so I thought we could explore our way to getting you fated, perhaps experience being a family." She sauntered back up to him.

She was very good, he noticed. He would not deny he was getting aroused. That body would arouse anything living. But he knew he could control any urge she would throw his way. Before she could toss her arms around him and lock onto his lips, something they had done hundreds of times over the years, he stopped her. "I am not comfortable with you here. You didn't announce. You can't just appear. We are not fated, and we never will be."

Maya frowned, twisting her head to the side. She crossed her arms and quickly pulled off her red satin top, revealing a lacy red bra she would never need. He knew it was for him. He had a fondness for fancy underwear on his women and she delighted in showing them to him any chance she got. He stood there looking at her and noticed his arousal did not deepen. This was not love. This was lust. Small compared to the feelings he had for Anne.

"You have no effect on me. Cover yourself up. This is why you are not welcome here." He turned and began walking up to the house. She followed him.

She traced in front of him, her shoulders glowing in the morning sun. "You said you would try. You aren't giving us much of a chance. Come on, Marcus." She walked to him and let the tips of her nipples that showed through the red sheer fabric rub against his shirt. "Can't you try just a little bit for the both of us? For Lucius's sake?" She rubbed her hand against Marcus's pants. "No need to hold yourself back. All can be forgiven." She rubbed her mound against his bulge. "All can be as it was before. Remember, Marcus, how right we were together? Don't you miss those days?" She leaned into him further and raised her lips, but he pushed her away in disgust.

"Get out, or I will tell the council."

"The council will be told you are not even trying to fate me. They will be none too pleased with my report."

"I am pursuing the honorable path, doing what I think is best. You must not interfere. You are bridled."

"Yes, I must keep my distance from the woman. But I can't stay away from you. Would you be able to stay away from her, Marcus? That's how I feel."

"Your decision to move to Healdsburg is a bad sign."

"Yes, it is. I don't like to be turned down. I don't lose gracefully. You know this. I can wreak a lot of havoc. But if you were willing, and a little compliant . . ." She started moving towards him again.

"Then I will ask for an injunction. I'll get it, Maya. They'll let me have this."

"Very well." She walked away, backwards. She waved her fingers, then disappeared.

Marcus was worried for Anne's safety, even though Maya had been bridled. He hoped Maya had enough sense not to go against the council's wishes.

He spent the rest of the morning doing chores. Hard work helped him think. He worked on one of his tractors, then experimented with the sugar content of the fruit at the ridge overlooking his villa. Harvest would be soon, and he was ready. He hoped there wouldn't be a late rain. The conditions this fall had been perfect.

He went into the kitchen refrigerator and drank the procured blood from the blood bank.

He sat on the stone balcony that overlooked the valley floor and thought of Anne. He could see the very spot he had laid the blanket down, where she had drunk from him. He did this on purpose. He wanted to see the site every morning of every day he stayed here. He was going to take the grapes that surrounded the little area and make his own special wine. He wanted to drink from the fruit that had watched their love blossom for each other. That elixir would be priceless.

He entered his bedroom chambers, through ornately carved oak doors. When he had bought the property, he had decorated the house with her in mind. There was a pink marble-topped vanity that was hundreds of years old, probably older than he was. He had bought a gold mirror and brush set and which sat on the top of the vanity, waiting for their mistress to come and use them. He touched the engraved letters AM, for Analise Monteleone, the name he would call her, the name he would use when he claimed her. She would have his family's name and would bear his children here, overlooking the vineyard and the place where she had first tasted her fated love.

He eased himself down in the rose colored high-backed chair in the corner, and with his elbow on the chair arm, he rested his fingers at the side of his cheekbones. Anne hadn't called him last night and he missed her, so he traced to her bed and watched her sleeping.

Like a sentinel, he watched her rest, making sure her sleep was uninterrupted. He watched the reflection of moonlight against the flowers in her bedroom wallpaper. Fog covered the street and blurred the dull light from the corner streetlamp. Her face was smooth as alabaster, a light blush at her cheeks. Her lips formed a smile as he kissed them softly, being careful not to awaken her. Did she sense he was watching over her? Was she having any second thoughts about sending Robert away? Had Maya contacted her at all? Her body was getting used to his blood, to the fating that would surely take place soon. So he waited, certain it would be any time now. As she rose to the bright yellow sunlight, he left her to her morning routine.

Anne had gone back to bed after the scene with Robert and slept until the next morning. She hadn't slept this deep in months, but suspected the evening before with Marcus and the fight with Robert had something to do with how soundly she had slept. Her dreams had been vivid, sensual. Marcus had been everywhere around her, kissing every inch of her body. They had flown through the night sky to the temple. They had made love over and over again in rooms she had never been in before. Big rooms, with beautiful views of ocean and greenery. Her dreams felt like visions of her future spread out before her.

Only thing stopping that future was Robert. His refusal to release her would delay the mating ritual she so desperately wanted with Marcus. What a time for Robert to finally come to his senses, even though too late. What would have happened had Robert realized his flaws earlier in the year and had made reparations? She might not have been so attracted to Marcus.

Somehow, that was not a logical thought. Loving him was the most natural thing in the universe. And for once, she was ecstatic to know she would live forever.

Yesterday, she'd almost thrown all Robert's things out on the front porch but had stopped herself. She wanted him out of her life but didn't need to punish him or destroy his possessions. She didn't want to be cruel. Cruelty

wouldn't get her the desired result, especially if it made him fight the release she needed.

She stretched, still wrapped in her fuzzy robe, naked underneath. She felt groggy but wonderful. She wished Marcus were here with her. She was hungry. She decided to shower and then give him a call.

As she was rubbing herself dry, she noticed blood left behind on the towel. She looked all over her body for an errant bite she hadn't noticed. Then she felt the dullness in her lower belly. Cramps. She was bleeding.

She looked at the pinkish red stain again. Not a lot of blood, but something she hadn't seen in two months, ever since the rehearsal dinner. She wondered if that meant she was fertile. Thank God nothing was wrong with her. She couldn't possibly be pregnant since she hadn't had sex since before the wedding. But now perhaps she could get pregnant.

She brought her phone to bed with her and pushed the number. Marcus's instant response told her he had been waiting for her call. After he greeted her, she said, "I sent Robert away with some of his things. But he wants to work it out. He wouldn't release me."

"I see."

"I feel sorry for him, but my mind's made up. Can I come stay with you while he moves his things out? I just don't want to be around him."

"I'd rather you asked it another way."

"You and your questions. I can't believe I've only known you for a few days. Can you come over here?"

"Not safe, Anne."

"Why do you say that?" Anne could tell something had shifted. "Is there some kind of bad news?"

"No. I must wait for an appointment with the council. I've requested it, but there are more pressing matters."

"I thought you said . . ."

"Patience. Plus the fact that every time we are together it is all I can do to keep from . . ."

"Why can't I come over there? I need you now. I'm starving. Are you on the other side of the world or something?"

"No, I'm right here."

She looked up to see him standing at the foot of her bed. She threw herself into his arms. The pink robe opened up the front to expose her breasts to his hands, and then his lips. He pressed her down and peeled back the robe as slowly as he could, as if she was some fragile china doll. She watched with greedy eyes, her breasts moving up and down from her heavy breathing. The muscles between her legs twitched. He kissed her hip, her bellybutton. He kissed down her stomach, moving lower and lower until he was at her puffy, hairless lips. She inhaled as he extended his tongue and licked her sex.

He grew tense and sat up. "You bleed."

"Yes, I noticed that this morning. It's the first time in almost two months. She watched him as he thought. "Is this a bad thing, Marcus? I mean, you said . . ."

He was serious now. "Get yourself packed. I think I have a solution to your problem about staying here."

"We're going to your place?"

"No, I have to go somewhere. You are coming with me, if you are willing."

He smiled as she squealed with delight and writhed on the bed. Going on a trip with Marcus, just the two of them? How exciting.

He was next to her in an instant, his mouth covering hers. He rolled to his back, pulling her naked body over him. He tugged his shirt away at the collar, exposing his jugular. "We haven't much time. Feed. Then pack your things and meet me at Starbucks, as soon as you can, okay?"

She nodded, then popped his buttons off, laid her breasts against his bare skin, and dug her fangs into his neck. They both groaned. She took him fiercely, needing to feel his blood course through her. Marcus laughed until he cried.

She spotted Marcus's long, lanky form while he leaned against the Ferrari, a cappuccino balanced in one hand. She parked the bomber by itself in a deserted area, not knowing how long they would be gone. She wanted to protect the car.

She wasn't going to kiss Marcus and make a scene, but she saw in his eyes that he expected some display, so she ran headlong into him, causing him to juggle the coffee without spilling it on either of them or the car. He felt warm and hard for her. His dark eyes smiled at the corners all the time now. It was thrilling to see him so happy and to know she was partially the cause.

"You going to teach me how to trace with baggage?" she asked as she sunk into the Ferrari's leather seat. He slammed the door and quickly came around to the driver's side. He got in and leaned over, then planted a quick kiss on her lips.

"No, we're flying this time. I have things I have to bring as well."

The Ferrari kicked in and her head slammed into the headrest, something she was quickly getting used to.

"Don't you ever drive slowly?"

"Why?"

They both laughed. Instead of heading to San Francisco to the big airport there, they drove up 101 to the Sonoma County Airport. They parked the black beast and were greeted by a short man in a pilot's uniform, who gestured for them to follow. He knew Marcus.

"No ticket?" she asked.

"Not when you own the plane."

Anne raised her eyebrows up, impressed.

Marcus leaned into her. "There are things you can do on a jet you can't do when you trace."

"Oh." Another new experience.

All by itself, a sleek white jet stood on the runway. They headed straight for it. A cabin steward who asked if they wanted something to drink greeted them.

"A little red wine, I think, or would you like champagne? I have an excellent Merlot Champagne, gorgeous color." Marcus was waiting for her answer. Anne had always loved champagne. She had not had any since her wedding day.

"Is it okay to have alcohol?"

"Sure, as long as you don't have too much." Marcus took her arm and led her to the back as the steward dispatched to get the glasses and the bubbly. There was a desk with computer console and telephone, a combination printer/fax machine, and swivel lounge chairs done in butter frosting white that had the smoothest grain of leather she had ever felt. He took her hand and showed her a full bathroom with shower and double vanity. Two fluffy white robes with an M emblem on the breast pocket lay at the lip of a substantial tub. Anne's eyes grew wide as she looked over everything.

Marcus grabbed her hand and took her to the very back, which was a bedroom. He pulled her to him with a huge hand around her waist, hungry for her. She always felt he was hungry for her. She wanted to do nothing else but please him and give him back her love in return.

His mouth covered hers. He knelt before her and pulled up her top. He kissed her stomach, his long fingers reaching under her bra. She took her top off and showed him the black piece she had bought at Victoria's Secret.

"This is nice, very nice. I know some places where you will be showered with lovelies in every color. But I like you best like this." He released the clasp of the bra and black silk fell to the ground.

The captain spoke, signaling they were about to take off. The steward had left a chilled bottle on the table in its holder and two poured glasses of the ruby colored drink beside it. Marcus handed one to Anne, then took a seat in the recliner, holding his glass and motioning her to join him. Topless, she sat, leaning her back into his chest as he strapped them in with one long seatbelt, securing them for takeoff. She turned slightly to lay her head against his chest.

"A toast?" he asked. "I am parched." With their arms entwined, the two flutes touched with a ring. "To us, may we love forever."

"Yes, Marcus. To us forever."

The bubbles made her nose feel itchy, and she rubbed it. The sensation of drinking something other than blood was odd. But she had to admit it was pleasant.

"Do we get drunk?"

"Not really. Takes an awful lot of alcohol. We usually get sick before we can get drunk. We are immune to most the effects of alcohol, but we can enjoy the taste. I'm actually going to make some very good wine."

After they were airborne, he unhooked them and brought the bottle over for a refill. "I've always wanted to do this. Indulge me, okay?"

He held the flute up to Anne's breast and pressed it against her nipple to wet it with the red mixture. Her nipples hardened from the cold liquid, but glistened and quivered. He put his mouth over the nipple and sucked the champagne from her body. Anne felt the place between her legs gush.

"Shall I do the other one?" He kissed her, searching for her tongue and pinning it down with his own.

"Yes," she moaned into his mouth. "Please."

He dipped her other breast into his flute, spilling some on her pants. He feigned horror. "Oh, my, you have soiled your pants. You must remove them. Jason will wash them for you." He slipped his fingers along the waistband, unhooked the clasp at the front, and pulled down the zipper one bit at a time, kissing her, wiping her lips with his tongue.

Anne was about ready to pass out. Marcus was the best kisser she had ever known. He was skilled in the art of seduction, doing things she didn't even know existed. She was grateful for his experience, for he would be his last lover.

She stood and let him remove her jeans. There she was, in the black thong with just enough lace to drive him crazy.

"Ah, I like this view very much," he said. He knelt in front of her, kissing her through her panties.

"Marcus, I have always wanted to do something. Indulge me, okay?"

He smiled at her imitation of his play.

She bid him to stand. Then she kneeled and undid his trousers, slipping the zipper down his front, kissing the opening. She smoothed his pants down his legs to his ankles, then prodded him to step out of them. She removed his silk boxers. His erection was throbbing, lurching with each little touch of the back of her hand, her fingers, or her hair. She gripped him in one hand and held her champagne flute in the other, holding it up to him.

"More." He reached for the bottle and emptied the contents into her glass. She guided his cock to the flute, and with delicate fingers, dipped him in the cool red bubbly. He jumped at the cold. Anne's eyes were fixated on his velvet shaft. She wet her lips, set her glass down, and covered his head with her mouth, sucking the champagne from him.

"Mmm. This tastes just wonderful. You taste so good." Marcus was almost overcome. She stroked him, massaging his scrotum with her hands, sometimes kissing and sucking. He slammed his hips upward, thrusting his cock deep into her hungry mouth. The tip of one of her fangs nicked him and she tasted just a drop of him as his bulbous head shoved past. At last he came into her mouth, filling her. She shuddered as she took every drop.

He took her hand and led her to the bathroom, then drew bath water. He held her the full length of him, his cock still hard, pressing against her lower belly.

"How many times can you do this? You don't get soft? Ever?"

"Not with you, pet. I've never had my fated female. Nothing else compares, my love."

He slipped off her thong with one long forefinger, which then found the hot spot between her legs. God she wanted him there, but his finger would have to do for now. He picked her up and set her on the granite vanity surface, her back flat against the mirror, raising her knees to over his shoulders. He stroked her now with two fingers.

"I want your cock inside me, Marcus. Please. Please, can I have it?" She felt him inhale. She almost thought he would ram himself into her at that moment, but he moaned and sank to his knees. He spoke the ancient words. Anne could feel the insides of her body vibrate to the rhythm of his voice. He played her like an instrument. Every part of her sang. She felt the long smooth orgasm send radiations of pleasure all the way to her fingertips.

"Ah, my pet," he said into her ear as he raised and kissed her. "I want to so bad, so bad. Help me be strong. We mustn't."

"Why? You said so yourself we are fated."

"It would be unfair of me. I have to ask permission."

Anne frowned at him. "Permission? You need to have permission to have sex?" That was about the most ridiculous thing she had ever heard.

CHAPTER 15

Laurel cut fresh flowers from her garden, then wrapped them in newspaper after tying them together with a rubber band. She placed the bouquets on top of an envelope addressed to Paolo, her oldest brother. It would be good to see him. It had been almost seven years. She missed his warm, gentle ways. He always maintained contact with her, in secret. None of the other family members, his two other sisters and three other brothers, had anything to do with him, not even Marcus. But she was able to pass on to Paolo family news. His own news stayed with her alone.

She heard his light tap on the front door of the villa. She eagerly ran to the door, pulled it open, and was greeted with a blast of warm sunshine and Paolo's big grin, full of startlingly white teeth.

"Paolo." She whispered into his shoulder as he hugged her fiercely. "I have missed you so much." He smelled of the woods, his favorite place to be.

"Yes, my favorite sister, I have missed you, as well."

"Can you stay awhile? Marcus comes, and he brings his fated female. He will be here tonight."

"Maya?"

"No, her name is Anne. She was mortal when he met her, but he knew right away."

"She is no longer mortal?"

"No." Laurel felt her face fall. She looked down to avoid eye contact.

"I see," Paolo whispered. Laurel looked up to his thoughtful frown and ushered him in.

How can I explain things? Everything has changed since Marcus met Anne. Laurel fixed her hair, bringing the fine strands that had escaped the tortoise shell clip she wore at the back of her neck back under control. It felt like wiping the cobwebs of doubt from her mind.

Paolo stepped into the hallway, then stopped, scanning the carved ceiling covered in gold leaf. Laurel remembered the balls they had attended here, first as children and then later when her brothers were eligible bachelors. She had watched the beautifully gowned ladies her brothers courted. One by one, each of them had found their fated females. Except for Marcus and Paolo. Two of her other sisters had married over a hundred years ago. Their children were now having great grandchildren. Almost two centuries had passed before Paolo declared he'd had enough. It broke her heart that he left their family to seek his own way, to live among mortals. He never had children, but she knew he had married. Three times.

"How is your wife?"

"She is fading, but free from pain at least. This one is living longer. She's seventy now, but still as beautiful as the day I met her."

"You are a good husband to her, I just know it."

"The best. She is my third, you know. This is the painful time for me." Paolo had lost both his other wives when they were young.

"Perhaps you will find your fated female in our kind, then you won't have to go through the heartache again."

"No. That won't be. I don't believe in the fate. Look at the mess it's made for Marcus and yourself."

"I am patient. Mine will come, and I shall wait for him. Perhaps he is yet human and hasn't undergone the change. In the meantime, I have my bachelor brother I must tend to. Come, I have something for you." She took his hand and led him into the kitchen. She handed him the flowers and then the envelope. He smelled the bouquet while dropping a kiss on the top of her head. Then he went to the thick envelope.

"What's this?."

"A surprise. Open it."

He broke the seal and his eager fingers flushed out several old pieces of paper. They were letters. Paolo looked up at Laurel, a question in his eye.

"Father wrote these about his choice to stay mortal," she said. "I thought you would enjoy them. I found a whole trunk full of many of his writings. I had no idea he had written so much. He had opinions about everything."

"Yes, he did."

"He saw in you a big part of himself. You should read what he wrote, Paolo. In the end, he wished he had chosen differently. But Mother would not be swayed, so he chose to stay with her."

Their parents had lived as mortals, something their kind could choose. Upon puberty, they were given a choice, to remain mortal, or become a golden vampire. The Monteleones had both held off the decision until they were sure, something they encouraged all their seven children to do as well. The parents chose to remain mortal and passed on almost two centuries ago. All seven of their children elected to become vampire when the choice came to them; they were so affected by the devastating loss of their parents after they died within one year of each other.

But Paolo had regretted his decision, almost from the day he had turned, Laurel recalled. He had fought it and had been tormented ever since. Finally, he'd had to leave.

He'd returned for a visit, requested by his mortal wife who wanted him to consider reconciliation with the family at the wedding of his younger brother's granddaughter. And then he'd abruptly left again. It had been at a particularly difficult time in his "mortal" fantasy life.

Her nephew Lucius entered the ballroom. He came to Laurel's side and leaned into her, holding her skirts.

"Don't be shy, Lucius. This is my older brother, Paolo." The boy's eyes were round and large. He had the dark features Marcus had, the unmistakable sensual Monteleone nose and lips. Even his hairline was like all three of the brothers, with a slight widow's peak at the center.

"Maya and Marcus have agreed to let him stay with us for a spell so he can become acquainted with the family, in case—" Laurel stopped, sharing a conspiratorial stare with her brother.

"In case of what, Auntie?" Lucius asked. Even though Marcus had not openly admitted the child was his, Laurel allowed Lucius to call her Auntie. And she loved it.

"In case your mother has to leave for extended periods of time." Laurel sighed and looked again into Paolo's knowing eyes.

Lucius stepped forward and extended his hand to Paolo. He had been trained well. Laurel was proud of him.

"Nice to meet you, sir."

Paolo squatted and looked at the boy. Their eyes were at the same height. He shook his hand. "Nice to meet you too, Lucius." Though Laurel had told her brother about the boy, this was the first time Lucius and Paolo had met. He touched the boy's cheek. Lucius pulled away. He didn't appear comfortable with being touched. Especially by a stranger. Family or not.

Paolo chuckled and stood. He mussed the top of the boy's head and then left him alone.

Laurel studied her brother. "He's a wonderful child. Very smart." Lucius scrunched up his nose upon hearing this. "Good with numbers. He's already gone through all the books I have up to the seventh grade and he is only six."

"Six point two-five."

"See what I mean?" Laurel laughed. Paolo nodded, smiling. "He reads practically day and night, don't you?"

"I've read the Twilight series four times," Lucius said with pride.

Paolo tented his eyebrows and whistled. "Impressive, young man."

The youngster basked in the admiring light between Laurel and Paolo.

"We were just going to do some gardening," Laurel said. "Later I have to run him over to his grandmother's house. Why don't you two go pick some apples? You could take some home to your wife, Paulo. She would love them." The Monteleones gave away most of the fruit they raised, since they had no need. It gave them some good will with the community. Laurel baked berry pies for Lucius every week. It was his favorite food, other than ice cream.

"Show Paolo the orchard, and the berry patch." She knelt before him and poked him in the chest with her forefinger. "Sweet pea, try not to get berry stains on your shirt, okay?"

She touched his cheek. "Your beautiful skin we can wipe off, but the shirt could get ruined."

Lucius took the initiative and shyly grabbed Paolo's hand, then pulled him across the terrazzo floor to the back. Laurel watched her brother run in little steps with the boy, bending down to make himself shorter. They were instantly in conversation, but never out of earshot.

Paolo occasionally looked at Laurel, who waved back at him as she continued to work in the garden. She probably heard all of Lucius's questions. Paolo thought he did a fairly good job of answering them. The two had put up a ladder, and Lucius was at the top, Paolo holding onto him.

"You don't have to hold me, you know. I won't break, and I never fall." Paolo was struck by the boy's confidence. He realized perhaps he was being a little too protective.

"Alright. But I know your mother, and if anything happens to you, well, let's just say my life in this universe would cease."

"Yeah, she's like that." The boy laughed. "How well do you know my mother?"

"Oh, we all grew up together. But she always had her eyes on Marcus. She only danced with me to make him jealous."

"Did it work?"

"I can't even remember. It was a long time ago." Paolo sighed and looked at Laurel, who stood up and massaged her lower back, then looked their way.

"Paolo, can I ask you a question?"

"That's a very grown up way to say it. Good job, young man."

"Marcus told me to ask permission before I ask something someone may not want to answer."

Paolo stood still, searching the boy's face as Lucius poured apples from the basket he had made with his shirt into the bucket Paolo held.

"Okay, shoot. What is it you want to know?" Paolo leaned in and whispered so Laurel would have a harder time hearing him. "You're too young to have the sex talk."

Lucius burst out laughing so hard he almost fell off the ladder. "Sex, sex, sex, everyone's always talking about sex, whatever that means."

Paolo thought how grown up Lucius was. Old and comfortable in his body, at his age. He wished he had some of the inner peace this little-six-year-old had.

"Exactly, my man. People make too much of it. Way too much. Lucius, my friend, we've just found the first point of agreement between us."

"Yes, gentlemen should find more agreement than disagreement."

This sounded just like Marcus. His brother had done well influencing this young lad, Paolo thought. Just when he thought he'd been able to avoid a query he wouldn't be able to field, Lucius remembered his question.

"Is Marcus my father?"

"Ah, why do you ask that? What has he told you?"

"My mother's told me he is. But he never calls me his son. If he were my father, wouldn't he want to do that?"

Paolo was suddenly heartbroken for the boy. This must be a very trying situation for Marcus, being such a responsible person. And he felt the little heart beating in the six-year-old's chest, still a mortal, still trying to figure out his life and where he stood. It touched Paolo. The pain was identical to what he experienced as a mortal child, not knowing where he belonged in the scheme of things. The sense of not belonging only increased after he chose to become vampire, wishing he had made a different decision.

Paolo also knew Maya would use Lucius for her own ends, and this made him angry. She was not a proper mother. He hoped Marcus would just claim him and take him away from her, for the boy's sake. But until that day, Maya would use this boy as her pawn in a giant chess game. *Not vampire. Must be witch.* Her whole family was a thorn in their side, all of them.

"Lucius, I would trust what Marcus tells you. I would believe him. I presume you've asked."

"I'm afraid to."

"Afraid? Why?" Paolo took a few more apples from the boy's small hands.

"I want him to be my father. I really do. He says he loves me. But I'm afraid he's not my real father." Paolo could not help but melt when he saw the lone brave tear fall down the boy's red puffy cheek. He grabbed Lucius off the ladder, almost scaring him, then held him close for several minutes as the child's little feet dangled off the ground. The boy struggled at first, then buried his head in Paolo's shoulder and sobbed.

Paolo drove Lucius over to his grandmother's house. He felt better about leaving Lucius with his mother's family after learning Maya was in America, chasing after Marcus. She wasn't expected back any time soon. The shared arrangement meant Lucius was to spend half the time with each family. But now there was talk of sending him to California to live with his mother and be closer to Marcus, who now spent all his time there. Laurel gave Paolo strict instructions not to mention Marcus coming to Italy.

Paolo enjoyed the time he spent with Lucius. They had picked berries, and a warm pie was setting in a box in the back seat floor, something Lucius would have all to himself, as all others in the household had no need, being that they were all vampires.

Maya's mother, Aurora, wasn't particularly happy to see Lucius or Paolo. She was not quite as beautiful as her stunning daughter, but she had the same dark, sultry look. *Witch blood in there, eons ago.* She turned her nose up when Paolo offered her the pie, like he was handing her a dead cat. In fact, Paolo thought she might have preferred a dead cat to a berry pie. She made it quite clear where her tastes lay.

Paolo figured her lack of culture would cause her to drink blood in front of the boy, something considered low cast. Or worse yet, feed on a farm animal or some helpless human. God, he was filled with visions of what this boy's life might be like. He squeezed his fingers so tight he almost drew blood from his own palms.

"So now Marcus has his substitute bringing him over." She looked Paolo up and down. "A poor substitute at that."

"Nice to see you too, Aurora."

She hissed and showed her fangs to him, luckily out of sight of Lucius, who had run into the house with the pie he had snatched from his grandmother's hands.

"May I come in to say goodbye to Lucius?"

"No." She slammed the door.

He hated them, absolutely hated them. He decided to stay a few more days to talk to Marcus. He knew his brother had requested Lucius go back to Maya's, and although she didn't say it, Laurel implied Anne did not know about the boy. He wondered how long Marcus could keep this secret.

So many secrets . . .

So many lives ruined.

CHAPTER 16

Anne was angry. She sat in an overflowing bubbled bath all alone, at 39,000 feet in a jet that cost twenty-five million dollars or more. And the man who had plopped her into the tub without ceremony, the man who owned this jet and a vineyard in California as well as a villa in Italy, the man who had confessed she was his fated female, the man who had waited three hundred years for her, refused to have sex.

This was beyond unbelievable. No way would she be able to tell her friends. But then, not much of Anne's current life and lifestyle could be believed either.

What was Marcus doing? Why had he abruptly left her panting and wanting? She snuggled under the warm bubbles that smelled of lavender and melted into the scented water. She rubbed a sweet citrus gel over her breasts as she massaged them. She swirled the lavender liquid between her legs. She didn't feel she was bleeding, but some cramping continued.

She hadn't bought any tampons with her. The thought of having to wear one now disgusted her. Draining a human didn't disgust her, but wearing a tampon did. How her life had changed.

The mirrored bathroom door opened and Marcus stepped in, wrapped in a white towel, naked to the waist. The front of the towel pushed out like a tent.

"May I join you?" He didn't wait for her answer, and instead dropped his towel and showed Anne his huge erection. She swore under her breath. *So not fair.*

"Are you going to tease me or please me?" She pouted, but didn't take her eyes off his cock.

"I think a little of both." He stepped over the tub's lip and sat in the bath, facing her. He slid his legs under her thighs to rest along her hips. The look of him, the smell of him and his blood force, so male, so tall, surrounded by light purple bubbles, almost made her laugh. Her chill was thawing.

"I have never done this before." He smiled, his face filled with wonder like a schoolboy. His hulking lower body disappeared under the water—all except his knees, which perched high above the bubbly foam. The tub was obviously too small for him. Anne could somehow believe he'd never shared a bath with a lady, for all his three hundred years.

So much for experience. She liked being his first.

Although she wanted to ravish him, Anne waited for him to advance to her. Her cheeks felt pink, her thoughts scattered—the effects of the delicious red champagne. Anne moved just out of his long reach, leaned against the back of the tub, and squeezed her breasts. She called to Marcus's dark eyes that followed the movements of her hands, which traced up the side of her neck and covered her lips.

By the sight of Marcus's flaring nostrils, she could tell he was barely in control. It was delicious knowing he could handle anything she could give out and she wouldn't have to be careful. She wanted so much to demonstrate to him she could handle anything he wanted to do to her as well. This need burned inside her belly, increasing in intensity the more she was around him.

"Are you hungry?" Marcus stopped before his chest touched hers. She felt his warm breath. He looked so sweet with his concern for her. She felt the last vestiges of her anger evaporate.

"Aren't you worried I'll get fat if I drink too much?" Anne curled her lips up at the sides. She sat up, still facing him, and scooted her slippery body over to rest her sex against his lap, making him touch her entrance with the head of his penis. "There is only one need I have at the present time. Please, Marcus. Let me have it."

He leaned into her, and with an arm around her waist, pulled her higher up to rest on his thighs. She wrapped her legs around him. He kissed her neck as she pressed into his chest. She turned to the side, made her neck long. She craved his bite. "For you," she whispered, then bit the top of his shoulder.

"Anne." He brushed her ear with his lips, then nipped her earlobe without breaking the skin. "I give you all that I can."

She drew back to look at him, then kissed him hard. His tongue worked into her mouth, his urgent pressure causing a little blood and a tiny drizzle of pain. She wrapped her arms around his neck and held as tight as she could. If she could possess his body, she would have done it right then and there.

"Please take me, Marcus. Feed from me."

"Would you give up a lifetime of forever for a few minutes of pleasure?" He looked at her without flinching. The dripping water faucet broke the silence of the room.

Anne shook her head and sighed.

The council would have to decide. Some stupid body that was probably made up of old crones and shriveled ancient-long-black-finger-nailed-vampires she had yet to meet would determine her fate. Would they have to run their gnarled hands over her pure white flesh to inspect her menstrual blood? She knew this was important evidence of their fating. Why was this so important?

"Come, pet. Feed, then take a nap in my arms."

He moved her with ease to switch sides, then lay back against the tub's edge. Anne leaned forward and took from his neck, undulating her body back and forth, maneuvering her clitoris against his marble hard cock. The sensation of his blood in her veins and the heat of his body against hers sent her into an orgasm, and her last drops had to be taken with short quick breaths as her body sizzled. She stroked him while she finished up her feeding. Her breathing was ragged. She was just getting started.

Far from satisfied, she moved to place her mouth over the head of his cock and encircled him, moving up and down in slow rhythm. "Give me what you can give me. I will take all of it," she whispered as she let her lips rub the length of him.

"At this rate, I think I might make you fat. I think you might be the first fated female to gain weight from her male's semen."

Marcus securely held Anne. She was so much shorter than him; her feet were not able to touch the end of the tub. She have could have floated except for being bound by his embrace. *My female trusts me completely. She sleeps as I protect her.*

He was thinking about the council meeting scheduled for the next day. First, he would introduce Anne to Laurel and get a tour of the villa. Then he would have to instruct her on what would likely happen at her council interview. He shuddered as he thought about how important this meeting was. He could not bear to think about a life without Anne now. And, if he had to choose between a few stolen hours with her followed by certain death or a life without her, he would have to say he would pick the first. His life was not real without her. He hoped they saw it the same way, that her bleeding would convince them.

But there was the boy. He felt guilty for not telling Anne about Lucius, but he wasn't exactly sure what he should say, not knowing what was truth. He didn't trust Maya. That the boy looked just like Marcus, there was no question. He hoped the council didn't make him choose between the boy and Anne. *Another tough decision and path.* Perhaps a lesser man would choose a course of being on the run from the council and their long reach, constantly living in fear. This would be a stupid choice. No, better to face them, and then deal with the circumstances accordingly.

He pushed it all out of his mind for now as he felt her breathing, smelled the wonderful scent of her hair, its silkiness against his chest. Nothing in the world had made him feel so complete as to have her feed from him, to lie here in his arms. He turned the hot water on with one of his feet, careful to be delicate so as not to awaken her. The little trickle of hot water did its work, warming the lovely womb they lay in together. He sighed.

How he wanted to be able to plunge into her pink nether lips and make her scream his name. And do it over and over again. As a new vampire, her lips would swell, turn rosy red.

As much as he felt their fating, he would only know for sure once they had sex. He had not told her about that. If they weren't fated, they could remain great sexual partners. Some of his vampire friends had chosen to follow this path rather than raise a family with a fated female. But then, eventually, the true fated female would appear, and everything would change. For him, it had taken three hundred years, not the longest duration to wait for a fated female that he had ever heard of, but definitely a rare number. Maya had been a most pleasant sexual partner during the last part of that, and he treated her with the respect that came with it, being exclusive only unto her, considering that perhaps for him, there would be no real fating. In fact, he'd almost resigned himself to it.

He had lots of opportunity to pick a mate, not only in the golden vampire species, but with the darks as well. Mortal women, especially little witches with their secret spells, had even tempted him, but he'd kept to Maya, with the need to keep things uncomplicated. It was curious that he had not felt any form of jealousy when he had learned Maya had been unfaithful to him more than once. He allowed her infidelity, perhaps as proof to himself they were not actually meant for each other.

Maya was known for her scenes, something she inherited from her family. She was wild and exciting, no denying that. But he did not feel the fate. Perhaps she had spelled him, like Laurel said. It was rumored her family had some witch blood in them from some ancient ancestor.

But time for all that later. First order of business was to meet his sister, then prepare Anne for the council interview. Each would have to face the council separately. With any luck, once Robert released her vow, Marcus could have his fated female in every sense of the word. Just thinking of it made his cock rise and push against this woman's buttocks, seeking release. His cock tickled her and roused her from her deep slumber. He chuckled deep in his chest. He had such a selfish cock, a very independently thinking cock. *Soon, my little friend. Behave and you will get a treat.*

Anne woke up in Marcus's arms, still feeling the luxury of the warm scented water. One of his hands was on her breast, the other rested on her lower belly. She guided his fingers between her raised knees. She moaned and arched her back, rolling her head from side to side, exposing her neck to him again. His fingers entered her and she began to shudder with pleasure. His other hand squeezed her nipples, one at a time. He licked her neck, letting her know he wanted to bite her there. He kissed her with gentleness, as if she was as delicate as a snowflake. It sent her into waves of ecstasy. Soft or hard, everything Marcus did to her was pure pleasure.

Anne knew it would be like this until they got permission. He would never let them go beyond a certain point, and Anne would not get enough of him in the meantime. If only they had a month to themselves. A precious life without interruption. Staying naked. Getting cleaned up, then getting naked again. No having to get up to eat, to prepare dinner. So much more efficient being in love with one's host. This tall vampire could satisfy all her needs. She laughed.

She'd probably come back from a month alone with him even more addicted to him than she already was.

The plane touched down in Genoa at sunset. The pink ring on the horizon looked like a watercolor stain. Marcus admitted to himself he had a fair amount of trepidation. Meetings with the council were sometimes dangerous. The decisions the council made could be arbitrary, and were always final.

The driver met them at the airport. They sped off south towards Naples in a black Mercedes sedan. Anne cuddled against his chest, looking out the blackened window at countryside and village scenes. They traveled on a two-lane freeway, through several roundabouts and then through a town center back out into the country. At the rise of a gentle hill, they turned into a crushed gravel driveway that stretched out behind iron gates, which opened as they neared them. The sign at the gate said Monte Olivio. They drove under large pine trees that stretched almost as wide as they were tall.

Marcus pointed to them. "These are from the oldest trees in the world. They came from trees alive during the time of Christ."

Anne watched how his face turned soft and sported a smile, though she knew he was under some stress. A woman at the entrance to a large stone villa stood waving.

"And that would be my sister, Laurel. You will recognize her." He smiled again and kissed her with tenderness. "Welcome to my country villa in Tuscany, my pet."

Anne's heart ached that he didn't say "our" home. Some of her frustration returned. God, if Robert didn't release her from their spoken vows, she would kill him herself. And then the reality of what she said fell upon her and she was suddenly ashamed. Marcus loved her for who she was. She must always keep her word and be trusted to do the right thing. Always. It was dangerous to be thinking even in jest about taking shortcuts, even if it meant freedom from Robert.

The purring of his chest when Marcus talked to her softly, when he pointed something out, when he brought her along into his world, sharing more of himself, when he held her body in the warm scented bath, when he kissed her and made her body pulse, when the aliveness of his blood inside her veins turned her into some magical creature, gave her one tiny slice of Heaven. And she was not ashamed to say the more of this life she got, the more she craved, could not live without.

The car stopped. She reached up and touched his cheek. "Marcus, I know this is an important time for us. I want to thank you—for everything, even before we do this, I want to thank you for giving us a chance like this. I—" Tears welled up in her eyes. All she could say was, "I am so grateful you found me—whatever happens."

"Yes." He kissed her. "Always remember I love you. You can trust in that. No matter what happens, please know that. Never forget that, Okay, my pet?"

"Yes, Marcus. Even if I find out you spend every waking moment away from me looking like a green lizard, I don't care. I love you and nothing will ever stop me."

"We will be tested." He traced her lips with his forefinger. "Our love must survive no matter what."

Marcus's sister came up to the car and tapped on the rear window. Anne looked up and gasped. Laurel was the nurse who had treated her after the attack. The attack that had changed her life forever.

Marcus exited the rear door and embraced Laurel, who jumped into his arms. She showered him with kisses and he laughed. "Careful, careful, Laurel. Anne will get jealous of my own sister. How scandalous!" It didn't stop her from kissing him further.

Marcus held a hand out. Anne let him help her out of the back seat. She stood not more than a foot apart from them. Laurel, who surprised her when she reached out and pulled her to her chest. "Welcome, Anne. It's so nice to see you so healthy, so beautiful. You glow with inner love."

"Yes, I think anything Marcus loves blooms." All three were silent for a bit. "I want to thank you for taking such good care of me that day. I have questions maybe you can answer."

"Later." Marcus said into her ear. He wrapped his big arm around her waist and began walking, almost carrying her to the stone structure.

Through large carved doors, they entered an enormous hallway. Ceilings frescoed in colorful paintings in bright colors warmed the room, which looked several hundreds of years old, with a few faded watermarks. Oil paintings of family members, some of them colorful, some of them very dark due to age, surrounded the walls, affixed to thick plaster walls.

"We have a strange ancestor." Marcus pointed to the frescoes on the ceiling. Anne couldn't see what he was pointing to. She saw some monkeys and banana leaves, birds, plants, and people with short pantaloons and shoes with pointed toes and square buckles. She shrugged and looked back at Marcus.

"Look at their chests." Anne looked at the monkeys and sure enough, they all sported large breasts. So did the birds. And the women were bare to the waist and had enormous breasts as well. She laughed, covering her mouth.

"How old are these?" Anne thought it was hysterical.

"I think about four hundred years, give or take a hundred. Maybe more, right, Laurel?" He looked at his sister.

"I think easily four hundred." She shook her head from side to side. "Marcus, of all the things you could show her . . ."

Marcus picked Anne up and whisked her up the stairs. "That's all of a tour you get for now. It's dinnertime!"

Anne waved to Laurel, who returned the wave just before she and Marcus disappeared through a high archway into a bedroom the size of Anne's place. The dark walnut ceiling was carved with monkeys with large breasts. He set her down and cupped her, then bent down to kiss her. "I have never brought a woman here to this room before. I have never bed a woman here. You will be the first, and the last."

It was a simple statement. Anne felt her heart would burst. However important their fating was, especially to Marcus and someday to her, no matter how urgent it was that she be able to have sex as a true partner with him, her life was now complete with these simple words coming from this man's lips. Everything else in her life would pale in comparison. She was certain her life would begin and end here. With Marcus, in his arms, in his bed.

Later on, Marcus explained some of the rules she would need to know. The blood was never wrong. Fating meant that the couple could have children. Otherwise, the sexual union would not produce any offspring.

And not every golden chose this kind of life. He told her his brother had chosen to live with mortal women and would continue to outlive them. He also explained that children born would be born human and were given the choice at puberty whether they wanted to go forward as a human or a vampire.

He explained his parents had chosen to stay mortal. But all his brothers and sisters had chosen to eventually become vampire.

A blood relative could only do the turning, so it was critical a teen stay close to the biological family in case a turning was required. It was rare for them to stray away. And any turning had to be approved by the Council.

"So why was I turned?" Anne asked.

"That was a violation."

"I don't understand."

Marcus kissed her. "Enough questions. We need to focus on the interview with the Council. I will answer all your questions later. There is still a lot for you to know."

CHAPTER 17

Robert fingered the note Anne had left. She'd demanded he be out of the house by the weekend. Well, his name was on the lease too. What the hell was she thinking? She couldn't just do that.

And then he read over the part where she said she was asking for him to publically renounce the wedding vows, even though she acknowledged they were technically not married. *What's up with that?* This sounded like something legal. Maybe he should consult Gary.

But he probably wouldn't.

Robert decided he wasn't going to go down that quickly. What was the point? Things weren't really so different than they'd always been. Anne was the one who had changed. *He* hadn't. It was just that he'd gotten caught. Even with her change, things could have remained the same between them. Maybe they could have even stayed married, *if* he hadn't gotten caught.

Damn Monika and her cherry flavored condoms. He'd be the only lonely ex-married man on a condom diet. Lambskin was just fine, thank you very much.

So why would *he* have to go to all the trouble to move out? That wasn't the Anne he married. She had changed ever since she'd come back from Italy. Now she ate like a bird but wasn't getting skinny. She used to be a cautious driver and now she was wicked fast. The neighbors told him she'd taken to gardening in the dark. Said it was so she could see the critters eating her flowers. Now that stuff was just weird. Even Gary thought it was weird, and he should know.

He thought about his friend Gary's taste in women. That one last night with the red bedroom, for instance. He didn't remember a lot of the encounter except for everything being red: her clothes, her bedroom, her bed, and—was there blood too? He tried to focus, but all he saw were her ginormous breasts and the red—that was it—red satin sheets, or deep pink sheets with red stuff.

Fuck me.

This mental fog was starting to piss him off, because he really wanted to get his money's worth. That was one time he wished they'd been in one of those rooms you could put on video. Bet she had some moves. Almost like it was a waste of the hundred bucks. Gary said it was a terrific deal, but not if he couldn't remember anything other than her letting him take a taste of her tits and then giving him that kiss that almost hurt. She really wanted him too, he could tell.

Gary had awoken him on the couch later. The woman had tossed him from her bedroom like sloppy seconds after they were done, and had locked her door. Helluva bedside manner. *Not very fucking professional.* Next time he'd tell her "no, thanks."

They helped themselves to another beer on their way out and compared notes as soon as they were alone in Gary's truck. They had their wallets, and Gary's cross and Robert's wedding ring were still in their possession. They decided they should take a dose of penicillin he had just in case, and a good, hot shower. They both smelled of burnt feathers, and each had figured it was the incense she burned that made their eyes water. He'd heard somewhere smelling burnt feathers was a sign of a brain tumor. Not likely something like that would occur to them both at exactly the same time, so Robert ruled it out.

On the way home, they both discovered their dicks hurt, which prompted a quick trip to a Starbucks bathroom. Screw that little punk with purple hair and the lip piercing for thinking they were gay. But when they both dropped their drawers and examined themselves, they both had two holes in the side of their dicks. They didn't look anything like pimples or a reaction to some cream he'd had in the past. Something very kinky had gone on there. That's when he found out Gary didn't remember screwing her either. They were of a mind to go back there tonight and ask for a goddamned refund at first. And Gary had set this all up. Who can you count on if not your very best friend? *Dickwad.*

He shook his head and realized his neck no longer hurt. He looked at himself in the mirror. There was very little of the purple mark left from the day before. Good riddance. Finally, he'd caught a break. Now if he could just lose the little holes too. He was glad the swelling in his dick didn't interfere with his urine stream.

Thank God for small favors. Now if I can just get my marriage back together.

Robert jumped into the shower as soon as he got home. No way he was going to get an infection and have his cock get all swollen, turn yellow, or drain puss. He'd seen that before, to someone else on his baseball team who had a lost weekend in Mexico. So, try as he might, he could not remember a single one of his hundreds of sexual partners who had ever done this to him. What exactly was it, anyhow? A bite? *Jeez.*

The phone rang just as he stepped out of the shower. Dripping wet, he hobbled over and answered it.

"Meester Robert. You got a lady," Elena was underscoring the word *lady* with emphasis she didn't normally do. This could not be good. "She want to see you right away. Joo close by?"

"Um, who is she?"

He heard muffled voices as Elena asked the woman for her name.

"Mr. Robert, her name is Maya Monteleone. She's looking to talk to you about your wife."

"Anne?"

"Yeah. Dat one. Joo comin' down here right now?"

"I can't get there for at least an hour." There were more muffling sounds, and over Elena's protests, a new voice came on the phone.

"Robert, this is Maya. We met last night, remember?"

No, Robert didn't really remember. But he knew who she was just the same. His dick lurched under his towel. *Fucking traitor.*

"Robert, are you there?"

"Yes, I'm here." He wanted to shout, *and what are those goddamned marks on my pecker?* but he didn't.

"How do you feel this morning?"

"How do you think I feel? Like a lab experiment."

Maya laughed. She didn't sound so dark when she did that. She actually sounded a little like Monika. And then he got worried the holes would make a scar. What would he tell Monika when she had her change of heart? He was sure she would. Maybe Anne wouldn't, but Monika could always be counted on.

"Listen, Robert. I have a business proposition for you, something I think you will be interested in." She lowered her voice to a whisper, no doubt trying to calm Elena's death stare. "I also thought I could make it up to you, if you like."

He didn't like, but his cock did. He felt like slapping it but that would make it worse. "I'm out of money." That was true, after all. Lawyers were expensive.

"You silly. I'm looking to help you *make* a little money. You interested?"

Robert wondered if she had in mind donating blood again through his dick. Maybe he had some rare blood type they would pay thousands of dollars an ounce for or something. Then he thought of Gary and knew this wasn't true.

"What about Gary?"

"He had his fun. This is between you and me." Elena was making lots of noise in the background. "You better tell your secretary it is okay we speak."

"I'll tell her tomorrow. What kind of business thing are you talking about?"

"Can I see you?"

"Um, I'm not coming in today. I've got some things I have to do at home."

"Okay, I will meet you there. What's your address?"

There was a pause. Robert knew it was a mistake to give the address out. Wouldn't be the first mistake he made today. Certainly wouldn't be the last.

She wore red again. And damn, she must have been a faster driver than Anne, because it only took her about five minutes to get to the door. He didn't even have his clothes on, just his shorts. She noticed. She didn't ask to be invited in, but walked up to him and slid against his chest, right past him into the living room. That was all his traitorous body part needed. It was very clear who its master was.

She scanned the room, even raised her nose as if to smell the air. Robert smelled under his arms. He'd just showered. Was part of the experiment learning what kind of shower gel he used?

"Is your wife at work?" she asked as she stepped to face him, touching her breasts against his chest. She rubbed them from side to side. The traitor under his shorts liked it. He was making a real fuss down below.

Robert stepped back, a little cautious. "She doesn't work. I think she's at the place she volunteers at today."

"Oh." Maya's eyebrows arched. "When will she be home?"

"I'm not sure. What is this about?"

"What is this about? What is this about?" she mimicked as she closed the distance between them. "This is about how much time we have before she comes home."

"Uh huh."

"So, how much time do we have?"

"Ah. I'm not feeling too good right now. Something *bit* me last night, did you know that?"

Maya smiled and looked at the bulge in his shorts. She squeezed it through the cotton fabric with one hand. God, she had strong hands. He didn't dare move. Wasn't anything like Monika, even on one of her "frisky" nights.

"I hope I didn't hurt you."

Robert was thinking that yes, she was hurting him a little bit right now. Traitor hadn't figured it out yet. This wasn't going anywhere good. Besides, how did she know the bite was on his dick?

"So, you admit to biting me?"

"Yes." She massaged his dick, being gentle now. That was more like it. Traitor purred. "Let me see what I've done. I am so sorry. I want to make it up to you." She got on her knees and slid his shorts down to his ankles.

"No biting." Like he could stop her.

"No biting, unless you want to bite me." She slid his cock in and out of her mouth and he lost his shame and fear all at once. "Do you want to bite me, Robert?"

"I don't bite."

"Maybe you should try. To get even with me, hmm?" She licked the length of his shaft. Her dark eyes begged him to come all over her face, but something told him she wanted something else. "Oh, Robert, you taste so nice."

He jerked a bit. Had she told him the very same thing last night? A vague memory surfaced, a memory of hearing the same words from under his jaw line, as she'd been *biting* his neck! Holy cow!

"I'm, I'm not sure what's going on here." He backed away from her. His cock bounced in the air, starved for her stroke, trying to stand up like a drunken sailor. He quickly pulled up his shorts. Maya was still on her knees, watching him. Then she slid the straps of her red top over her shoulders, but stopped before her breasts were completely bare. She lowered her eyes to look at her hands folded in her lap.

"You don't like me. I'm sorry." It was a whisper, so faint, but it was as effective as a shout.

Robert lifted her pure white chin with one hand and looked at the closed eyes and pouting red lips and knew he would get lost in them. He looked at her like how he looked at Monika asleep in the limo on the morning of his bachelor party and felt compelled to be tender, to try to give her back some of the pleasure she gave him, gave all of them.

"No, honey, I like you just fine." He thought she looked sufficiently grateful. He liked grateful sex. He liked feeling like the best lay in the county. Maybe he could surprise her with some moves of his own.

And yes, maybe he would bite her.

What the hell.

CHAPTER 18

R obert was rock hard again. This was too good to be true. Something about this woman, Maya, brought out all the best in his maleness. He bet he'd showed her a few things. He was so satisfied, lying in his bed feeling like he was eighteen again and horny as hell. He looked around and noticed Maya was no longer next to him

He got up and slipped on his shorts. He found her in the bathroom. She was sniffing one of Anne's bottles of perfume. She had found Anne's robe hanging on the peg behind the door. Robert wasn't sure he liked this. Even Monika would *never* do that. Not like Maya was anything like Anne. He decided he just attracted strong female types and loved Monika for the wanton variety she was.

"Oh, hello there." She greeted him with a smile. She didn't hide what she had been doing.

Robert leaned over and took the perfume from her hands. "This belongs to my wife."

Maya let the open robe slip to the floor and stood in front of him, naked. "Spray it on me so you can think of her when you fuck me again."

Robert thought this was a strange thing to say. Certainly a twist he hadn't run across before. It irritated him for some reason. He picked up the robe and put it back on the peg.

"If you need clothes, I can give you something else to wear." He turned to walk away, but noticed she had removed the robe and put it on again. He sighed. *Pick your battles carefully.* He had to admit, this one was real different.

"Come on, Robbie, let's talk." She tried to grab his hand but he yanked it free. "Don't call me Robbie. Call me Robert or Rob."

She sauntered over to him and placed his hands on her breasts. "How about I call you big boy. How about Superfuck?"

Now that was nice of her. But all the same, he could tell she was lying. There would be no outsmarting this one. Better get ready and let her have her way, and then maybe she would leave him alone. But damn, he felt great. Really great.

"You want another taste?" She bared her neck and, sure enough, there were human bite marks there, two rows of them, even spaces for some of the molars he'd had pulled. So he hadn't been dreaming. And it looked like his bite had broken the skin, too.

"I'm so sorry, Maya." He was shocked at his behavior. What in the world was happening to him?

"Oh, don't be. You only gave me a little bite. I think you got maybe one or two drops. You were just having fun punishing me, remember?"

He felt her breasts, then moved his hands down and behind to encircle her waist and pulled her to him. "I wanted to be tender. I didn't mean to hurt you." His statement was genuine. He wasn't some animal, after all. He looked at the mark, rubbed his fingers over it. He could see it almost disappearing right before his eyes. He looked at the end of his finger. Nothing there. Maybe he had a healing touch. Who knew?

"You see, you didn't hurt me." She ground herself into his crotch. "I like it when you taste me."

"Well, I'm not used to tasting my ladies' necks. I prefer other parts." His voice became husky again.

"Oh. That's nice too. Want to try it?"

He nodded as he kissed over the remains of his punishment. She moaned and melted into him.

"But, Robert, one thing. If you taste me, you have to give me just a little bite, okay?"

Robert wasn't sure whether she liked the sex or the bite better. Just his luck he managed to find someone who he could hurt and would heal so quickly. He was thrilled.

"So, we have to talk now."

God, Maya was beautiful. Seemed to become more and more beautiful every minute he spent with her. Robert loved kissing her everywhere. Her skin was so white, so completely white. But her nipples were deep red, as were her lips. And the nice slit between her legs was blood red when he peeled back the petals and tasted her, bit her. She came when he did it. He thought that was what he liked doing most to her.

"Robert?"

"Yes." He lay next to her, looking up at the ceiling. He couldn't concentrate when he looked at her.

"Do you know where your wife is? You don't seem to be very afraid of having her come home and finding us naked together. What's going on?" She rolled over, then propped her head with her arm.

Robert inhaled and then decided to just tell the truth. "She kicked me out. I have to be out this weekend. We're splitting up."

"What?" Maya sat up straight and looked down at him, a sneer on her face.

"What difference does it make?"

"All the difference in the world." She whirled around and presented her back. Robert rubbed her there. Her skin was so pale, and smooth. Like alabaster. He leaned over and kissed each of her ass cheeks and the base of her spine, moving up.

Maya stood and put on Anne's robe again. She sat in the chair Anne sat in three days ago, when she'd told him it was over. Same robe. Same chair. He hoped the message wasn't the same as well.

"You have to tell me where she is right now."

"How should I know? For all I know she's gone to visit her parents in Portland, or over to a friend's house. I don't think she will be back over here today."

"What makes you say this?"

"Her suitcase is gone."

"Damn."

He could tell Maya was thinking hard about something. "Um, Maya. Why all this interest in . . . in . . . Anne. I thought you and I . . ."

"Oh, shut up and let me think."

This offended Robert's sense of dignity. He felt like he was the last one in on a dirty little joke. Maybe the joke was on him. "Wait a minute. What the hell is going on? I need to know right now." Robert thought that sounded pretty strong. Manly.

Maya flew off the chair and landed on top of him, pinning him to the bed. She almost knocked the wind out of him. He was suddenly very afraid. She looked down at him with her dark eyes. A golden ring began to form in the middle. Robert squinted as her expression changed from docile kitten to ravenous beast.

No wonder she liked the bites better than the sex.

Bile rose in his stomach. Maya turned her head at an awkward angle and smiled at him. Her mouth looked like she was working hard to keep her lips covering her teeth. She sat still, her eyes closed, and sighed. All of a sudden, she was calm. None of the wolfish face remained. Robert was a little relieved.

"Did she take a big suitcase or small one, dear?" The dear part was added a bit too late. Like she was masking something, feigning affection.

"Big." Robert didn't care if she saw he was shaking. He had the urge to pee.

"Thank you." She traced his lips with her forefinger. "And where, Robert, does she keep her passport?"

Robert couldn't speak. He pointed to the dresser. In an instant she was off him, rummaging through the top drawer. Then through the next one, then the bottom drawer. She wasn't putting things back. Anne would be pissed. He was thinking what he would say to her if she found out. Of course she would find out. He was the one leaving. She was staying.

Robert sat up, making sure to cover his crotch. What did he know about this woman? Nothing! Nothing except she was wicked fast, wicked strong, could light candles faster than anyone he had ever seen, worked in an adult bookstore, and took men home to her red bedroom. And she liked to bite, in strange places, too. And . . . *I bit her!*

His stomach gave up on him. He put his palm over his mouth, bolted for the bathroom, and almost made it. What he threw up on the floor didn't make him happy. His bile was black, and it seemed to burn holes in his brand new linoleum. There was that burnt feathers smell again.

Shit, what have you done, Robert?

Maya stepped behind him as he was wiping up the mess. She didn't look surprised at the damage to the floor. When she bent over to touch his back, he leapt up and pinned himself against the opposite wall, protecting his privates with both hands.

"Don't touch me." He didn't care he was sounding like a first-rate coward. He had gone along with everything, the biting, the blood stuff, but now he was poisoned as well. And this bitch was looking for his wife! His *wife*!

As if she read his mind, Maya held up his cell phone. She extended it out in front of her while spearing him with that look in her eye. Robert flinched. He carefully took the phone, not wanting to touch her skin as he did so.

"Call her."

"Who?" He sounded like a fifth grader. He swore to himself.

"Call your wife. Ask her where she is."

Robert was going to say no, but one look at Maya's face told him that would have dangerous consequences. Not lethal, but more than likely painful. Well, hell, it was *just* a phone call. Not like he was going to set a trap for Anne or something. He had to have time to consult Gary, who would know what to do about this situation. And then maybe they would go to the police, or visit his friend who was a security guard at Wal-Mart. At least his friend owned a gun and knew a lot about law enforcement, although Gary *had* flunked the police exam.

Maya was still wearing Anne's robe. She was not in a sexy mood. "I said call her, or I will make you call her. Do it now, before I get mad." Maya walked up to him very close. He felt trapped, helpless. "You really don't want to get me mad, Robert, do you?"

CHAPTER 19

Paolo stepped into the entryway and perused the bags by the front door. A cell phone chirped in the pocket of a jacket hanging on a hook by the door. The jacket didn't look to be Laurel's, so he took it to be one belonging to his brother's woman. He fished through the pocket, grabbed the phone, and noticed the name "Robert" flashing on the screen. He put it back without answering it.

Laurel joined him.

"Are they upstairs?" He pointed to the ceiling.

She nodded.

A smile graced Paolo's lips as he thought about his brother in love at last, after all this time. Perhaps there was hope for him, after all. He wondered if Marcus ever really loved Maya and guessed not.

"What's she like?"

Laurel looked up for a minute before answering. "Anne is beautiful, but then, Marcus has never been interested in anyone but real beauties."

Paolo nodded. This was true.

"She's small, petite. They look nice together." She stared off into the distance, through kitchen windows to the orchard. "I have never seen him bending over so much. He shows her things and almost kneels down to her eye level. It's very sweet. He's so tender with her."

Both he and his brother had a fondness for small women, made even more is distinctive by the fact that they were both so tall.

"Nice."

"Yes, it is. Nice to have lovers in this house again. You notice how the air smells better, the flowers seem brighter?"

"Yes, we are basking in the glow of their love." Paolo hoped she didn't pick up his sarcasm.

"You will too, some day."

"I love my wife now." He looked at his hands. "But it is different. Not like this."

Laurel hugged him, burying her head in his chest. "Promise me, brother, your next choice won't cause you so much pain. You should choose from your own kind."

"I am not human, but I choose to live and love that way."

"At what cost?"

"She is worth the price. Any price."

"Why not bring her here, let her meet the rest of the family?"

"She's ill now. Cannot travel. Maybe if she gets better I will, but I think this may be the end for her." Paolo sighed and stroked Laurel's hair. "Does he know I'm here?"

"No. There wasn't time."

Paolo smiled. "That anxious to get upstairs, hum?"

"Afraid so." Laurel broke their embrace and looked into his eyes. "We must be happy for him, Paolo. He mustn't see our pain, our loneliness."

"Agreed." He said this as he nodded.

The cell phone in the jacket rang again.

"Who's Robert?" Paolo asked. "He seems to be calling Marcus's woman."

"I don't know. Marcus would. Should we bring it to them?"

They looked in each other's eyes and both shook their heads.

The door to the master opened and Marcus descended the stairs with Anne in tow.

"Paolo! What a surprise." Marcus almost crashed into him as he gave his brother a big hug and slap on the back. They stood at the same height, eye to eye, regarding one another, looking for changes that would never occur on their faces.

"This is Anne," Marcus said, presenting her hand to Paolo's bow.

"Enchanted." Paolo kissed the back of Anne's knuckles and traced a lovely citrus and vanilla fragrance. He instantly wanted to bite her.

Anne giggled.

He dropped her little pink newly turned fingers and noticed her face flushing. She seemed bashful. Paolo could read the sigh of contentment in his brother's demeanor.

Marcus beamed, looking at Anne, obviously proud of his new love. And protective. Then Marcus became serious. "How long are you staying, Paolo?"

"I leave tomorrow. Sorry, but this was just a quick trip. My wife is ill, in her final stages of cancer."

"I'm sorry."

"Where do you live, Paolo?" Anne seemed genuinely interested.

He knew he and Marcus could pass for twins if it weren't for his sandy brown hair compared to Marcus's black locks. Did this female find him attractive as well?

"South of France."

"Beautiful countryside. I was there earlier this summer." She dipped an arm around Marcus's waist, adding a seductive look that Marcus returned along with a caress to her cheek, followed by a little kiss.

How Paolo longed to have a female look at him like that. He was suddenly filled with need. It was difficult to see the flesh of his human wife whither and gray before his eyes. And the pain of watching her age was probably more difficult for him to bear than it was for her. How would it feel to have someone love you who was so young, who would look budding and luscious forever?

"You going to finish the tour, Marcus?" Anne's eyes were bright as she looked up at her man. "Paolo, you want to come?"

The flash in her eyes quickened his pulse. He hoped Marcus didn't notice. This female was indeed intoxicating. He looked at Laurel, who was fanning herself and shaking her head.

Yes, my sister. Some things never do change.

"Actually, Marcus, let's have Laurel give her the tour. I need to speak to you alone, if you don't mind."

Before Marcus could reply, Laurel took Anne by the arm. The two women got into quick conversation, their heads bowing to each other as they walked through the hall to the kitchen and out the back door.

Secrets. Women always had secrets, and whispers. Were they talking about him?

"She's lovely." Paolo said as he watched the women.

"And she's mine."

"Of course." Paolo smiled at the slight verbal slap on the cheek.

The two brothers went into the study.

"Something to drink, Paolo?"

"Two fingers, please."

They retired to the leather chairs in the corner. Marcus handed Paolo the tumbler with the hundred-year-old whisky without ice. "So, what's up?" Marcus asked.

"I met the boy today. He's a handsome one."

Marcus's brow furrowed but he nodded his head and took a sip of the deep amber liquid.

"Does Anne know?"

"No. Not yet."

"What are your plans?"

"First I have to meet with the council, so we can marry. I will ask Maya for permission to adopt Lucius, if Anne will agree. I think she will. I hope she would grow to love him, as I do."

Paolo looked at his glass and nodded, a faint smile toying with his lips. "You're probably right. You are sure, then?"

"What, about the fating? I am sure about being fated to Anne. I have no explanation for the fathering of that child. But I sense he is mine, just as I feel I was meant to wed Anne and not Maya."

"How can you feel for the boy and not for the mother?"

"I don't know, but that's the truth of it. I just hope the council sees it the same way."

"Marcus, I wanted to speak to you because I feel you must decide to raise this child as your own no matter what the council says. He shouldn't be allowed to spend any time with Aurora and the rest of Maya's family. You know they are long suspected of having part witch blood. I cannot think any of them would ever make a proper guardian. All those women are deadly to the boy. I even fear for his life." He looked up at Marcus, feeling the weight of the difficulty of his position. "That boy needs a father. Deserves a father."

"First things first. Once Anne is approved and accepted, anything is possible. I think she will help me do this."

"Yes, I hope so too." Paolo remembered the ringing phone. "By the way, who is Robert?"

"Robert?"

"Yes, Anne's cell phone has gone off twice. I noticed someone named Robert was calling her. Does that name mean anything to you?"

"He's her husband."

"Excuse me?" Paolo wasn't sure he heard correctly. *Marcus has fated to a woman who is married to another?*

"They pledged their vows. That's partly why I need council permission."

"Marcus, you've made a mess of things. For once, you've outdone me!"

"Robert's not worthy of Anne. And he's mortal. She knew that before we became close."

"So, you are not bedding her?"

"And risk separation forever? Hell, no."

"When do you see them?"

"This afternoon. We have an appointment in one hour." He stood up. "I think we should get ready. I need to prepare her for the inspection."

"She bleeds?"

"She does indeed." Marcus looked proud.

They said their goodbyes.

As Marcus walked out to the garden to get Anne, Paolo watched him. Was his brother man enough to do the unthinkable, be fated to two females at the same time? Was that even possible? And what would the council decide?

CHAPTER 20

On the way to the council meeting, Marcus took Anne's hand and kissed it. "Your hands are freezing."

Anne had been looking at the countryside as they passed by. The gently sloping vineyard rows and red rocky soil looked familiar. She felt an odd connection to this strange land. The driver behind the clear partition of the big Mercedes limo paid no attention to them.

Marcus always rode in style. She would have enjoyed it except for being so nervous. Who were these people on the council, and what power did they have over Marcus? Over her? Their entire future depended on what this panel of elders decided.

She still bled, but there was hardly a trace. She was slightly concerned it had dried up completely.

"Marcus, I have a bad feeling about this meeting."

"Don't, my pet. You will see. They just need to learn who you are. We have to follow the rules so we can enjoy the *benefits* of our society." By benefits, she took it to mean they could have sex. Unlimited sex. Nothing less than that would do. She'd never had to ask permission for this before.

He nibbled on her fingers. She knew he was trying to get her attention, trying to seduce her again with those dark eyes. All she had to do was look at him, and she would do anything.

God, she loved watching him take command of her body, and of everything else around him. He owned it all. She craved the maleness of him—the way he smelled, how his huge dark form enveloped her, devoured her. She wished they were just going wine tasting or on their way to the jet or going on a road trip. Something fun. Not something she dreaded.

What would she do if she somehow didn't pass muster? Was her life in danger? Was his?

He gazed at her now with that look that said he needed her, that he needed her kiss, the reassurance she was up to the challenge of facing them. She leaned forward and made her lips as soft as she could, then pressed them against his lips, flesh on flesh. He went deeper with his tongue, as if he could not resist. His hands—his wonderful big hands—covered and squeezed her breasts. He was totally hers.

If the council allows it.

"May I, just a little taste?"

She loved it when he begged. "I'm thinking, Marcus."

"About what?"

He explored the valley between her aching tits. His tongue was hot and snaked under the black bra he had bought her for the occasion. The one with the matching panties that had the hole down the length of the crotch. She tingled with the thought of what his tongue would do as he nuzzled and found that opening. *Make him beg a little more.* She wanted to feel the fullness of his need.

"Just a little of you on my tongue."

Yes. She nodded as he bit her breast in the dark fold underneath, so it wouldn't show.

His body shuddered as he supped her precious drop of blood. He and whispered, "My sweet, sweet Anne."

How glorious it would be when she could completely surrender to him. Maybe she could get Robert to give her that freedom tonight, if she and Marcus were successful with the council.

A vision popped into her head, forcing a smile. She saw Marcus with her naked, his cock just at the folds of her sex, ready to enter and blast her to heaven and back, and her dialing Robert on the phone. The phone would ring, the anticipation fueling the passion. Just as Robert would be about to say he'd agree to release her, Marcus would thrust inside her. In just that second, she'd be free. No longer than a second. It couldn't come soon enough.

The panties were handy for Marcus's fingers as well. He stroked her. Anne saw the driver's gaze fastened to the road. He was discreet and never looked back at them. The possibility that someone was watching heightened the danger of it, though, made her even hotter. She would have let Marcus do more, but he withdrew his hand.

"What were you thinking about just then, hmm?"

"About how it will be, our first time together. Having sex."

He kissed her. "Me too, pet."

"Taste me again," she whispered with barely a sound.

But Marcus could hear. He watched the words form on her lips, leaned to her neck, and licked her pulsing vein. "Soon, very soon now." His hot breath and one sharp fang slowly slid up her cool flesh, following the vein throbbing underneath.

Their lips claimed each other again, and she nicked her tongue on his elongated canine. He inhaled when her blood dropped onto his tongue, then rubbed the blood all over the insides of their lips. He pulled away and held her gaze without blinking.

"I have not told you something you need to know. They are going to have to inspect you. Inspect your bleeding. Just like at a doctor's office."

"Okay."

"Someone other than I will need to witness, as well."

"Like one of the directors?"

"Yes."

"Perverts." She was not looking forward to this at all.

"You're unbelievable. Wicked and strong. I like this in you." He gave her that smile, all white teeth, just showing the tips of his fangs. Just the look of his fangs could get her wet now. How her life had changed in such a short time.

She offered her wrist to him for another taste.

He took a small nip then said, "Thank you." He licked the wound, blew on it, and rubbed it with his forefinger, accelerating the healing process.

"You should take more. I could live with wounds of your love all over my body."

"In time, my pet." His voice almost purred.

She saw the euphoric effect her blood had on him. His red lips puffed up, full. She knew his manhood was equally swollen. She knew they would do this when they made love. He would become so engorged from drinking of her. And her lips would swell from the drinking of him. Her muscles contracted in waves as she thought about them enjoying each other all night long. Unspeakable pleasure.

"You must feed now."

Anne knew he was right.

He drew her to his chest. She peeled back his unbuttoned shirt and bit him just above his nipple. She resisted the urge to straddle him, her favorite position now when she was feeding, so she could rub him against her sex. That's why they always had to feed in private. It was as intimate as making love.

She pulled away.

Marcus whispered, "Take more, love. You need your strength. I want them to see you fully sated on my blood. I want them to see the effects of our fating. I want them to smell the chemistry, the blood between us."

The car descended to the council compound. Anne noticed Marcus's glow had faded. His eyes squinted, as if in alarm, and his body tensed. He grasped her head between both his hands, and while smoothing over her lips with his thumbs, looked deep into her eyes. "Just answer all their questions truthfully. We have nothing to hide, right? You can tell them about Robert. You can tell them we have not had sexual intercourse. You'll want to tell them what it feels like to be vampire. They need to know these things."

She nodded. She knew there was something he wasn't telling her. Was he worried they wouldn't rule they were fated?

But how could they deny this evidence? She decided perhaps Marcus was just overly cautious.

"I will tell them how much I need you, crave you, Marcus. Surely they will recognize signs that I am fated to you."

He was silent, watching their fingers entwine on her lap. "Whatever you hear, know that I love you. Whatever they ask you to do, you must do it. Please do whatever they ask."

"But, Marcus, what if they ask something of me I cannot do?"

He looked down. She could tell he was thinking about that.

"My pet, I hope that you are able to do anything they ask you to do, please, for us. Then we can be together, forever."

"Yes. I will do it."

"Remember that I love you. I would do anything for you."

"Yes, I will remember. You can't tell me anything more?"

"What we are asking has never been done before."

They were ushered into the drawing room where they were instructed to wait on opposite sides, facing each other across the large spans. He was summoned. As he came over to give her another kiss, the messenger hissed at him and he was forced to follow, denied Anne's touch. She did not like this one bit. Her bad feeling grew worse.

And then she was summoned.

The room was dark and had a smell she found disgusting. *Vampire sweat.* Old vampire sweat. All of the seven council members were ancient. Two of them were especially hunched over, looking barely alive, sitting in wheel-chairs, which squeaked and echoed off the walls of the enormous hall lined in mirrors.

How can these be immortal? They look like they are dying.

She guessed this large room had been the scene of many great pageants and celebrations over the centuries, but now was covered in cobwebs. There was no music, no laughter. Just cold marble statues and dusty two-story high mirrors in heavy baroque gilt frames.

The two sick council members had IVs of red liquid attached to their arms. All of them wore deep red robes. She could see Marcus nowhere.

"Welcome, child." All but the two infirmed stood as she approached the long raised table. The two who didn't stand grunted and frowned. The vampire in the middle motioned for her to have a seat in the red leather chair in front of them.

Anne's first reaction to all the red and the smell was to be sick to her stomach. How could Marcus abandon her to this group? They appeared disinterested and dangerous.

After she took her place, the leader began the questioning. "So, my dear. You are a conversion, is that correct?"

"Excuse me?"

"You are not a naturally born vampire, right?"

"Right."

"And tell me about that experience." His eyes turned to slits as he leaned forward to hear. "And you must speak up because several of us have hearing problems."

Anne thought one had already fallen asleep. Odd. Very odd. This vampire appeared to be mortal. "Well, I was bitten, by a woman. I was told later it was Maya."

"Who told you this?"

"Marcus."

Two of the members grunted in open disgust, nodding to each other.

"Go on."

Anne wasn't sure what to say next. "Well, she bit me, and then I woke up in a hospital room, or what I thought was a hospital room. I was released the next morning, and they said I was okay, free to leave, and that I hadn't been harmed."

"Who are 'they'?" the robe next to the leader shouted.

"The nurse." She decided to leave off the fact that it had been Laurel. No sense getting her into this mess, though she was probably already involved.

It worked, as the heads bobbed while they conferred in whispers. When they looked back at her, she realized they were expecting her to continue the story.

"I drove from Genoa, along the Mediterranean all the way to Spain, then went by boat to Majorca. I had my first urge to feed four days after the bite. So I did."

"And how was that?"

Anne remembered what Marcus had told her. She decided to appeal to their maleness, if that was still present under their wrinkled skin and somber demeanor. She thought she would use a little helpless charm.

"It went awful. I got blood absolutely everywhere."

Several of the vampires chuckled.

The sleeper woke up. "Is it over?" he blurted out.

Someone reassured him he hadn't missed anything. They stared back at her. She figured she'd continue talking until they asked her to stop. Her time to show what she was made of, perhaps. Maybe this was what Marcus had meant.

"I ruined a perfectly good pair of jeans that cost me $140."

She got no reaction. Maybe they didn't know about jeans.

"I was embarrassed, ashamed at having caused so much of a mess. My intention was not to draw so much interest. And I felt sorry for the man I essentially murdered." She kept her eyes lowered in a sorrowful demonstration. But it was an honest depiction of how she had felt that day.

One of the leaned forward and opened his mouth, about to say something. The man next to him stopped him. "You have fed many times since then, right? No problems?"

"Yes. Until recently, I preferred doing my feeding in the shower so I could wash up afterwards. I'm sorry, but I don't like to walk around with blood all over me. Besides, buying new clothes is expensive."

She saw some faint nods again. Maybe this was working. "One thing I do not like."

"And that is?"

"I really don't like taking lives just to eat."

"But when you were human you sacrificed animals to eat, no doubt."

"But they were raised for food. I don't see the human population as being raised for food. For us."

More nods. "Go on."

"I work at a home for battered women, as a volunteer. I have taken to feasting on some of the awful men I have heard about. I am careful. I try to choose people who have no redeeming qualities. People no one will miss. But do not mistake me, I still believe every life is sacred."

The room was silent, except for the vampire on the end who snored.

"I want to ask you about Marcus," One of the council asked her, leveling a bony finger in her direction. His voice was irritatingly shrill.

"Yes. I love Marcus. He has told me about the fating that goes on between golden vampires mates. I do feel we are meant for each other."

"But I understand you are still married."

"No, not legally. We had a wedding performed, but I am severing all my ties with him. He has never honored our bed. I cannot live a life where I have to worry about where he is, and with whom he is sleeping."

They were nodding again, so Anne added, "He does not honor me. Why should I continue to honor him?"

"Do you want him eliminated? Have you asked Marcus to do this?"

Anne's stomach clenched up. She gripped the arms of her chair, indignant at the insinuation she could ask Marcus to kill off her no-good husband. And how could they think Marcus was capable of such cruelty?

"What?" She squinted her eyes in anger. Had Marcus told them that? "As cruel as Robert is to me, I would never wish my ex-husband harm. Never." She was shaking. She hoped the fervor of her feelings didn't interfere with their decision.

"One more question, if you please." A new visitor came into the room. Handsome, tall, though not as tall as Marcus. He appeared to be the younger vampire. The whole room deferred to him, seemed to center around him.

"Praetor. We are honored with your presence." Most of the council bowed in deference.

With a swagger that told Anne he was used to bedding any woman he wanted and could get away with it, he looked her up and down, resting his eyes on her breasts, then lower to the place between her legs. He licked his lips and sighed. She instantly didn't trust such a powerful, sexy man.

I hope you can do whatever they ask of you. She remembered Marcus's words. What if he asked for . . .?

"I understand you bleed now." His expression was serious.

"Yes, I am bleeding now."

"When was the last time you bled before now?"

"It was before my wedding day, about two months ago."

He smiled and nodded his head, turning to the council. He shrugged.

"Fine." The middle robe stood up. "I have no further questions. I am satisfied. Let's get on with the inspection."

Oh, God, an inspection? With these creeps and this gorgeous male?

Now the reason for her black lacey things with the slit up the middle made sense. Marcus had known. *Damn the man!*

The leader rang a silver bell. Two young girls dressed in harem costumes came into the room to stand by Anne's side. They eased her up from the chair, one on each arm. Anne saw Mr. Handsome peruse all three of them, hand under his chin, stroking his lips like he was studying something. She didn't like being on display. The council members who could, stood up and watched as she was escorted out of the room.

She was taken down a tiled corridor to an exam room. After undressing and putting on the familiar paper dress, she had to suffer through a gynecological exam performed by an elderly doctor as Praetor stood in the room, observing.

Remember that I love you. Marcus had told her to do anything they asked her to do. God damn him. He didn't tell her because he knew she would never agree to it.

The doctor excused himself with the swab, now tinged red at the tip. She sat up and snarled at Praetor. "I find this whole process revolting, sickening. Barbaric, even."

He bowed slightly. Anne could see he perhaps agreed, but did not say anything.

"So, what happens now?"

"He is confirming it is menstrual blood. If that is verified, I'd say you and Marcus could have *a little party.*"

There was something about how he said the last part that made her suddenly catch her breath. *Could we be that close?*

"They've accepted me?"

"They believed your story."

"That's because it's true. All of it."

The doctor returned. "It's confirmed, and now Praetor, you have witnessed it. It is menstrual blood. I will go inform the council." He was almost to the door when he turned. "She is not to be left alone. Bring her back to the chambers once she has dressed."

"Of course."

The physician left. Anne slid off the table, being careful with the placement of the paper wrap and skirt. She glared at Praetor, raising her chin in defiance, aware that although covered, she was naked from the waist down. He broke the silence.

"I see what Marcus has found in you. I only wish I could have seen you first."

"You don't believe in the fate, then?"

He smiled. "It's difficult to believe in something that hasn't happened yet. I, like Marcus, have waited a long time. Let's say I have faith, but I do not believe yet, no." He abruptly turned around to let her finish dressing.

Anne, donned her skirt, muttering to herself about the ridiculous panties. She straightened her hair, making a fuss, harrumphing and gasping, hoping she showed her indignation at the ordeal.

"I have a question," she said.

"Ask me anything."

"What's with the old council members? I thought all vampires are immortal."

"We are not immune to all disease, contrary to folklore. And sometimes there is an errant ancestor of questionable parentage. Some of us age, but age slowly."

"Will this happen to me? Because I started out human?"

"No way to know, my dear. Not a question of your humanity. It's a question of bloodline and breeding."

"The children . . ."

"Can die of normal childhood diseases. Very sad. Very sad indeed."

She stopped. She understood why the children were so important. They were rare. And they were fragile. It was sad.

Anne continued to dress, fiddling with the buttons at the back of her blouse so that she didn't have to ask Praetor's help. It was something she knew he would gladly assist her with.

"Okay. I'm done."

He turned around and looked her up and down, drinking in every curve, every valley. Unashamed to let her see how tantalizing he found her.

"Stop that."

"Stop what?"

"That. That thing you are doing. I don't belong to you."

"My dear, you don't belong to Marcus, either. I don't think you ever will."

He brought her back to the chamber room.

A brief statement was read into the record, verifying all the facts. And then it was over. The directors filed out, including the two sick ones in their wheelchairs. All but Mr. Handsome. Praetor had an expression that was hard to read. She couldn't mistake the tease in his eyes, the invitation to show him some affection if she chose.

She wanted to set him on fire.

He extended his elbow in her direction. "Come, Anne. There is someone dying to see you."

"Where are you taking me?" she asked.

He put his finger to his lips. "It's a surprise."

He waited for her to put her arm through his. She didn't want to do it, so he grabbed it and put it there himself. He patted her hand that rested on his forearm, leaving his hand in place over hers. "Don't worry. Everything will be alright." He hesitated, then turned to face her. His large brown eyes were as beautiful as any woman's eyes Anne had ever seen. And he clearly knew it. "I know my place here, my dear. But, if you ever tire of Marcus the Magnificent, I have some skills that would make your soul tremble. The door to my bedroom is always open to one such as you."

"I'll have to ask Marcus if he thinks that would be such a good idea. He doesn't seem to think I need much instruction. But if I did, Marcus is an excellent teacher."

He was surprised with her boldness, Anne could tell. But she was careful he didn't take it as a slight. That would be a mistake.

They walked through a door to an anteroom, an auxiliary soundproof chamber. Marcus instantly sprang up, hesitating to come over to her. Stress was written all over his face. And when his eyes fell over Praetor and Anne locked arm in arm, he frowned. She couldn't remember when she had seen his hair so disheveled. The room was littered with chewing gum wrappers and cans of Red Bull. He looked miserable.

"Praetor. How nice to see you." Marcus's speech was measured.

"Marcus, I'm afraid I have some news . . ." Praetor started.

Suddenly Anne was overwhelmed. She disengaged from Praetor and ran to Marcus, burying her head in his chest.

"I passed."

Marcus picked her up with ease, holding her sideways. He nodded to Praetor, then tore off down the hallway, headed to the outside. Anne clung to him, her arms wrapped around his neck, looking over one broad shoulder at the handsome vampire who stood behind them, watching them leave.

Praetor raised his hand up and waved with a couple of his fingers, as if to say, *I'll still be here if you change your mind.*

CHAPTER 21

Robert picked himself up off the floor as soon as he came to. He was covered in blood. His cell phone was shattered. Little pieces of the blue plastic and silver parts littered the bottom of the tub where Maya had thrown it. God, that woman had a temper. For the first time in his life, perhaps he had misjudged a female. Maybe that wasn't quite right. Maybe it was the first time a female *scared* him, like the bullies at school had scared him, like the gangbangers who walked past his job sites scared him.

He'd passed out after she bit him, and, damn, yes, she'd actually drawn blood there. He looked at himself in the half-broken mirror. Sure enough, two puncture wounds stood out on his neck, just like the ones on his dick two days before. No question about it. This one was an animal.

And she was so interested in Anne. Why? Anne had never hurt a fly. All she ever did was work at the women's shelter, helping those ladies get their lives back together. Everyone loved Anne. She was like a mother lion with her cubs. Hard to figure one of her clients would be this angry. No, it must be something else.

He wondered how Anne could meet a woman like Maya. He doubted Anne had ever stepped foot inside the Double Eights. The whole thing just didn't make sense.

He placed the pieces of his phone in the trash and removed his clothing. His dick had healed. Thank God for small miracles. Well, now maybe Monika would take pity on him. He jumped into the shower. The wounds on his neck really hurt.

Afterward, he wet down his shirt and used it to clean up some of the blood on the wall and bathroom floor. He tossed his clothes, including his socks, into the washer, added extra bleach and detergent, then turned it on.

With fresh clothes and a shower, he sure didn't look as bad as he felt. He hurt all over. *All* over. Like he'd been beat up when he was unconscious. Like how he felt the day he had woken up after having his wisdom teeth pulled. That day his cheeks had been so swollen that he could have sworn the dentist had taken aim and punched him just for fun.

First, he would try to call Anne and tell her about this crazy lady, and then he would see about having Monika help him with his stuff. If she'd have him back, that is. And if all else failed, well, he could always promise Gary a night of drinks and a free dinner. Hell, Gary owed him at least a place to stay, after all the trouble he had caused him. If it wasn't for Gary, this bitch wouldn't be stalking Anne, he'd have a cell phone, and he wouldn't feel so tired and drained of energy. He just hoped there wasn't some medical condition that would spring up at an inopportune time. Like that time he and Gary went down to Mexico. That would really suck.

Robert picked up the landline and dialed Anne's phone. All he got was voicemail. Again. He left a message asking her to call him on the house phone, then he called Monica. Monica sounded annoyed, and when he asked where Anne was, she called him a dipshit and hung up. He called Elena and told her he wouldn't be in, then sat down to wait. Surely Anne would call sometime today.

About an hour later, he got a call from Anne.

"God, you sound far away," he said. "Where are you?"

"Umm the connection just isn't very good here. I'm at a friend's house. They live in Healdsburg."

There was a lot of background noise. He could hear someone talking and the peel of church bells. He didn't remember hearing bells before in Healdsburg.

"Well, I've missed you."

"Umm."

Robert knew she wasn't listening to him, or she would have protested his sentiment. There was the sound of something rustling in the background.

"Are you okay, Anne?"

"I'm perfect." More rustling. "Ah, Robert, I need to ask you a very important question."

"Shoot. I'm all ears."

"Will you renounce your marriage vows?"

This was not what he expected. Anne was going to go through with this.

"Please, Robert." She sighed one of her very best, long, sighs. "If you have ever loved me, please say you will fully release me."

Should he set her free? Should he say no? "Could we talk about it? I'm real sorry about everything."

"No, it's over. Let's face it, you love Monika. Go be happy with her. I want you to be . . . happy." She gasped. "Please, please, just tell me you agree to end our marriage. Release me, Robert."

"But in my own way, I love you Anne. I know if we went to counseling, we could revive our marriage. I've learned my lesson."

"Please, Robert."

"I can take anger management classes. I think I'm a sex addict, Anne. There are twelve-step meetings for this. I'm willing to become a changed man."

"I don't want to change you," Anne said. "I want you to let me go. I've released you with my full heart. Please do the same for me. Please, Robert."

It was against his better judgment, but it was the right thing for Anne. He'd messed up things enough, put her through enough. He could do this.

"Okay," he whispered, surprised the word came out of his mouth.

There was a pause. It sounded like she was whispering to someone.

"Okay, what?" Anne said breathlessly.

Had she been running? "Okay I release you! Jeez, that sounds funny. But I still love you."

He was crying, actually crying when he heard her say, "Robert I did love you too, once. Thank you."

He knew Anne thought she had hung up the phone properly, but the line remained open. Robert could hear the passion play going on and could not help but recognize the moans of his young wife being completely sated by someone else. Another man. Someone named Marcus.

It was a fitting end to his short marriage.

After a few minutes, he softly laid the phone back on its cradle. He looked at his crotch and wondered if he ever would feel aroused again.

Then he remembered he had not told her about that strange woman with the oral fixation. Well, if she was with a man, perhaps that guy could protect her. He should at least warn her.

He redialed the phone and got her voicemail.

"Anne, forgot to let you know. There was some woman here who wants to know where you are. She is a real bitch. Uh, honey, I want you to be happy and I'm sorry. I'm gonna need a few days to clear out everything—" Then the line on the other end went dead. He wasn't sure his message was left, after all.

Perfect.

They lay on the massive four-poster walnut bed. Anne loved the feel of the deep red satin quilting against her bare back and buttocks. She spread her arms to the sides, and Marcus found them. He pinned her fingers with his and then brought them back to his lips. His warm body sheltered and protected her, covering her torso and thighs. She knew he tried to touch her flesh with as much of him as he could, and what he couldn't touch he had kissed over and over again.

She stared up into his coppery eyes, committing to him for all eternity. She was so willing to become the mate he had searched for his whole life. He had pleasured her with his mouth, whispering incantations to her sex, making her quiver as he lapped and sucked her juices. She wondered if the blood was still there. God, she hoped so. She hoped so that she could be fertile for him. That she could be the vessel of his passion, the keeper of his progeny, the holder of his soul.

Her breasts glistened in the late afternoon Italian sun. She barely could remember the events of earlier today. She was in his home, the home of his ancestors. He'd brought her here, flying through the large mullioned windows overlooking the family vineyard, placed her on the bed, and walked around back and forth. She had disrobed button by button, hiking her clothes up here and there. He'd refused to touch her, making her remove each item of clothing until she was writhing on the bed naked with a need between her legs as deep as the Grand Canyon. That's when he'd asked her call Robert.

He was lapping between her creamy thighs when she sat up with a little "Oh" like she did sometimes when the excitement of his tongue was too much for her. But this time she held the little phone out to him and asked Robert to repeat something so he could hear it.

"Okay, I release you! Jeez, that sounds funny, but I still love you." She could have kissed the man. Marcus laved the space between her thighs, then whispered something she felt take hold inside her womb, where it stayed warm and coiled. Some magic glam or spell that waited to receive him and his seed.

With reverence, he stowed the phone on the side table. She felt the muscles at his back move under his tanned flesh, felt his torso press her breasts against him. He wrapped his arms around her and pulled her hair from her neck. He licked the length of her as she moaned and wrapped her legs around his waist, arching up to meet him. His long kiss claimed her again, as they both pricked each other and drank the combined blood, their tongues washing over teeth and gums, covering all the surfaces of their mouths with the elixir of their love.

"Marcus. At last, Marcus."

He groaned and whispered something to her she didn't understand. Words in a dialect she didn't recognize, something ancient. And she heard music between the timbres of his deep voice. Was she dreaming this? She felt him press against her slick opening. She needed to be filled with the strength and power of him.

He looked down, then kissed her eyes, the sides of her face, under her ears, and in the valley under her chin. "Will you fate to me forever?" he breathed. She could smell the blood on his lips. "Will you love me, allow me to give you my seed, protect you? Will you share my bed, my pleasure, my family, my life for all eternity?"

"God, yes." It was everything she'd always wanted. He was everything she'd ever wanted in a mate. She added demands of her own. "Will you love me forever? Will you let me give you children? Never leave me, Marcus. Hold me for all eternity."

"Yes. I claim you for my own, in the ancient way, as you own me. You are . . . mine."

He pulled her hair aside, angled his own throat for her hungry access.

"Now," he groaned.

She bit down at the same moment she felt his fangs sank into her neck, at the same moment his cock thrust inside to the hilt. His plunging entrance sent her body into spasms as her insides stretched to receive his huge gift. His blood was sweet, tinged cinnamon. It awoke every cell in her body. His scent warmed her heart, made it flutter as the blood filled all her cavities. She drank without holding back, loving the sound of his ravenous sucking, feeling the strong muscles of his back and shoulders as he took her blood into him, as he ground into her and rhythmically played her sex until she felt a glow below her waist. His deep thrusts demanded she give him all of her. Passion ignited a flame long held low in her belly—something that had been lurking there her whole life. The warmth traveled up her spine, made her thighs and knees tingle, made her press her neck into his hungry mouth. She wanted to be taken, and it wasn't anything like what she'd felt before.

He stopped, brushing thumbs over her cheeks, wiping the tears of joy from her eyes. Awash in the scent of their love, she felt him spasm. Every drop of his seed refreshed and coated her willing womb.

They kissed, barely touching, tenderly speaking a language she didn't realize she spoke, nor did she understand, but when his eyes filled with tears, she knew he heard her ancient message to him, the male of her life. For the rest of eternity. He continued to thrust into her.

"My beloved," she said as she angled her neck. "Take all of me. Take as much as you can. I give myself to you in every way possible."

He was staying hard inside her and she could sense something was happening. Perhaps he was going to come again. All of a sudden a golden light shone from their joining, enveloping them in a warm electric pulse of energy. Marcus shuddered. Anne's muscles clamped down on him and her whole body began to shake in a wrenching orgasm that left her gasping for air. Their shouts echoed off the paneled ceiling surfaces. The faces of the monkeys overhead smiled down on them.

Marcus rolled over and pulled Anne on top. He held her body at her hips, moving her up and down his shaft as he arched into her, then filled her with more of his seed.

Her thirst for his neck brought her forward, breasts pressing against his chest as she drank at the base of his throat. His fingers urgently clutched at her hair, moving it aside again. His tongue warmed the other side of her neck as his fangs plunged in to mark her again. The twitching his cock made deep inside her forced a series of spasms. She lowered herself onto him, deep and hard. He brought her feet up to his shoulders and held her ankles while she rode his bucking frame. He bit her right wrist and took from her. He licked her ankle and fed from her there.

She wanted him to fill her from behind, something he seemed to understand without her needing to communicate to him. He smoothed over her rear with his large palm, turning her body on her knees so she could present her peach to him. He leaned forward and sunk his fangs into her labia, kissing and sucking, then lapping with his tongue. He placed himself at her violated opening and she felt a delicious pain as she took him in. He rode her, whispering ancient words that made every cell of her flesh tingle with delight.

At last they collapsed into a sweaty pile of arms and legs. She allowed her wet body to be crushed in his embrace. He wouldn't let go, even as she tried to tug the satin coverlet over them so they wouldn't get cold.

"I will do it. I will keep you warm," he said.

And it was true. As he tasted the side of her neck again and rubbed her breasts with his massive hands, she warmed to the touch of his flesh all over her body.

He'd pierced her body and drank her blood from numerous places, but she smiled to think she hadn't counted the wounds he had made.

I am indeed fully satisfied, sated.

A faint beeping sound interrupted their nap. Marcus grabbed her cell phone that lay on the floor, then raised it to her face so she could see the battery had died. He placed it back on the night table. She felt a twinge of regret that perhaps she had not dealt with Robert properly. There was a part of her that felt sorry for him. She had loved him, once. She was honest with that statement, at least.

She looked up at the man who gazed down at her, the mysterious man who filled her with wonder. Tracing the profile of his face along his hairline, she let her fingers dance across his lips. She rose to meet those lips. His strong hand held her, pulled her to him, and then let her head fall back. He kissed the arch of her neck that she extended for him. He licked the two little holes he had made in the heat of his passion, when he had claimed her, where she would have him claim her again an hour later, where she hoped he would claim her every day for the rest of eternity.

He drew himself to sitting position, holding her in his lap. She wrapped her arms around his neck, happy to be draped against his body. She inhaled his maleness, the scent of their lovemaking, and the scent of their blood for each other. She kissed his wound, stroking up the sides of his thick neck with her fingers.

His arms enveloped her as he bent his head to rest on the top of hers. "Ah, my pet. You are mine at last. Fully mine."

"Yes. Always, Marcus."

He produced a small black box. Anne was surprised at this, and looked around the bed to see where the box had come from. She searched his smiling eyes, then planted a kiss on his lips as he rubbed a hand along her thigh. He moved two fingers lazily along her flesh to find her wet opening and stroked her there while she popped open the box. His fingers stopped while she took a deep breath.

"Oh, my. Marcus. It's . . . lovely!" A large emerald glittered and glowed in an intricate setting. The ring looked very old. The stone was almost the size of the nail on her little finger, in a deep forest green color, surrounded by a circle of smaller diamonds.

"The stones are new, but the setting belonged to my mother. I think it belongs on your finger, now."

He took the ring and held it as she placed the fourth finger of her left hand into it. A perfect fit.

"I bought this very rare emerald while I was waiting to be able to come to you. It reminds me of your eyes, my love. I slept with it every night." He held his hand over his heart.

Anne looked at the physical evidence of their fating and what it meant to him. He had brought her his past and laid it at her feet. "Oh, Marcus. I am touched beyond belief. I accept this ring, but I have nothing to give you in return."

He didn't speak, but instead put a warm hand on her belly. She could feel his heat radiate up throughout her whole body. She knew she would bear him a child from tonight. The wheels of the future had been irrevocably set in motion.

She righted herself, then straddled him, clasping her arms behind his neck as she leaned her breasts to his bare chest and sought the heat of his mouth on hers. Her tongue tasted the soft breath of a moan coming deep from inside this man. She was overwhelmed with the rising tide of her emotions that were taking over her body in waves. Her heart felt stretched to bursting. She hoped there would never be an end to the way she felt this evening.

Marcus lay back as her hands traveled over the rippled landscape that was his chest. Her sex awakened to the knowledge of the need between her legs again as she rubbed against a growing hardness. She closed her eyes as she felt him move against the little knob that sought attention. His powerful hands lifted her up slightly and she sighed at the brief cold, parting between their bodies. Then he set her down on top of his shaft.

"Oh, yes, Marcus."

Anne's body rocked back and forth as he massaged her breasts, pinched her nipples, squeezed her buttocks, and caressed her thighs. Every inch of her was worshiped, explored, conquered, kissed, and caressed. The penetration of his shaft deep inside set off a long, undulating orgasm. Marcus was a demanding lover, but not easily satiated. He watched her experience the ecstasy that was theirs before he would allow himself to release again.

She was on fire with the touch of his cock inside her, where it needed to be, where it belonged, where it always had belonged. Every drop milked from him as he shot inside left her thinking it still wasn't enough.

They rested, Anne covering him with her body. "Do you have any plans for the next week?" She smiled, holding her hair back with the hand that bore his mother's ring.

"Well, we should announce the Council's decision to the family. I think you should meet my other brothers. And my other sisters. Perhaps we'll have a gathering." His finger outlined her nipple, and he watched as it hardened to his touch. When he stilled, it softened, and he played with it again. "And there is a fating ceremony we should plan after that."

"Is it a wedding?"

"It is an important acknowledgement of our fating, and recognized in the chapel. You know the one. Where I first saw you."

Anne frowned. "You saw me in a chapel? I thought you saw me in town."

"Yes, remember, when you came to the chapel in Genoa? You lit the candle and wrote a prayer? That's our fating chapel."

Anne sat up. "Wait a minute. You were there? The only other people there were—"

"Yes." His fingers laced down her spine. He stopped suddenly.

Marcus thought himself a fool. Things had moved along so rapidly, and in his haste to make sure the Council saw her fating blood, he had forgotten to explain to Anne about Maya and the claims Maya had on him. He had been so confident the Council's decision would have given him the right to pursue Anne in the fating that he had forgotten to tell the one person who did not know about the boy and the history of his relationship with the boy's mother. He could see Anne stiffen. He had made a very grave mistake, one he hoped he would not pay as dearly for as he deserved.

You are a rake. Consumed by your own selfish desires.

He'd told himself to be patient, thought he was, but damn, was she right? Had he used Anne in his haste to end the years of loneliness and lack?

Was it really the fating power, or my own hunger for a woman of my own?

Would a true fated partner not even consider the consequences of his omission? Of his lie? Had he hidden his relationship with the boy's mother from Anne, implying he was free to take her, join with her, just so he could spill his seed and perhaps create another progeny? Or worse yet, was he becoming the type of vampire like his dark brethren? The ones who used women as playthings and pastimes to distract them from an otherwise boring eternal life?

Marcus was beside himself with loathing. He returned his attention to Anne.

She was off the bed, seeking a robe, pacing back and forth in the room. Marcus donned silk pajama bottoms as he continued to watch her. Her head was down and he could tell she was counting the loops of carpet at the foot of the massive bed. This wasn't a good sign.

"Anne, let's talk."

He reached for her arm, but she shook him off.

"If . . . if you were in . . . the . . . chapel . . . you were there next to a woman." She looked up at him with tears in her eyes. "A woman, Marcus. You were *not* the priest. You sat next to a *woman*. You were *participating* in the ceremony with someone *else*."

"No, not actually *doing* the ceremony. We were planning—" He couldn't bring himself to say more. Panic seized him. Why had he been so stupid not to think about this? "Please, Anne, let's sit while I explain this all to you."

"You will goddamn explain it to me right now!" Anne's face was contorted in a nasty sneer he'd never seen before. Her cheeks were flushed and red. Red with the passion his blood gave to her as it circulated inside her body, giving her life. But her body had been taken over by a range he didn't know she was capable of. Her eyes were murderous. Accusatory. Devoid of the soft surrender he had just witnessed.

She squinted. "What have you done?" She walked to within a foot away from him. He could smell sex and the revulsion—a painful elixir of dashed hopes and dreams. "You have bedded me for your own pleasure. But you are already taken? You have done the ceremony with someone else! How could you?"

Anne flew to her clothes and began putting them on.

"Don't. Don't do this, Anne. You have to let me explain this to you. You don't understand anything. Oh, it's my entire fault. I should have told you sooner. I am not married or taken. Please believe me." He came over to Anne's seated frame. She was pulling on her boots. In kneeling position, he begged, "Anne, I love only you, and I can explain everything so you understand."

She looked down at Marcus with the coldness of death in her eyes. "Do you deny you were there? With a woman? You intended to be fated to another?"

"No, I don't deny it, but I can explain." He reached up for her hand and she slapped him across the face.

"Don't you touch me."

He ran over to the door, blocking her passage.

Anne pulled back and took a deep breath. Her face became red and splotchy. "Now you're going to force me, keep me captive? I am not sure how ugly you want to make this."

"I need to explain. Please let me do this."

"Move. I want out of this room now. I need to get away from your smell. I will come back later to get my things and perhaps you will explain, but not now."

Marcus moved to the side, heartbroken. Tears streamed down his face, covering his chest. He couldn't get enough breath to satisfy his parched throat. Everything inside him felt constricted, like he was dying. Everything but his heart, which was racing wildly, ready to burst from his chest.

She ran down the curved stairs into the foyer below, Marcus right on her heels. She yanked open the front door just as someone else burst into the room, almost toppling her.

Maya.

Oh, God, no. Not now.

The dark vixen stood her ground, seemingly pleased with her sense of timing. Her eyes flashed to Marcus. She raised her nose to the air.

"Ah, I smell puppy love. An afternoon of passion. And such a lovely little pup. You've created for yourself quite a little fuck buddy, Marcus. An enjoyable love puppet who will live forever. Was she as good as you'd planned? Hmm?"

Anne spoke. "You are the filthy bitch who turned me."

The vehemence in Anne's voice put Marcus on alert. In a direct attack, Maya would be able to defend herself, and she'd fight to the death. Anne's death.

Maya laughed with a cackle that must have been a throwback to her ancient ancestor. The echo reached all corners of the carved living room and made the monkeys smile. "Oh, this is too rich."

"Maya, I order you to leave this house immediately." Marcus was on his way to forcibly remove her from the foyer.

Maya hid behind Anne and whined into her ear, "So he has not told you, little one. *He* is your creator, not I. He lusted for your body, gave you immortal life so he could screw you forever. You are Marcus's eternal whore." Her laughter rumbled the glass windows of the whole house.

Anne's expression showed Marcus she was dead to him, as dead as she had been the evening he'd found her in the alleyway, after Maya had drained her of her mortal life. He watched as Maya's words settled all over his fated female like acid.

"Marcus and I have shared over one hundred years of passion. Did you know that? And, has he told you I bore him a child?"

Anne whirled around, venom spewing from her eyes. Her lips were pale and parched. He could hear the bile collecting in her stomach. Maya eluded her and ran into the middle of the ballroom. "Marcus and I danced together in this room almost two hundred years ago. Has he told you this? He held me tight and we danced and danced. We fucked everywhere we could find. Ravenous. He was ravenous for me . . ."

As Maya sang some tune and twirled, her arms outstretched, Anne turned to Marcus, obviously unafraid to show him the hatred in her soul. In a calm voice, she asked him the question he had not wanted to answer. "So, you have a child as well. Why am I not surprised?" Her sad face repeated the words.

Marcus came as close to her as he dared. He suspected she wanted to do him real harm, and he didn't blame her.

"I am not sure the child is mine," he whispered.

"I thought you said the blood never lies." She eyed him with steely conviction, and yes, some hatred.

"I never felt the . . . the . . . fating with Maya," he begged.

"Well she bled. She bore you a child. What else is there? I find the fact that you never told me any of this to be all too convenient. You are a liar, Marcus Monteleone. No doubt your night of passion with her felt equally as . . . as . . . stirring." Her eyes filled with tears.

He reached out to grab hold of her, to reassure her, to ease the pain he knew she was feeling in her soul, but she drew away. He cursed himself. With the backdrop of Maya's swirling and cackling, Anne barely spoke, but Marcus could hear every word.

"I will be returning to California. The only thing I ask of you is to help me get there. I do not want you to follow me. I do not want to ever see you again."

Anne cried all the way into town as the limo driver brought her to a country inn and paid for a room. She thanked him, unable to tip him because she had no money. He informed her arrangements were being made and that in the morning some clothes and money would be delivered.

"And I do not want Marcus here. You must come, not him."

"Understood."

"And I won't take the jet back. I don't ever want to set foot on anything he owns again."

"Pardon me, ma'am. Just to be completely honest with you, he owns this inn, but he has told me in case I had to reveal this, not to worry. He will not come to you again. You can feel safe in that, at least."

She nodded.

"So sorry, ma'am. We all are."

Alone in the room, without audience, she collapsed. Suddenly she didn't want to live any longer. And then it hit her.

She was immortal.

All the way back on her first class flight to New York, Anne tried to sleep. Every time she woke up, she started to cry. She began to wonder if she would have to start feeding on the plane because she had cried so much. She had cried herself to sleep on her first trip to Italy, on her honeymoon, and now she was bawling again on her way back to California.

She was exhausted. She tried to watch the movie. She adjusted her sleeping chair, closed the window, and put the eye patch on. She drank more whisky than she ever had before, thinking maybe she could get good and drunk and then be able to sleep off the horrible pain in her chest. There was a hole where her heart should be.

She hadn't figured Marcus for the cad type. But, judging from her past taste in men, she shouldn't be too surprised. She hadn't seen anything but innocent randiness on the part of Robert. But his appetites clearly stretched long and deep in several very dark directions.

No, what she needed was something else in her life. A new start. And she needed to be alone, away from anything that reminded her of the wine country, Italy, or from her former life with either Robert or Marcus. She would need to get a job, an apartment, and a new passion for life. And in that order, too.

In the JFK airport, waiting for the flight to San Francisco, she walked down the halls between the shops, noticing the families. People were going to or from vacation destinations all over the world, or were like her, waiting for their next flight, carefully marking time until the next adventure. She saw the faces and happy chatter of children and the mothers and fathers who loved them.

Something I'll never have.

Once again, she was grateful for her first class ticket to San Francisco. She noticed no one had a seat next to her and deduced two seats had probably been booked for her so she would be left alone or not risk the chance she would meet some millionaire or handsome prince that would sweep her off her feet. Funny, how in such a short period she had begun to know how Marcus thought, how he orchestrated everything in his life. Even as she was leaving him forever, he was controlling her every move.

She sighed. He would be hard to forget. But she would. After all, she had spent the last three years of her life letting someone use her. Nothing could be more difficult than facing that again. And, if she were with Marcus, she would have to turn a blind eye to the fact that she had been used. While Robert had stolen her trust, Marcus had stolen her mortal life, and that could never be recovered. A broken heart then was something that could be fixed. No way was she going to be human again.

Marcus could go back to Maya, his true mate, just as Robert was to go back to Monika. Good riddance to both of them.

A car waited for her at the airport. She hadn't planned on that. The sign had properly read, "Anne Balesteiri." She looked down at her hand and saw the emerald she had forgotten to return. No doubt Marcus thought this to be a hopeful sign. But it wasn't.

The ring was a reminder of what could never be.

Her eyes filled with tears. Perhaps she was mourning the woman who used to own this setting, the woman who had decided to remain human and die a human death with her husband. Anne also mourned the woman who had accepted the gift and thought her life would be perfect forever. That woman was dead as well.

Casualties of life. Casualties of love.

The two beautiful Italian leather suitcases were deposited by the front door of her old house. Robert's truck was not in the driveway, but his green bomber was. She smiled in spite of her misery. She had missed that car. Anne tipped the driver from the wad of hundred dollar bills she had been handed in a perfumed envelope with her name written in Marcus's distinctive script. She was at last home. Alone.

Marcus had put her keys in the matching carry-on bag, along with a few things she had at the villa in Genoa, including a small bottle of her favorite hand cream that couldn't be bought in the US, and the sample bottle of the Carpathian perfume she loved from Capri. He was funny about the details. Of course, everything was thought out with Marcus. Which was further evidence he had planned her seduction, the making of her new life. If she had stayed with him, she too would have become a jealous vampire female consumed with hate as he found another, and then another and another new bride to add to his collection.

She could almost sympathize with Maya. Anne just wasn't going to stay around for that chapter. The humiliation of being discarded. She wouldn't be able to take that. Again.

Her house was strangely comforting to her. Everything as it was before. Robert had taken a few things. She decided to let him have it. Sort of her present to him and his new life, too. Everyone would go on with their lives. Everyone would find their way. She had to be optimistic.

Her top dresser drawer moved smoothly, revealing her favorite nightie. After drawing a bath and removing her clothes, she added lavender bath salts, remembering the bubble bath on the jet. With Marcus. And then came the tears again. But they didn't last as long this time. The pain was getting easier to bear.

The warm water soothed her bones and washed away the travel grime. The steam caused her face to sweat. She felt a delayed reaction to the whiskey she had on the two plane rides. Maybe this was how it works. As a vampire, she still would feel the effects of the alcohol, but perhaps it took longer to arrive in her system. So much she still didn't know. She and Marcus had gotten so caught up in their "fating" that he'd forgotten to show her how to live as a vampire. Typical. He'd figured he would always be there to take care of her, show her everything. Arrogance. Total arrogance.

She fell back into a warm, deep sleep.

Anne awoke when the water was cold. She dried off and slipped on the white satin nightgown with the soft lining. She liked the way it hugged her body. She went to light candles in the bedroom, but omitted lighting the garnet red votive with the blood orange candle in it. Instead, she moved it to her dresser. She would throw it out tomorrow. Tonight, she just wanted to rejuvenate her body.

No decisions tonight. Just get a little sleep. Maybe get up early and feed. Back to that again. One thing had not changed, at least. There were still probably plenty of bad guys out there who deserved to die. Perhaps some of her revenge could taste sweet after all.

Her cell phone rang. She picked it up. Monika. That meant Robert. Good for him. Glad at least he has someone to share his life with.

"Hello?"

"Oh, hey, I thought I was just going to leave a message for you. You sound not so far away. You back from Healdsburg?"

This actually caused Anne to smile. Her first genuine smile. She surprised herself.

"Yes, I'm in the house tonight."

"Uh, Anne, I kind of know you have a new guy. Can't say as I blame you. So, I was wondering, would it be okay if Monika and I move into the house?"

"Sure, Robert." So he had heard, after all. Well, thank God for small favors. She wasn't upset. No reason to tell him "the guy" was in Robert's league. No sense giving him that satisfaction.

"Gee, Anne. You're being really great about this. Monika says thanks. And she's really sorry too about how all this went down."

"Yeah, Robert, I bet she is." Anne shook her head. She partly blamed herself. Her own twisted logic created a world where Robert never belonged. So now he was reverting to the person he was meant to be, with the person he was meant to spend his life with. Things were going to work out just the way they should.

"Well, honey. You have a good rest. We'll talk more about it tomorrow. You don't have to rush on moving things out. Just get to it when you can. She still has three weeks left on her rent here at the apartment, and we're fine here until, until, until you're ready, okay?"

"Have a nice evening, Robert, and you too, Monika." She knew her ex-maid of honor was listening to every word.

Anne set the phone down on the dresser, next to the burgundy candle. She brought the votive to her nose. Why did she think it wouldn't smell so sweet?

She decided to unpack and then finally return to bed.

When she unzipped the larger bag, there was a letter with her name on it in Marcus's handwriting, lying on top of the neatly folded clothes. She sucked in breath at the sight of it, then quickly rezipped up the bag. No way was she going to read that until she had some decent sleep and a good feeding. Wouldn't be fair to her.

She set the leather bag on the floor, next to the smaller bag. She pulled back her comforter, pouring herself into the creamy linens that smelled of lavender. Finally surrounded by her own environment she fell asleep, with the faint acknowledgement she would have to wash the sheets tomorrow to remove the traces of his scent.

She never wanted to smell it again.

First thing she saw when she woke up in the morning was the dark form of another vampire standing at the foot of her bed.

Praetor.

CHAPTER 22

Anne wasn't about to let Praetor make the first move. He'd already let himself into her house, *into her bedroom,* without permission. That in itself was crossing an invisible line. Although numb from the long plane ride and the fretful night of sobbing herself to sleep, a tiny ounce of self-preservation remained.

At least she still felt *something.*

Fear.

Pulling the covers to her neck, she wondered how long he had been there. What had he witnessed?

She knew Marcus could trace, and had half expected he would come to check on her from time to time, though she had asked him not to. Perhaps he had sent Praetor in his place.

Was the handsome golden vampire standing at the foot of her bed here to protect her, or help her forget? He was a completely unknown element in an already complicated life. The reality of finding a new place to live, a job, and some means of going on without Marcus suddenly hit her, bringing tears to her eyes. Did he see?

He smiled.

Can he read my mind? His eyes said no. She needed to figure out Praetor's intentions. Could she trust him? But if Marcus had not sent him, what was he here for? What would the rules of engagement be?

But still the most important question of the morning was the one hardest to figure out. What did *she* want? Did she want another friend, someone to take her mind off Marcus? Or did she want to be left alone to figure out everything on her own? Exhausted from the emotional pain she'd been suffering, she didn't have an answer. That put her at a distinct disadvantage with this handsome, sexual being who clearly had given her signals before he was interested in doing more than escorting her into the arms of her then love, or watching her eyes in an exam room.

Careful. Must be very, very careful.

She was not about to make the same mistake she made the first time she'd met a large alpha male vampire.

"Under the circumstances, I'm not sure if I should say good morning to you, or throw something at you. I've given you neither permission, nor encouragement to just show up when you feel like it." Anne tried to sound disinterested and strong, but she heard the waver of her words as they crashed together.

This struck him, and he yielded a crooked grin and gave a slight nod of his head. "Then *I* will say it. Good morning, Anne."

"What made you think I would welcome you here without asking?"

"Your need."

He said it like he had whispered the words into her ear as she rested on a pillow in a soft bed after a night of lovemaking.

"I think you are mistaken." Although her pulse had quickened, she understood part of it was plain fear. She did not want to be hurt, and right now she was vulnerable.

"Oh? I believe you need to feed, my dear. Why, what were you thinking?" He smiled again. This time, she felt her cheeks flush.

Far too confident. Her stomach pitched and growled, feisty and temperamental. Her mouth was parched. She swallowed and watched his dark form as he stood motionless, awaiting her instructions. His total focus was on her eyes, except for one glance down to a space underneath the covers where her breasts lay covered. Had he been able to see them?

Or could he?

Or worse yet, did he?

"If you came to offer yourself as a meal, you could have picked up a phone and called me. Or slipped a note under my door."

"True. I prefer to do it *this* way."

"Well, I don't. You are acting like you got an invitation I did not extend. Am I clear?"

"Quite. Now, would you like to feed?" He began unbuttoning his shirt.

Anne found herself inhaling, her eyes wide with shock at the sight of him baring his neck and upper chest to her. She could not help but lick her lips at the sight of his large pulsing vein. She got the impression he would be tempting her with it all morning, until she partook. He waited again, his dark eyes boring into her flesh, bringing out a warmth in her chest that caused her to perspire. She could smell him, the muskiness the younger males had. He didn't smell of lemons, like Marcus. He smelled like the wind.

"I will not ravish you. You may feed without worry. Come, I think your lack of nourishment is clouding your judgment." He held his hand out to her.

She found herself reaching out to take his fingers. He pulled her toward him. She walked on her knees as he guided her to the end of the bed. With a slip of his hand around the small of her back, he brought her to stand. He stepped back, took an appraisal of her body beneath her gown, then grabbed her fingers and led her to the living room. He did not let her go as he sat in her leather couch. His eyes asked her to join him there, while his fingers entwined in hers. He was not going to pull, but he did not release her hand, either.

She sat crossways on his lap, suddenly conscious of the closeness of his mouth, his strong jaw, and his chest open and waiting. Her hair touched him just underneath his chin on her way to his neck and he groaned, tensing slightly. His hands lay on the couch, palms up. He did not try to touch her as she bit into his neck and took the sweet elixir he offered.

She stopped, just to make sure she could. He exhaled, and then inhaled deeply when she reapplied her lips and drew more of him. One hand came up to her back involuntarily, and after grazing the satin fabric of her nightgown lightly, fell back to the couch.

She withdrew, leaning forward as her tongue finished the remnants of his blood on her lips, her eyes closed.

It did not feel the same.

Then she realized she was not fated to him. A huge sense of relief came over her. The immediate sexual energy she received from Marcus's blood was not present now. She was sated, but she was not hungry for sex with Praetor.

He brushed her hair from her eyes, untangling it behind her neck. He left his long probing fingers there, rubbing the muscles at the top of her shoulders, which felt wonderful. She had been so tense. She turned to look at his face, finally. He spoke first.

"So beautiful, so delicate. Do you feel better now?"

She had to admit, she did feel vital, full of life suddenly. "Praetor Artemis . . ."

"Just Praetor, please. And I desire to call you Anne."

He touched her chin, raising it a bit, but he did] not kiss her. She was not sure she liked the possessiveness of his actions. Was every unattached vampire female his for the taking? She supposed this was something to do with his status.

"I'm sure you would not have appeared here, were it not for the fact that Marcus and I, Marcus and . . ." Anne could not bring herself to say it. She found her eyes welling up with tears.

He pulled her head to his chest, then patted her shoulder as she sobbed into the smooth flesh of his chest. She could not help it. The well of sadness opened in her soul and she just could not stop.

"I know, Anne. I know how you love him."

She sat up and looked at his eyes. They were still smiling down at her. He traced a forefinger across her lips.

"Yes, my dear. I know of your pain. I have felt the same."

"You do?" This did surprise Anne, after all.

"I have experienced loss, although not quite the same circumstance. My pain is in never having met my fated female. I grieve for a love I have yet to feel. So you see, you are much more experienced than I." He smiled as he stroked the sides of her cheek with the back of his fingers.

Anne felt she could trust him. She lay her head against his chest again and let him hold her, this time without her tears. His arm rubbed hers up and down through the fabric of the white gown. She was struck with his sense of tenderness and concern.

"Maybe we can help each other fill the loneliness, the void in our lives, just for a time."

Anne thought about that. A little warning bell went off in the back of her mind. But try as she could to honor her doubts, she was beginning to trust him. Within reason.

"Praetor, I have to tell you something."

"Go on." His voice was smooth as velvet. His hand movements did not change.

"When I fed from you, I didn't feel anything. I didn't feel anything for you sexually." She drew back to look at his full face, looking deep into his dark eyes.

"Nor did I," he whispered. "Although I was hoping I would. I really thought I would."

So it was decided. Praetor would help her get situated. He would be a loyal and true friend, help her with money and teach her things about tracing and what the capabilities and limitations of her new life were, things Marcus was unable to do because of the distraction of their fating.

She took a job at Starbucks. Praetor had insisted he pay for the rent on the new apartment she found. It was brand new. Marcus had never been there. Nothing about the place reminded her of either Robert or Marcus. It was hers and hers alone.

Praetor spent the night half the time. He never asked for her intimacy. They went to movies together. He learned to drive the green bomber, something he seemed to delight in.

"You never learned to drive a car?" she asked one day as they rode through the countryside on their way to St. Helena.

"Why drive when you can fly?" he asked. "And now you can too."

"Barely," she said. She was getting better. She had traced herself once into a treetop and had gotten stuck in the branches. He'd arrived shortly to release her from her bondage. But he teased her about her broom handle being bent.

"So you think you will ever find your fated female?"

"Perhaps she was born and died before I ever got to meet her. It happens. Some never find their true mates."

"Do some people marry without the fating."

"Pretend? Play house?"

"Yes."

"When the sexual chemistry is strong enough. Sure." He wiggled his eyebrows. "Tell me you'd like to try this, my dear."

Anne delighted in his joy. But she didn't want to ruin their friendship by sleeping with him. "If I change my mind, you'll be the first to know."

Two weeks into their arrangement, she finally began to feel settled. The pain in her heart was dulling by the day. She was grateful nothing in her life reminded her of Marcus or Italy. Praetor was sometimes gone for days at a time, but he never brought up any family business, never mentioned his communications with Marcus, if he had any.

When he returned, she welcomed him like a brother.

They laughed in private when Robert thought Praetor was her new beau. It was just easier to let him think that. No way would he understand.

Never was there the hint of sex between the two of them, though they took long walks down by the water, holding hands. The strong arm he frequently slipped over her shoulder or around her waist was comforting. Anne loved the fresh man-scent of him and the timbre of his voice as she listened to him speak—even when he was whispering. His presence made her tingle all over, but not in a sexual way. She was healing.

Anne could see herself being his sexual partner, though unfated. But he never offered himself to her again or suggested it, even in jest. Her life was beginning to return to a satisfying normalcy.

She helped the women at the shelter and chose candidates for "educational sessions," Praetor even helping her from time to time with suggestions. Nothing was more satisfying than terrorizing a wicked husband or boyfriend, then glamming him with the suggestion he should move away and stop causing problems. Some were harder cases than others, but she was careful not to eliminate the predators, though she felt they deserved it. Though she scared these men half to death, she justified she was doing a good thing for the women in her charge.

One day, a bloody towel appeared in her wastebasket. She didn't recognize the scent and made sure it wound up in the alleyway garbage cans. Then bloody T-shirts and rags started appearing in her trash. Careful to dispose of them, she wondered why someone who had a chronic nosebleed problem would use her wastebasket at work. She didn't like to walk into her office and have the smell of blood hit her between the eyes. Even though no one else could smell it like she could, she couldn't help thinking perhaps someone was trying to plant evidence at her expense.

She enjoyed being a barista, working in the public view, surrounded by the smell of coffee. Her one cappuccino a day fulfilled her in some magical way, as glimpses of a life she could lead formed. Life appeared to be perfect again.

Until one day Maya showed up, filled with murderous rage.

The vampire, dressed in red, as usual, was standing by Robert's old green bomber. Because Anne had been rushing, late for her volunteer shift at the Center, she almost ran into the woman. The vampire was flushed from a recent kill, red lips plumped and full, and fresh blood under her fingernails. Anne wondered why Maya hadn't bothered to clean up.

The look in Maya's eyes had something else. A glow. Sadly, Anne could only attribute this to the Marcus effect.

Though she tried, Anne could not stop dreaming about Marcus occasionally. His kisses felt as real in her dreams as if he were constantly there beside her. She knew a tiny part of her would always be his.

Praetor hadn't wanted to get very specific, but had told her Lucius had moved in with Marcus. He told her too, just so she would be mentally prepared, that sometimes Maya stayed over. She assumed there was going to be a fast tracking of their vows at the chapel, now that all the pieces had fallen into place.

So Anne was more than a little curious why the vamp chose to appear to her today. Anne could not be considered to be a threat any longer. So, why was the vamp here? Perhaps to gloat. Show off her wedding ring, or tell her how happy Marcus was in her bed.

"I am not in the mood, Maya." The gaze she got back from the vixen was predatory. She was watching every movement Anne made.

Maya's dark hair framed her face like a bonnet and her eyes were dark with a tinge of fire at their center that burned deep red. It matched her lips, her red form-fitting dress with the low bust line, and highlighted her tiny waist and ample bosom. It was showtime, and Maya was playing some deadly part in a diabolical play. Anne stiffened for the worst.

"No, I guess not. I can see you aren't especially happy to see me," the seductress answered.

"And you expected what?"

Maya nodded her head and studied her. "Does Marcus know Praetor spends so much time with you here?"

"Oh, you mean, like how you stay over at Marcus's?"

Her eyebrows rose. "You have your little spies. Very good." She leaned into Anne, letting their perfumes mingle as they studied one another. It took everything Anne had to keep from running. She wasn't going to call for backup. Yet.

"Actually, Maya, I could care less. What Marcus does is none of my concern."

"Oh, really? Are you sure?"

"Completely. I've moved on. I thought both of you had as well." Anne studied her face. "You two are well suited to each other." She wasn't sure why the vampire had an issue with her. Perhaps she was here to rub her nose in the fact that she and Marcus were together. There was something else on the tip of Maya's tongue. Anne didn't want to know.

"May I ride with you? I don't want to interfere with your daily routine—or your life."

Anne glowered in response. Her insides were boiling. "No. Say what you came to say and then get away from me. I think the order still stands. You are not supposed to contact me. And now I'm late for work."

It did seem like a slap across Maya's pretty face. For a brief second, her witch nature, the ugly side of a long line of dominating female predators, came to Anne's view.

There it is. That's what Marcus saw, too. She understood his unease.

Maya composed herself. "Not when I have to defend my fated male from someone coming between us."

Interesting.

"Worried about keeping your man? I hear that's a problem for the women in your family."

Maya's eyes sparked with flame and she bit her own lip, sending a trickle of blood to the side of her mouth. She swiped it aside with her tongue and inhaled. "You wish," she hissed.

Anne forced a smile in return. "I don't come between you. I am no longer interested in Marcus. He has told you the same, I'm sure. I have not spoken to him or seen him since the last day I saw you."

"I don't believe you."

"Not a requirement. You can rot in hell, for all I care." Anne liked her control and composure. She felt strong, powerful, and whole. The anger she felt towards Maya only strengthened her experience. She added, "Maya, you and I both know Marcus uses women. What makes you think he has not found another innocent mortal he can turn into—what was that you said?—his eternal whore? Maybe you should be looking elsewhere for the female coming between you and Marcus in his bed. It isn't me."

"Oh, really? I have seen him over here before."

Anne's pulse increased. This surprised her. Then she discounted the truth of it. "Impossible. I have not seen him anywhere."

But what about the dreams?

She added, "Look, would you two just leave me alone? I don't want to have anything to do with either one of you."

"My God, I actually believe you, Anne."

Anne opened the car door to get in. Maya stopped her from closing it. "He doesn't know he has lost you to Praetor. I can keep that a secret, if you like."

"Ah, so he hasn't traced here and seen Praetor leave my house in the morning. So he hasn't seen how me makes me feel in bed."

"But you aren't fated."

"No. Sadly, no. But we're working on it." Anne liked the effect this lie had on Maya's face.

"He has not bed you. I would know."

"My God, Maya. Now you want the *other* man in my life? You're bored with Marcus and now you want Praetor?" Anne removed Maya's arm from the car door. "That's out of my hands. He'd never be a pleasure partner of yours. And we all know you're fated to Marcus, right? So how come the roaming eyes, hmmm?" It was working. Maya's eyes were darting about. She developed a twitch at the side of her nose. Anne saw a red blotch form on her chest.

She's nervous about something. Maybe she was after Praetor, after all.

"I can keep your secret—your relationship with Praetor—from Marcus. I have no designs on Praetor. But if Marcus asked him to keep his distance from you, he would. You know this."

"You really think it's a secret?"

"I do."

"Why would it matter to me? There are others I can be with. I've learned to adjust."

"Perhaps you are thinking Marcus will come back to you?" The smile Maya followed her words with wasn't pretty. More like a grimace.

"Like I said," Anne began, "I think you should be looking elsewhere for the temptress who bulges his pants. I assure you, it isn't me. If you do catch up to her, tell her I wish her luck. I am done with this."

Anne stepped inside the cab and closed the door after Maya stepped away. She watched the dark-haired beauty from the tiny rear view mirror of the bomber. She knew it wasn't likely Maya would give up this easily and wondered what event had occurred to bring her back to California.

It was a busy day at the Center. The new director, Peter, had invited Anne to an early dinner, but she'd wanted to decline. Eating meals with mortals was tricky, at best, since she had to feign being sick to explain for her lack of partaking, or eat and then get rid of her stomach contents right away, which she detested. She saved those occasions for events she absolutely could not get out of, like a society gala dinner or private sit down party. She reluctantly said yes, then drank mineral water with lemon, citing she was on a special diet.

"They've done an investigation on some missing persons," Peter said. "These are people associated with some of our clients at the center. I thought I should share these details with you."

Anne's blood pressure went up. She scanned the face of her friend.

"What details?" Her interest was avid, but tried not to show it.

"They all are related to women you've counseled, Anne." He leafed through the spinach salad with his fork.

"I wasn't aware of that."

"Anne, they are looking for people who would want to see these guys dead."

"I would imagine that could be a pretty long list. Can't see why they are spending the time."

"Well, they wouldn't. Except it has come to their attention we've lost eight relatives of women at the Center during the past four months or so. That was as of yesterday. Today, they found another two."

She was filled with dread. Her perfect life was beginning to unpeel like the veneer on a dresser left out in the rain.

How could this be? She would need to ask Praetor. The timing of Maya's appearance and the deaths of relatives at the center were too much of a coincidence.

"Two more? Who?" Anne asked.

Peter handed her a list of names, the last two circled. All of them were boyfriends or husbands of her clients, just as he'd told her.

"All these men have died?"

"Yes. And these all have occurred since you came back from your trip to Italy." He looked back at Anne with sad eyes. "All of them stabbed."

Anne shuddered. "How awful."

"I'm afraid the police want to talk to you. I just thought I would give you a head's up."

Anne went instantly into high alert. She wondered if Praetor was lending a helpful hand—too helpful. He'd been good at his word, supplying her with his own blood, and told her he didn't hunt any longer. Did he have a sudden lapse in judgment? An urge he couldn't control?

She could see Peter noticed her concern. "Anne, I am one hundred percent positive you had nothing to do with any of these. I mean, how could you?"

She didn't want to look him in the eyes. She didn't want him to see that she had a theory, and that theory involved Maya.

This could be something Maya could do. And it would be something impossible for Anne to explain, even if they believed her about vampires being real. She needed to speak to Praetor. Surely he would be able to help figure something out.

But how could he control the local authorities if they came after her?

Praetor was grim when Anne told him of the finding. He said he would investigate who the victims were and what evidence they had. He was most disturbed by Maya's recent appearance.

"So, she says Marcus traces here occasionally?" he asked.

"Yes. Why can't I detect him?"

"Maybe it's a bluff. She could be paranoid, you know. Or, maybe he does and just doesn't want you to know. Maybe my presence here has alarmed him." Praetor was thoughtful. He tapped his fingers on the table as he mulled something over in his mind.

"He couldn't be responsible for the killings, could he?"

"No, impossible, Anne. He would never do that." Praetor tried to smile, but failed. Anne hadn't seen him worry like this before.

"Then who? Maya?"

"This is someone who is making it look like you are the culprit. That would never be Marcus. My bet is on Maya." He leaned forward and took Anne's hands in his. "I need to speak to Marcus in person, make sure we have not started a war between us."

"Perhaps Maya is right. What if he doesn't know you have been here?"

"And what likelihood do you think Maya will keep this information to herself?"

"Yes, I see your point."

"With Maya on the scene, I will need to send someone else to watch over you. I think . . ."

"No. I will be fine. She is bridled from hurting me."

"But not from hurting your situation or those you care about."

"Make your peace with Marcus, if you must. I will be fine here. She's mistaken if she thinks Marcus has shown himself around here." She chose not to tell him about her erotic dreams. "Once she learns I am truly not with Marcus, I have to think she will leave me alone. How could they accuse me of these murders? Surely there's no proof."

Then she thought about the bloody traces in her wastebasket at the office.

"I think you are too optimistic, Anne."

"She has a child to raise. Surely she has a life to live."

"You don't understand. Marcus was her life. You took that away from her. It sounds like that has not returned to her. Regardless if he finds another, you are still the one who stopped their fating ceremony from taking place."

Anne worried as Praetor's words echoed over and over. Her *perfect* new life was now unraveling. Even though she'd told him she would be safe, being without the protection of this kind friend was making her nervous.

Someone wanted her to be blamed for these murders, and she had a pretty good idea who that was. And now she would be completely alone.

CHAPTER 23

Robert and Gary left the Double Eights about eleven o'clock. Gary had too much to drink, so Robert drove his own pickup in order to drop Gary off at his apartment. He helped his friend get out of the truck and pushed him in the direction of the walkway. Robert thought he saw a shadow under the stairwell leading up to Gary's unit. His friend was babbling something about how unfriendly the girls had been tonight at the bar, and didn't notice the shadow.

"Not like I don't tip them. They're conspiring. Holding out on us," Gary said to the clear night air.

"Maybe they're tired of us, Gary," Robert said.

"Tired of this?" His friend brought his arms out to his sides and immediately was jolted by the blade of a knife that passed through his torso from behind. Gary tried to scream, his eyes bugging out with the shocked realization of his own death.

Robert saw Gary's mouth open one last time to let out a gurgling sound as he threw up blood and sank to his knees. Fingers clutched under his jaw and ripped a hole several inches long, nearly from ear to ear.

The movements were so quick, Robert couldn't make out who was the attacker. But he knew he had to get out of there as fast as he could. It was clearly too late for Gary.

Robert ran to the truck and nearly made it. The attacker had just smashed the driver's side window and had reached around to tear at his neck like he'd just done to Gary, when Robert's car horn went off. Momentarily stunned, the attacker hesitated, which gave him time to push the onCall button above the rear view mirror. He could hear the emergency phone ringing.

Then he couldn't answer the pert operator who wanted to know what the nature of Robert's emergency was because someone with black hair and boobs the size of cantaloupes was sucking at his neck.

With the squawk of the operator in the background, Robert felt a dark coldness descend on him. He was yanked from the cab of the truck and thrown. He landed on his knees, in excruciating pain. One leg had twisted and was under his torso at an odd angle. He'd also landed with his left arm tucked underneath him and he felt pain at his wrist and elbow.

He was aware blood from the neck wound was rapidly spreading over the asphalt.

And then mercifully, he passed out.

Anne was being questioned on a daily basis, and instead of it taking a few minutes, the interviews had lasted for over an hour. She lost her job at Starbucks. She was exhausted without Praetor's blood. She had to travel farther away to find victims to feed on.

Occasionally she saw a police tail. Her tracing abilities were not yet perfected and she couldn't trust doing it without winding up in some boiling cauldron or fire pit somewhere, ending her life. So she waited until she absolutely had to feed, and then ventured out.*Where is he?*

She was weary of the box that was beginning to close in around her as the days turned into nearly a week of hell.

Six days later, she was greatly relieved to find Praetor back in her living room when she returned late from a feeding in San Francisco. She ran to him and gave him a hug, genuinely happy to see him.

"I am sorry it has taken so long to get back to you. Council business has been neglected while I have been here with you. And I needed time with Marcus."

"So he knows?"

"Yes. I got to him just before Maya did. But he already knew. He was not happy."

Anne understood this reaction. But she felt Marcus had brought it on himself. He had caused the whole problem by lying to her in the first place.

"I have some news you are not going to like to hear, Anne." Praetor hugged her again. Anne felt tears well up in her eyes as she steeled herself. She had some faint idea it was going to cause more pain than anything she had felt previously. Worse than her leaving Italy without Marcus. Worse than Robert's infidelity. She sighed.

"Go ahead. I'm ready," she said to Praetor's' shirt.

"Marcus has announced he and Maya will be fated. The ceremony is being rushed. I will have to return tomorrow for the preparation. By the weekend they will be formally recognized, and the ceremony makes it final."

Anne's knees gave out. Praetor held her as she lay limp in his arms, unable to move. She felt as dead inside as that night in Italy. She had no will to live. She couldn't even cry. Everything was gone.

He laid her gently on the living room couch. She still couldn't move. But she could cry.

"Anne, there is something else, though." Praetor kneeled in front of her. "He has done this so that Maya will stop preying on you. I know about your ex-husband and his friend. Word traveled to Tuscany and the council is concerned. I have spoken to Laurel. She thinks Marcus sacrifices himself. She begged me to handle Maya myself."

She looked into his eyes, which firmly said the obvious.

"She doesn't want him to spend eternity in a loveless union," he said. He underscored the predicament they were in with his words. "As much as I would like to, if I did that, it would mean the end of me, and possibly you. I cannot interfere."

Marcus could do this, she thought. He could fate to Maya. Bind himself forever to the Queen of Hell herself.

She had not dreamed about him for several nights, which probably meant he was staying away from her, and spending time with Maya. He could bring himself to do this for her, he would try to appease Maya first, and then if that didn't work . . .

What an ironic twist of fate. She understood now just how deeply he had loved her, and what he would do to keep her safe. And now she knew how much she had loved him.

The reality of her barren life of forever without him loomed large. She inhaled and beheld her new reality, like she was walking up the steps to a hangman's noose.

Except that would have been merciful compared to what she was going to have to endure.

Anne was arrested the day after Praetor left to negotiate and arrange the fating ceremony. Another man had been found with his throat slashed, draped over the fence of his house, where a group of children found him on their way to elementary school the next morning. They were fourth graders, and because of their age, there had been an outcry from the community, causing the Chief to make a quick arrest of the most likely suspect.

Anne.

For the first time in her life, her picture was on the front page of the local paper.

As she sat in the cell awaiting her appointed legal counsel, she got the impression none of the guards or even the arresting officer believed she was the real killer. But too many things had pointed in her direction. The man who had been killed and left for the children to view had been the ex-husband of one of her clients, a man who witnesses had seen Anne argue with on more than one occasion. The circumstances were too compelling to ignore. Anne had to give it to Maya. That woman knew how to be diabolical.

Anne was glad Marcus would be in the boy's life now more than ever, so that the boy wouldn't fall prey to her family.

Anne's feelings were so raw and ragged she wasn't sure she could respond to anything. She was resigned to just let herself be the cog in the system. Let them take her away. After all, they couldn't kill her. She would be able to trace at night, so even if she was confined to a jail cell, she would be able to spend the night in a comfortable bed away from the dangers of prison life. She just needed a little more training. Surely Praetor would have the time to do this. The wheels of the human criminal justice system moved so slowly, she probably had years before she would have to think about it.

Her biggest concern, other than trying to repair the hole in her heart, was what the vampire coven would do to her as punishment. There wasn't much a human judge and jury could do to her, but the council was another story. If the human world thought she was guilty, why wouldn't the vampire world?

And perhaps this had been worked out with the council. Perhaps Marcus's capitulation to Maya included the agreement that Anne would be left untouched and perhaps banished by the coven, or at best, left alive in her vampire body.

Her eyes filled with tears as she realized this was perhaps the last thing he could ever do for her. She knew his fating would mean Maya would be placed before any other female in his past, present, or future. She would forever be his queen, someone he would defend to his own death, if need be. He would go on to father other children. One happy family, as if the day she came to the chapel never existed.

She spent the night crying her eyes out for the last time. Praetor traced her to his own bed. He held her all night long, stroking her hair, and when she closed her eyes, she pretended it was Marcus bidding her farewell. That somehow made it better.

She had come to see Praetor as her only friend in the world. Perhaps, if he would have her, if the scandal could be overcome in the coven, he would be allowed, would be willing to take her as his partner. She knew they would never be true mates. But not having the hundreds of years of experience, as well as a family unit in place to help, she was left at such a disadvantage that for the first time in her life, she felt she could not face eternity alone.

She asked him about it as they sat in bed and watched the peachy stain on the morning sky grow, and then fade into the bustle of the day. He'd have to return her to her cell before the guards checked morning rounds.

"I am honored, Anne. But then what would happen if I find my female? You would be discarded again, for the third time."

"Is there any precedent for people to grow into a fating? Marcus is truly going to try. He must believe something like that is possible."

"My honest opinion? The answer is no, regardless of what Marcus tells himself." He continued to stroke her hair and the side of her arm. "You should not make any decisions now. Wait until after the ceremony. Wait until you hit bottom completely." He kissed the top of her head and whispered, "And then you start to build back up. If you are mending, perhaps we can talk about it. But not now." He leaned her head back examining her lips, which she parted for him.

Anne could fall in love with him, maybe. Her eyes drew him to her and he softly complied. His tongue tasted her bottom lip but did not pry its way into hers. When she began to push into his mouth, he closed his teeth and drew his lips together, sealing her out.

"You don't feel anything for me, Praetor?" Anne asked.

"I love you like a sweet friend. As a most precious sister, or a long lost childhood crush. I think if you examine yourself, you will see it is the same." He traced her lips with his forefinger and smiled. "You are a wonder, Anne. Those hours you shared with Marcus I'm sure made him feel like master of the universe, to have someone such as you love him."

"And I think he did love me back. He did."

"Yes, I think you are right. But now we have to accept another reality. Not healthy to dwell on the past. Time to return you to your cell."

She was out on bail later that afternoon and came home to her apartment that had obviously been searched. She straightened up, cleaned some of the litter of multiple strangers who did not care about her or her things.

She went to the hospital to visit Robert.

He had a cast on each leg and on one of his arms. Bandages were wound around the top of his head. Someone had played a cruel joke on him and had tied the bandage around his neck with a big gauze bow right under his chin. Anne was most concerned about that wound, as she smelled fresh blood. She looked at him for signs Maya gave him vampire life, like Marcus had done for her. She decided he was healing as a human, not an immortal. Even a recent turn would have shown up.

She gave him a kiss on his lips, which were swollen and deep purple. "Are you in pain, Robert?"

"Uh huh. But I'm letting them blast me full of anything they'll give me. I might fall asleep. They have me pretty much wacked out."

"You go ahead and fall asleep if you need to. I'm just paying respects."

"I'm not dead yet."

That got her thinking. Had Maya intended on killing him or hurting him? Anne believed the attacks would stop, and, if she could survive the investigation, maybe she was finally at the turning point. The fating was scheduled for tomorrow morning. How nice it would be to just leave this all behind, have all the drama be finally over.

"You hear they are looking for a female who did this?"

"I'm not surprised. They have been questioning me non-stop. My contempt for some of these men was pretty well documented," Anne replied. "And people knew I thought Gary was a scumbag."

"Oh, no." Robert tried to sit up but let out a sharp groan as something hurt and he stopped. "Anne, I told them it wasn't you. I told them I met her, in a bar before."

Anne looked at him with what she hoped wasn't too much pity in her eyes. He was in enough pain.

"She's a weird one. We met her that next day after you kicked me out."

Anne remembered the jet plane ride, the lavender bubble bath. Robert could have told her he had screwed fifty women that night and she could have cared less.

"What did she say? Did she give a reason?"

"She told me she killed Gary. But she told me that she'd come after me over and over again until I jumped off the Golden Gate Bridge."

Anne looked out the window. Surely that was before Marcus gave Maya the news he was going to give in to her demands.

"Robert, I don't think you have to worry about her anymore. I think she has moved on to someone else. She's in Italy, getting ready for her . . . wedding . . . tomorrow."

"Hell she is. She came here not more than an hour ago. She untied this bandage and sucked more blood from me. I couldn't do a thing. Hurt like hell."

Anne looked at Robert's white bow tie.

So that was how it was going to be. Anne understood now that Maya would never give up. She was going to needle her for the rest of her life, and everyone around her. She would make Marcus miserable. She would ruin his life, ruin the life of the boy. She would turn everything upside down for all eternity.

But maybe Anne could stop it. Maybe it was up to her, after all. Everyone would get what they wanted, or close to what they wanted. Marcus would be free. The boy would have a father. Laurel would live to find her fated love and comfort her brother. Robert would survive to go on his eternal search or find in himself the good part Anne had seen in the beginning, and, at last make a good husband to Monika, perhaps have that family he wanted.

And everything would revert to where it had been when she lay in the cobblestone street in Genoa, drained of blood. That was the night she *should* have died.

But she had been given the miracle of finding love, or she would have died without it. She was never born to be vampire. But, God help her, she loved one with all her heart. And she had to feel grateful for having received this gift, precious and so limited as it was.

And if she couldn't have him, she could remove the devil in his life.

She was going to pick a fight with Maya, and she hoped the element of surprise would give her the edge.

Protecting Marcus might become her dying wish.

CHAPTER 24

Anne sat in the apartment reading a book, *A Hunger Like No Other*. She sensed movement downstairs. One quick glance to the street revealed the strikingly beautiful female in her best red, eyeing the car. She wondered if Maya coveted the beast because it belonged to her or because it would be a trophy she could bring back to Italy and make Marcus ride in it, proving once and for all her dominance over Anne. What a wedding present that would make Marcus, if Maya could figure out how to transport it before tomorrow. Anne smiled because she knew she was thinking about it. Could almost hear her thinking about getting her trophy, for her trophy husband.

Robert made sure the trap was set. He played the part perfectly. God bless his little cheating heart, Anne thought. For once, he got something right.

Anne couldn't really read Maya's mind, but people like her were not hard to figure out. She wouldn't be able to resist gloating over her victory. It was simply not in her nature. Win or lose, she'd be nasty to the end. Anne was counting on that nasty side to keep her distracted.

It was nice that Maya knocked on Anne's door, even though she had the ability to trace right through it. This indicated the element of surprise was still with Anne. If Maya sensed danger, she would spring into action and go for Anne's throat. But apparently, she thought she'd already won. Maya had decided to behave, for once.

Good.

Anne knew Maya didn't want to do anything to anger Marcus. After all, he had given in to her desire to mate for life. She'd gotten what she wanted, even though everyone knew he would have made a different choice. At least this is what Anne told herself.

But who cares, now?

When she opened her front door, Maya gave her a smile that had probably aroused Marcus the first and probably hundredth time he saw it. Anne thought about Marcus's large cock riding this woman who stood before her. About how he would kiss her. How Maya would ride him and writhe, squeezing her own breasts. How he would kiss her nipples until they hurt. Did he bite her next to her sex like he had Anne? Did he enjoy Maya's blood?

These images helped Anne feel the conviction in her soul. No one could resist Maya. And no one ever would. It would have to be a woman to bring her down, a woman who came at Maya from her blind side. A woman so desperate she had nothing to lose.

A woman like me.

Maya had made the miscalculation of her life.

"I see you got my message. Thanks for coming."

"The least I could do," Maya responded. Her grin was defiant. She was searching Anne's face for evidence she had caused her pain.

"Thank you for sparing the life of my ex—my almost husband," Anne said, allowing her lower lip to quiver sufficiently.

"On our tastes in men we agree. He is quite worthless. Untrustworthy. So unlike Marcus." Her eyes flared with the tiny red flames Anne had seen before.

"I trust he will be left alone now."

"Of course. You are free to have him. I give him back to you. I, on the other hand, take Marcus. Or rather, he takes me." Maya looked Anne up and down, and then added, "I will make sure his days are filled with every fantasy he desires."

Another evil challenge. Anne was sure she was doing the right thing.

"Come in." Anne said, turning her back on the vamp. She hoped Maya didn't see it as a test of her dominion. "I thought we could bury the hatchet between us." Anne led Maya into the hallway.

"Very civilized of you. I didn't expect this."

"And so good of you to come, so close to your wedding day. I'm sure you have a million things to attend to."

"I've been planning this fating ceremony for a hundred years." Maya frowned. "Under the circumstances, I felt it prudent not to invite you."

"No thanks. Weddings are a painful reminder of what we cannot truly have." Anne inhaled and began her prepared speech. "You won, Maya. I hope you and Marcus are filled with centuries of love and many brilliant children."

"Thanks." Maya slid beyond Anne into the living room, looking unmoved. She glanced around the room as if looking for someone.

"Still trying to rub salt into the wound? Didn't you hear me? I said you won. Marcus isn't here. Neither is Praetor. Come, look at your trophy. Can you see it in my face?"

Maya turned and gave Anne a sultry smile again after looking her up and down. "So, Robert said you had a wedding present for us. A car. That one?" She pointed outside to the bomber, which stood silent, innocent as a green frog. Deadly bait. Anne loved that car on so many levels. Now more than ever before.

"Yes, my car."

"Really? I am surprised."

"I can't drive it anymore, truth be told. Marcus and I made love in it several times. I realized yesterday, it brings back too many memories, unhappy memories. Marcus's smell is all over the seats." Anne hesitated and leaned into Maya to whisper, "And a little on the ceiling, if you know what I mean."

Maya's smile was long and deep, and wicked. Anne knew she was thinking about taking him for a ride in it, and the things they could do made Anne blush.

"See, that's why he has made the right decision. None of my memories of being with Marcus are unhappy." Maya walked over to Anne. "My body aches for him. And when I next bed him, he will belong to me forever."

"Yes. But I thought you would appreciate my telling you I have found the fating with Praetor even more wonderful. See, you will be taking Marcus away from me just as I am opening another thrilling chapter in my life. Have you ever had Praetor, Maya? He is centuries older. He hasn't been so prudish or exclusive as Marcus. His conquests number in the thousands. He has forgotten more than Marcus ever knew about sexual pleasure." Anne smiled for the effect she hoped it would have on the woman.

There was a split second where Maya's eyes got wide, then she looked into Anne's eyes with pure hatred.

That's when Anne struck. She reached out and grabbed Maya by the hair, and, with her other hand, grabbed her shoulders. She wrenched Maya's head from the top of her body like breaking a twig. She was surprised at her own strength.

Had Anne wanted to get even, she would have made it a fight so she could enjoy the conquest. But this was no conquest she would enjoy. It was an execution. Maya's headless torso almost danced, pirouetted in the room from the force of the twisting motion, spewing blood on the ceiling and walls as her arms flailed helplessly at her sides.'

Anne held the head up to her face and let the blood drip down her front. It stared back at her, lifeless. Anne liked the change in Maya's expression, and for the first time felt truly rid of the evil vampire.

Her front door burst open. Praetor and Marcus entered. Marcus shrieked, "No, No, No!"

Even Praetor was white with shock. His lips had turned purple, his forehead creased as he stared between the lifeless head of Maya and Anne, very much alive.

Anne wouldn't look at either of them. She dropped Maya's head with a dull thud and went into the bathroom to take a shower.

She took her clothes off behind the curtain, listening to the men shout and argue in the other room as they dealt with the reality of what she had done. Anne's insides were dead. She was washed of Maya's blood, but she had no desire to touch Marcus, to get any of the taint on him. Her only thought was that she hoped it would be all over soon. She hoped the council would act faster than their human counterparts were known to.

She stepped out and wrapped herself in the towel, her bloody clothes remaining in the shower. The man she once loved was bent over Maya's headless body, sobbing, no doubt grieving for his lost bride.

"You are free. You gave me life. Now I give you the same. We are even," Anne felt the chill in her soul as she spoke these words.

"No, Anne. We are *not* even." He rose up and stood, his hands and shirt covered in blood. He did not smile. Anne felt like she had put her own stake through his heart.

Praetor ushered her into the bedroom, instructing her to dress. "We are going to Genoa to secure your fate immediately. You must pack some clothes."

Anne dressed quickly. She got out the Italian leather suitcase, remembering she had never unpacked the bag Marcus had sent her home with two weeks ago. The one with the letter in it she had never read. She added her makeup kit to it, brushed her hair, and told him she was ready.

"I'm going to trace us there. We have little time left."

"I don't want to travel with Marcus."

"He'll come later, after he makes the arrangements for Maya. Her family will be all over this."

"Yes." Anne could only imagine the retaliation they'd want to foist upon her. Their darling child, dead.

Praetor added, "He needs to stay away from you, for obvious reasons. Come." He held out his hand. Anne reached out and he pulled her to him. She wrapped her arms around his body as they transported through the afternoon sky.

Anne felt dead inside. Praetor paced back and forth in the foyer of the great hall, jotting down notes. He was muttering to himself. She wasn't even counting the small nail holes in the wooden paneling on the walls.

At last they were summoned.

They stood in the exact spot where Anne had faced the inspection interrogation. The council sat, stoic, both infirmed members wide awake, and only one was on a blood IV. They looked disheveled, like they had been summoned in haste. They wore nightshirts under their crimson robes.

Praetor began his prepared speech. He brought out the piece of paper he'd written his notes on earlier.

"Most respected Council, I come to you today with distressing news you have no doubt heard. Our sister, Maya, has been murdered. She was savagely beheaded. The transgressor has done this deed, it is said, because of love. We in the coven know this cannot be the case. Only in cases of self-preservation can this be a justified crime. I find no such justification in this case. The person responsible for this unspeakable crime is one Marcus Monteleone."

"What?" Anne whipped her head around to face Praetor.

"Council, you need to know he has warned me that Anne would try to take the blame for him, but I saw it with my own eyes, saw the blood wash over his body and can attest to the fact that he is the murderer."

Anne was livid. "That is not what happened. They have conspired to lie to you. Your Praetor lies!"

"Silence!" The middle vampire held up his hand. "You are a conversion. You have caused us nothing but problems since you came here. I will not take your filthy word over that of Praetor Artemis, who has served the Council faithfully for centuries."

One of the other Council members spoke up. "It is well known Marcus was only fating Maya as a means to protect you. I would expect more gratitude towards him. Calling Praetor and Marcus both liars makes a mockery of their station."

And so it was decided. Marcus had been arrested, left in a cell underneath the great hall. Anne wanted to meet with him, but Praetor said Marcus did not wish her company.

The trial lasted only one day. Marcus was found guilty, by his own admission. Anne was not allowed to attend. She was desperate for the opportunity to speak with him.

But she was promised a night with him before his sentencing. The hearing being set for tomorrow, Anne would spend her last night with Marcus tonight.

Marcus sat in the room given him for his last night. It was not large, but boasted a large bed with fresh linen sheets and opulent satin pillows. He had been given warm blood after being given the choice for a human whore, which was something he flatly turned down. He was reading, strangely calm, and looking forward to his one night with Anne. Should his sentencing determine he would be given the death penalty, it was always carried out within an hour of pronouncement. He was encouraged to set his affairs in order, which he had.

He met with Lucius, who was beside himself with grief. Laurel promised she would be both father and mother to the boy, at least until she found her fating. Lucius was already sleeping in Laurel's bed, crying himself to sleep every night. Laurel said it actually helped her to have him there. It truly broke everyone's heart. Lucius's pain had been an ancillary casualty of the war between Marcus and his two women.

Marcus knew everyone wished he had taken Lucius into account before acting. But, Laurel would make a righteous mother to him and had let Marcus know she would tell him stories of his father and what a wonderful man he was, and how his honor in the end had been his undoing. And Marcus told her he was going to ask that Paolo help out as well. Laurel agreed. Paolo had been conspicuously absent during the trial and pre-trial ordeal, called to the side of his dying wife.

Marcus was visited by his other brothers and sisters on this eve as well. The women cried. The men were angry. He made them promise to accept Anne as part of the family that he would never share in. Reluctantly, they agreed, but none of them came away with anything but contempt for her.

Paolo finally came on his own after the rest of them had left.

"You look well, Paolo. How is your wife?"

"She has passed on. She is no longer in pain. I am sorry, I was attending to the affairs of her household and could not leave before now."

"No worries. I'm sorry for your loss."

Paolo shrugged. "Nothing compared to yours. I knew this would be the outcome for me. You, on the other hand, had a life of eternal love snatched away from you. It's not fair."

"It's entirely fair. We are only as good as the rules we have crafted for the benefit of us all. I will not have my family mock the Council's decision."

"You know they have no choice but to sentence you to death."

"I am hoping they do. I can't live with myself. I've murdered someone who was to be my fated female."

"You can't be serious."

"I am. Paolo." Marcus stood up, walking to the one tiny window, with bars on it, overlooking the front entrance of the compound. "I have thought about this many times. You have now lost your wife. I was going to ask you something, one last request before I slip away and am no more."

"Ask me then. It will be granted before you even finish."

"I want you to take Anne. Love her, as I would have. She doesn't understand our ways. She feels for Praetor Artemis, but they know they are not fated.

I ask you to pretend you feel something for her, that you feel a fating. I don't think she would question you."

"Marcus, this is insanity. Are you of right mind?"

"I am entirely."

"I can't do this."

"Too late. You already said my wish was granted before you heard of it. It is done. I need to hear it from your lips."

"Marcus."

"Say it, damn you!" Marcus stood and boomed so loud it shook the building.

Tears streamed down Paolo's face. "Brother, you cannot ask me to watch you die, then take that miracle that brought you such joy after years of loneliness. Take Anne for myself?"

"With one exception."

"Anything, Marcus. Tell me you were joking, playing some kind of morbid hangman's game."

"I will bed her one last time. Tonight."

"Of course. I'll bring her within the hour."

"I do miss that woman. I do miss her touch. I'll not tell her of our agreement. You must make it appear completely natural. Do I have your vow?"

"My heart is breaking."

"Do I have your vow?" Marcus said, raising his voice.

"Yes. Yes, brother." Paolo answered with a whisper.

"And you will raise the boy. All three of you will see to it he is showered with love, yes?"

"Marcus, I wish I could speak longer with you about this."

"No, brother. I miss my female. You must bring her to me now. If she won't come, tie her up and bring her. I will not die without bedding her one more time. It's for her I die tomorrow. Do not refuse me."

Paolo didn't have to tie Anne up. She fell at Marcus's feet when the door to the bedroom chamber was opened. He instantly kneeled before her, holding her head between his hands, which shook slightly. She noted the binding bracelets on both his wrists, their coppery dull glint catching in the late afternoon sun, clinking as they touched their counterpart on the other wrist. She held one of his wrists with the band in both hers, tracing the ancient symbols embedded in the metal with her fingers. She bent and kissed his wrist, kissed the band, then drew it to her heart and pressed like she could absorb it there. As if she could dissolve the restraints and set his soul free forever. She turned her face up to his.

"Love, you cannot do this. I never took this on expecting you to pay the price for my indiscretion."

"Anne, it's my indiscretion. I never should have agreed to the fating with Maya. I killed you just as if I had dismembered you the night I promised to fate her. I knew it almost instantly, but tried to make her feel I would honor my word."

He covered her mouth with his, then drew her to him with strong hands that pressed her chest to his. "I just couldn't sleep with her, even kiss her. She knew she would never have my heart. Only you have that. Only you ever will."

He kissed her again. Anne melted into him, leaning her body against his torso. Her arms came up around his neck. She had been crying so long it seemed like the natural state to her.

"Come, love. Let's take what we have left."

Anne knew the difference between this embrace and the embrace Praetor had given her. The kiss was different, too. Marcus prepared her mouth, bringing his tongue to her lips, over her teeth. He let her hook her tongue over his fang. A huge drop of blood fell squarely into his mouth, causing him to shudder. He was urgent with his need to taste her, nibbling on her lips and pulling them into his. She felt he consumed her.

Anne then opened her dress to him, to let him taste the rosy tips denied him for too long. He was brave. He did not cry, but shuddered as she kissed his forehead, his ear, his neck, as he played with her nipples. She came as she straddled his thigh, rocking on him with urgency and burning need. Marcus thoroughly enjoyed her breasts. She whispered into the soft curly hairs at his temple, "These were to be yours for eternity. They will always be, even . . ." Her voice broke.

She could tell he was pushing out the visions of tomorrow. For right now, his head would stay connected to his torso, long enough to feel the texture of her white skin, the salty taste of the flesh that needed his tongue and his lips.

He would take from her all her moans and sighs. He would secret them away to a place deep inside his heart, and would take them with him forever.

His lips on her bud caused her to burst into tears. "I will not be able to live without this." He whispered how he regretted his decision to join with Maya. He should have stolen Anne away to some island somewhere they could love until the Council found them. He would have stolen her away forever, would have willingly taken on the pressure to watch out for Council guards coming after them so she could sleep in the pink tenderness of the morning, in his arms. He whispered how he loved her, had always loved her, and would always love her, somehow.

"How many days could we have had? Maybe one or two more? It would have been worth it." His sigh made her tingle. "We could have had a few days, until they found us. Maybe we should have."

Marcus spoke the ancient words to Anne's womb. Her body constricted and she took in air, involuntarily reacting to his mysterious words that celebrated the life force that would grow there. He spoke as he gently kissed and sucked the juiciness of her fruit of life. His body knew hers and how to make her insides come alive. He would remain, a part of him would, inside her forever. Anne knew that she carried his child, created from the first time they made love.

For now, the most beautiful love in the universe would have to end come morning. Marcus hoped as he placed his cock inside her warm folds, that Paolo would learn to worship this holy place as he had, that he would feel something like he did as he thrust inside her, stroking and fueling her passion, and covering her insides with his seed over and over again. Perhaps, on the eve of his death, he could give her a child. If there was a God, and he never had believed in one before, this God would find it in his heart to give her a child she could love and remember him by. Just one more miracle. He needed just one more.

Anne could not be sated. She drank from him in long feedings that nearly caused his vision to disappear. Blackness came upon him. He saw how she felt the energy and the golden fating come over them both. More tears. He drank liberally from her, biting her as the claiming ritual demanded, on her neck. The holy elixir filled his body with a glow that numbed the reality of their short time left.

Anne convulsed, then silently wept as he claimed her neck.

"Not now. You must not cry now. Love me, Anne. Love me enough for the centuries we will be apart. Maybe there will be a time we will be together. Humans have this, maybe there is a place for us, for our love."

She was trying to be very brave. But it was difficult to look at her eyes and not see the utter sadness there. "Bear me a child, my love. Bring a child into the world for me. Can you do this for me? Just one more thing I ask of your body? Bring to the world something made from us both, together."

She nodded. "You will have your wish. I will get big with a healthy child. I will watch him grow up and marry. I will watch our grandchildren. You must understand I will make this happen, Marcus. This will happen, love. They will know and love you as I have. They will know of the wonderful lineage from which they came."

He nodded his head. "I give . . . you . . . life. . . . I leave my love with your womb."

There were no more tears to cry by morning. They had fed from each other, made love more times than even Anne could count. They watched the orange tint fade, and with it, their time together.

"No tears. I go a happy man that I have loved you."

"I am fulfilled, Marcus. Anything else is bonus."

They parted as Marcus prepared for the sentencing.

CHAPTER 25

The great hall was filled to capacity. Half the audience, those from Maya's family side, were hostile, huffing and flouncing in obvious disapproval of the entire proceedings. They aimed nasty stares at anyone related to Marcus, the coven's admitted Golden Boy, the man who was the object of desire for any unattached lady, vampire or otherwise. Young females grew up hoping, in fact, that they would come to puberty and discover their fate was tied to Marcus.

Maya's family didn't appreciate the show of relief coming from other goldens that Maya was gone. She had caused trouble with the group for decades. Her demands were loud, her decisions arbitrary. She got her way most of the time, like her mother, Aurora, because fighting either of the two women was more distasteful than just agreeing to their terms. And it was rumored they cast spells and were more witch than they openly admitted.

Now Marcus would pay for Maya's death with his own life.

Aurora gathered her family members like a mother hen. Her sorrow was very public and loud. Maya's father was still alive somewhere, but even Aurora's fated male could not stand to be in her company and had sought the arms of other women far away from Genoa and rarely came home. He did not do so today, either. Not that any of the coven blamed him.

In contrast, Marcus's side was reserved, except for their quiet sniffling. In mourning already, many of them wished the ordeal over and felt guilty for those thoughts. At Marcus's request, Lucius was allowed to come to the hearing, something Marcus had promised the boy on his final visit. At six years of age, Lucius was going to have to understand quickly his part in this passion play. And running from it, at any age, was never Marcus's style.

But the sight of Lucius was difficult for all of Marcus's family. In their final show of support for their favorite son, they stood by his decision, and each braced him, hugged him, told him how brave he was and said, though they denied it on the inside, they were glad he was there.

Anne sat between Praetor Artemis and Laurel. Paolo sat next to Lucius, who insisted on sitting behind the seat Marcus would take when he was led in, a spot traditionally saved for the mate. It was obviously the right choice, under the circumstances.

Marcus entered through a side door just ahead of the council in their red robes. Young female attendants, who, thankfully, were more respectfully dressed in robes, wheeled in the two infirmed ones. Anne looked up at Praetor and he managed a smile.

Marcus found his seat, but first leaned in to kiss the boy then shake Paolo's hand. His eyes connected with Anne's and she tried to look satisfied, but at last it was impossible. She broke from the row and ran to his arms as Maya's side of the aisle let out gasps of outrage.

"We agreed. You need your strength. Don't trouble yourself." Marcus leaned in to her ear. "I can feel the life I started in your belly. Bring him up with love, not hate. Don't let him avenge me, Anne. Raise him to be strong, but raise him to love as I have loved you."

She nodded before they were asked to separate. Marcus gave a bow to his family in a general greeting, and sat down. This last action caused the side of the room behind him to stir. Several were sobbing. Anne sat up as straight as she could, staring at the back of the man she might only be able to see for a few more minutes.

Looking old beyond his time, the Council leader rose. "We are gathered here this day to pronounce sentence on the convicted murderer of one Maya D'Alessandro. Will the condemned please rise and hear sentence?"

Marcus rose, his white silk shirt billowing out behind the tail tucked into his dark pants. He wore his tall leather boots. Anne realized, with sudden horror, that Marcus wore the same outfit he'd worn that day she had met him in at the Starbucks, not so long ago. She remembered his tall lanky frame in those boots as he got her coffee. She swallowed the salty tears, choking on a sob. Praetor stretched his arm around her and brought her head to his chest. Laurel clasped Anne's fingers and laid her cheek against the hand on Anne's shoulder. Anne was grateful for the support, feeling like an old book carefully placed between two substantial bookends.

"Marcus Monteleone—"

"Excuse me, Head Council." Paolo stood up. "I have something you must hear."

Maya's side of the room burst into shouts and catcalls. Anne knew they took this as an offense, so eager were they for Marcus's blood. They didn't want to be denied one more chance to show their indignation and outrage.

"This is highly irregular." Several of the Council conferred in whispers and nods. "This has to do with the sentencing?"

"I believe it does." Paolo hadn't waited for an invitation. He made his way up to a lectern at the middle of the center aisle, with Lucius in tow, who looked just as confused as Marcus. Laurel squeezed Anne's hand. When Anne looked at Laurel, she saw Laurel give a faint smile to Paolo.

The audience gasped when Paolo raised Lucius up and set him on the top shelf of the lectern. He held the tiny hands in his large ones. Paolo's face was lined with tears. Lucius began to cry openly, his lower lip quivering. The poor boy was scared silly. Marcus moved, as if about to come to his aid, but Paolo gave him a glance and a gesture with the palm of his hand, telling him to stop.

The Council members were stunned into inaction.

"Lucius," Paulo began, taking a deep breath and releasing it. "I am your father."

Both sides of the room erupted. One of Maya's male relatives grabbed Paolo and tried to wrestle him to the ground. He was restrained, but not after ripping the sleeve from Paolo's dark coat. Paolo recovered, soothed his sleeveless jacket, and then resumed his conversation with Lucius as if the two of them were alone in a room somewhere.

"Your mother and I were fated lovers, for a short couple of days. I ran away afterwards, not knowing you had been conceived during our mating. I was married at the time to a human woman who needed me and whom I loved, although not in the same fating way. She was a good woman and didn't deserve my indiscretion. It was confusing for me. I am truly sorry."

The audience had hushed. Paolo hugged the boy on the lectern. The whole room could see the boy did not hesitate to hug Paolo back. Lucius closed his eyes. Paolo pulled away and put his hands on the sides of Lucius's face. "I am ashamed of my actions, Lucius. I have caused pain and death. I have robbed you of a home and a father who loves you dearly. I ask your forgiveness. You are the only one I live for now, my son."

Aurora stood up. "This changes nothing. How touching. This only goes to prove what a depraved family we have here before us. You will pronounce sentence now and wipe this man off the face of the earth. And as contributory, you should take the scum Paolo as well!" She pointed a red tipped long forefinger at Paolo.

The Council was clearly in disarray. It was obvious they did not know what to do. Praetor Artemis stood and addressed them, his hand remaining on Anne's shoulder.

"Council, it appears we have two crimes here, but only one trial." He leveled a glassy stare at Paolo. "And we have one crime of unspeakable cowardice, which will have its own punishment."

At this, Paolo sadly nodded. He hugged Lucius again, who tried to steal a look at Marcus.

"Praetor. Explain," Council Chairman requested.

"Is it not a crime to come between two fated mates?"

"It is," Council Chairman replied.

"And I have been told Maya fed on this female as a mortal, draining her, actually set off to kill her after she heard from Marcus's lips she was his fated female. This is part of the record. I wrote it so several months ago."

"You are correct."

"Maya knew the boy was not Marcus's. She had felt the fating with Paolo. But, faced with a life of raising a child by herself and spending the rest of her life with a mate who refused her, she did only what she was trained to do." Praetor gave a harsh look to Aurora, who stood immediately.

"He disrespects me and my family. The Council has spoken already and convicted this man by his own admission."

"Silence," the Chairman boomed.

Paolo looked at Laurel and Anne noted the two shared a nod and a smile. She wondered if this was true, and, if so, had Laurel known?

"I think we will have to adjourn so the Council can take this new finding under advisement," the Chairman declared.

"Excuse me, Chairman," Praetor began, "if I may perhaps speak for the entire Council in recommending Marcus Monteleone be exonerated, under the circumstances. I think these families have suffered enough."

"Outrage!" Aurora screamed so loud it made Lucius jump and grab hold of Paolo.

Amid catcalls and shouts from the family members beside her, the Chairman raised his voice and commanded, "Have this woman removed from these halls!" Immediately, guards by the door forcibly picked her up, restraining her as she tried to scratch their eyes and kick them. Seeing Aurora contained seemed to calm Maya's other family members. Before she was ushered out the door, Chairman stopped them.

"And, madam," he said as he stood. "Let me declare to you that you are bridled from causing any harm to this man or this woman." He pointed to Marcus and Anne. "Nor any member of their family." He rubbed his fingers through the air in a sweeping gesture, addressing the general side of Marcus's family.

"And if any member of *your* family, madame, is responsible for causing any harm to any member of this family, I will hold you, Aurora, responsible for it one hundred percent. Do I make myself clear?"

Everyone in the room looked at the red face of the Chairman.

"Do I make myself clear, ladies and gentlemen?" he shouted again.

At last, several of Maya's family turned down their heads and nodded. Aurora's chin stood upright in quiet defiance.

The Chairman pointed a finger at Aurora. "I can hold you until you agree. Your freedom is contingent on your vow."

Aurora tore her arms from the guards. On her own, she nodded and whispered, "I agree."

"Now, remove her." The guards picked up the wild-eyed woman, who still spewed hatred towards the Chairman. But, she was led outside without further incident.

Marcus at last turned to look at Anne. Her heart was racing, the pulse in her veins quickening, unafraid to show her need of him. She saw him call to her in the ancient way her fated male would call to her, through his dark eyes that looked into her soul. From afar, he kissed her there.

The Chairman again addressed the crowd. "I thank you for your words, Praetor. And you, young son, your bravery is noted. Paolo, you have much to answer for, but I see your course is tracked. I wish I could physically punish you, if I could do it without hurting the boy. Your punishment is of a different nature, and I hope you pay the price forever. Please be seated." As Paolo and the boy made their way back to their seats, Marcus stopped Lucius and gave him a hug the boy returned. Then Lucius kissed Marcus on the cheek, and smiled.

The Chairman looked at the other Council members, many of whom nodded in a silent agreement. "Marcus, please rise."

He did. Anne wanted to run to his side, but held her spot between Laurel and Praetor. She leaned forward, placing her hands on the back of the seat in front of her, next to Paolo. She patted his back.

"Although I regret we cannot take back the pain that has been caused by this proceeding, I find that, in light of the fact that you did everything in your power to protect your fated female from her attacker, this homicide is justified." When the shouts from the opposite side of the room died down, he continued. "I want to say we do not condone violence. This is never the solution to any problem, as I'm sure this illustrates. We should always seek to find another way. I am not sure in this case, though, it could be avoided. Marcus Monteleone, you are exonerated and are free to go."

Shouts of joy rang through the room. Marcus's family descended upon him. He was wet with tears, covered in lipstick, jostled with hugs and slaps on the back. His hair came untied and hung loose around his face. Anne stood back, but could see his eyes scanned above the crowd.

"Anne? Anne? I want to see Anne."

Anne pushed her way through the crowd, who took no notice of her. She wedged herself between body after body until at last she broke through to the front of the circle of well-wishers surrounding him, and ran into his arms.

"At last. Forever and forever. We have forever now."

She had no words and no tears left. She collapsed into the chest of the man who loved her with the intensity she loved him.

CHAPTER 26

They walked down the rows of green fruit that hung below slender vines. Anne looked out the Dry Creek Valley to the vineyards on the flats below, Marcus's warm hand in hers. The verdant view took her breath away. She watched the vines grow in front of her eyes, the liquid from their fruit like the blood she and Marcus lived on. This place was her sanctuary. Her mortal life had ended on a cobblestone street so far away, but her new life had begun right here, at the place where Marcus had laid the blanket down when she tasted him for the first time. The time she'd felt the fating. And here again, her new life was starting over as she watched Marcus lay down the same blanket, stretch out the long lean length of his body, and call to her with his eyes.

Anne wore a peasant skirt and white top she had seen once on a gypsy dancer in Spain. It was comfortable in her present condition. Her enlarged belly needed room. She gave herself many lacy petticoats for Marcus to get lost in on his quest for her opening. They mussed his hair as he explored. He took his time, though, catching on the rhythm of the game, peeling back one layer at a time, as he brought her closer and closer to the familiar core of her passion.

She had decided not to make him work too hard and had not worn panties. When he found this, he dipped his tongue into the pool of her sex and, looking up to her eyes, whispered, "Thank you."

Licking the sensitive fold next to the lips of her sex, he whispered a question he didn't need to ask. The way she was splayed out for him should have told him the answer, but she loved hearing him beg for her anyway. She loved that he respected her body. Though he had the keys to every door in her heart and soul, he would always ask permission, never take what was not freely given.

"May I taste?"

"Please. You can have any part of me you wish to devour. Every part but the child I am carrying."

He licked her again with a warm tongue, his touch, vibrating over her white skin as if to calm her flesh and prepare it for the bite. The punctures through her skin stung and then dulled into a sensual glow that radiated out from it, making the lips of her sex quiver and release its juice. Marcus suckled her blood, and then suckled the juice of her passion.

He was whispering secrets again to his child, to the womb inside her, making the child strong. He could hear his son's strong heartbeat. The sound of his father's voice quickened it, along with his mother's.

Marcus raised himself up to take Anne's lips that she parted for him. He moaned and gave her his hot breath.

"I am yours. Forever." Marcus bit her earlobe.

"Yes, my love. And every cell in my body belongs to you."

Long male fingers inched their way under her blouse, stopping only to squeeze the taut nipples and warm flesh of her breasts. He delicately raised the white blouse off her and sighed at the new red satin and lace bra he'd bought her. She knew he liked it when she dressed inappropriately for him. She even liked doing it in public, making his pants tent in front of lots of people, making him nail her in his mind against any available wall. She wanted to always have this effect on him, and she knew she would.

"Are you going to punish me for not wearing the matching panties you bought me?"

"Under the circumstances, this is a violation that deserves punishment, don't you think?" He kissed her neck, then followed his lips with exploring fingers up and down her pulsing vein.

"I am truly sorry for my sins. But I fear the punishment will bring me too much pleasure." She liked that he smiled and showed his white teeth, the tips of his fangs.

"Then you have no choice but to bring the executioner of this punishment into your body and show him. To be truly punished, he needs to know all things about you to exact his measure."

"I hope his measure is lost inside me and never wants to return to his body again."

"Ah, but only for the delicious bridle of it until it is free to exact its punishment again. The yearning is delicious."

Anne loved the whispers they gave each other. She looked at the vines surrounding them. They knew. The grapes knew. They were indeed witnesses to their love for each other. Marcus's maleness was so strong he could exact juice from the grapes at her sides. Everything in the world deferred to him.

She sat up, then helped him off with his shirt. She kissed his chest, working her tongue over his nipples. She bit him gently and took a drop. Her tongue wanted more. Her mouth ached for him as her sex dripped for him.

She unbuckled his jeans and helped slide them down his long legs. His erection was fully red and glistened in its velvet goodness in the afternoon sun. Anne covered him with her wet lips, working her tongue over his head, letting the warm shaft bulge further and throb for her.

One knee grazed his thigh. She dipped her sex and rubbed herself up and down on his flesh as she leaned into his chest and sucked on a nipple. Her round belly pressed against him and she watched his pleasure as she rubbed their offspring against his tanned abdomen. Then her knee reached over his other thigh so that her wet sex hung over his balls, his erection pressed against her and lost in her petticoats. She raised the lacy fabric so his cock could find its home, then looked at his dark eyes as she raised herself up. She set herself down upon his shaft in one long motion as his hands gently massaged her belly.

"Ah, this is how it is done, my son. This is how your fated female will make you feel," Marcus whispered, and then looked at his wife.

There were no words for how Anne felt. His shaft thrust from below into her belly, reaching to touch all of her insides, seeking to create pleasure wherever it pressed. His cock was demanding and hard. She would remember this mating for centuries, this sunny summer day when she was large with his male child. Full circle in a life that started out mortal and became immortal, and in time, legendary.

Anne's muscles began to twitch as she lowered herself down to his neck and claimed him in her orgasm. He did the same, claiming her with a new strength and urgency to shoot his seed she had not felt before. They were life force for each other as their bodies tangled in the mating where there wouldn't be satisfaction, but a growing need for each other and the love they shared. They would bloom together. Not grow old. They would just grow.

And they would drink the wine of their love forever.

The End

OTHER BOOKS IN THE

The Golden Vampires of Tuscany Series:

Purchase on
amazon.COM

BOOK 2

BOOK 1

The Guardians Series

(Guardian Angels, Dark Angels)

Purchase on
amazon.COM

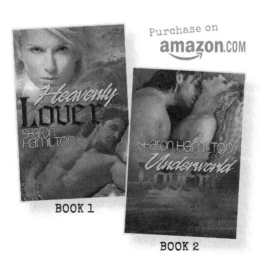

BOOK 1

BOOK 2

SEAL BROTHERHOOD SERIES:

BOOK 1

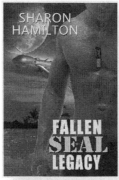

BOOK 2

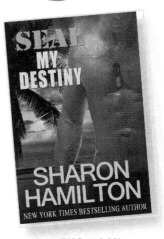

COMING SOON:

SEAL MY DESTINY,
BOOK 6 in the
SEAL Brotherhood
Series

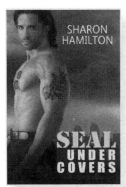

BOOK 3

BOOK 4

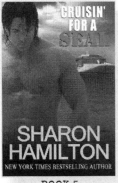

BOOK 5

Connect with Author Sharon Hamilton!

sharonhamiltonauthor.blogspot.com

sharonhamiltonauthor.com

facebook.com/AuthorSharonHamilton

@sharonlhamilton

http://sharonhamiltonauthor.com/
contact.html#newsletter

Made in the USA
Charleston, SC
19 April 2015